The Crooked Queen
Daniel A. Crane

Copyright © 2023 by Daniel A. Crane

All rights reserved. No part of this publication may be reproduced, distributed, or transmitted in any form or by any means, including photocopying, recording, or other electronic or mechanical methods, without the prior written permission of the author, except in the case of brief quotations embodied in reviews and certain other non-commercial uses permitted by copyright law.

This is a work of fiction. Any characters, businesses, places, events, and incidents are either the products of the author's imagination or used in a fictitious manner. Any resemblance to actual persons, living or dead, or actual events is purely coincidental.

Printed in the United States of America

Hardcover ISBN: 978-1-959096-99-3
Paperback ISBN: 978-1-961624-00-9
Ebook ISBN: 978-1-961624-01-6

Library of Congress Control Number: 2023941320

DartFrog Plus
A division of DartFrog Books
dartfrogbooks.com

To the Portuguese people,
who gave me many of my earliest memories.

Chapter 1

SAINT ANTHONY'S FEAST

A young woman slouched in the back corner of the Café Luís de Camões, sipping indolently on a *galão*—three quarters milk, one quarter coffee. Up until early afternoon, she would have ordered a *meia-de-leite*, half milk, half coffee. She had been tempted to do so even now when it was pushing five o'clock because it was Saint Anthony's Feast, June 13, and Lisbon would be bright for hours to come and pulsating for hours after that. But she was on the job, and too much caffeine could make her giddy. So *galão* it was.

On the other hand, Lacey Papparin never had a problem with sugar, either giddiness or diet, so an enormous *bola de Berlim*, sprinkled with coarse sugar and bursting with golden *crème pâtissière*, sat half eaten in front of her. When Lacey had gotten the Lisbon assignment, she had spent an hour reading the food section of the *Fodor's Travel Guide* before turning to headings like "culture" or "attractions." There was a good deal too much about codfish—*bacalao*—and such a mess of pork preparations that Lacey judged it a culinary obsession suggestive of a compromised national character. But the promise of delectable pastries—custard tarts dropped into flaky pastry shells, white bean and almond cakes dusted with powdered sugar, egg yolks spun in sugar nestled in rice paper casings, and enormous balls of fried dough exploding with crème—had more than sealed the deal. So, Lisbon it was.

Now duty called; the *crème pâtissière* would have to learn patience. Reluctantly, Lacey shifted her focus from the *bola* and glanced across the café. It was nestled in a tidy room with fifteen small glass tables and a serving bar in the rear. Terracotta floors reflected the bright June sunlight that streamed in through the storefront facing the Praca Camões. A solitary waiter brooded behind the bar, scowling at the seven patrons and daring them to pray for his attention. In her week in Lisbon, Lacey had learned—the hard way—that Lisbonese waiters considered it the patron's humble duty to supplicate for service.

The patrons: When she had entered the café fifteen minutes before, Lacey had quickly assessed and created mental files on all of them. There was the university student, probably studying marketing, judging from the book he was reading, and dateless for at least three months, judging from the greasy hair, dirty jeans, and the fact that he used the café's cloth napkin as a handkerchief. The older couple had been married for at least thirty years and had spent the morning at the beach, although the husband had gotten out of the sun earlier because he had a history of melanomas (and secretly planned to grab a beer) and the wife resented him for leaving her to get sunburned. He was now explaining in no uncertain terms that her sunburn wasn't his fault. This was clear, even though Lacey couldn't hear what they were saying and, in any event, spoke no Portuguese. The portly businessman from Porto was in Lisbon overnight and was treating himself to two—*two*—pastries, because his wife wasn't there to nag him and would ask no questions about his travel diet once he told her that he had closed the deal on the municipal water pumps. So much for the background noise.

It was the two men seated at the table farthest from Lacey and farthest from the exit that commanded her attention. The older of the two was pushing fifty and hailed ethnically from somewhere in the southern Caucasus region. He sported a gray, double-breasted suit and a paisley tie that might have been fashionable in Paris ten years ago. He also had ordered a *bola* and was trying to eat it politely while carrying on an intense conversation with the younger man. That, of course, was impossible. Grains of coarse sugar and flecks of *crème pâtissière* lodged in his Stalinesque black mustache, creating a vivid contrast. From time to time he discreetly flicked them away with his white cloth napkin.

The younger man was probably not yet thirty, but he had already seen something of the world, and the world had seen something of him. He was thick of neck, square of jaw, bearded, and bovine—evocative of the extinct European aurochs—and might have outdone the sunburned woman for beach time. A white linen shirt was open three buttons down from the collar, revealing a corded gold chain and a crucifix the size of Jerusalem bobbing against the man's painfully scarlet chest. The words of Lacey's Bible college chaplain suddenly came to mind: "There is an inverse correlation between the size of religious jewelry and the piety of the person wearing it." As if to confirm this maxim, the younger man's right hand fidgeted nervously with an expensive cigarette lighter as he spoke.

From across the café, Lacey could not hear any of the men's conversation, although when she had walked to the bar to claim the *galão* and *bola* that the surly waiter had seemed uninterested in delivering, she overheard snippets of English and a word or two in French. From the interlocutors' frequent use of hand gestures, Lacey surmised that they were not comfortable in the same language. And they were arguing about something. Whatever the something was, it had an immediate physical instantiation in the form of a leather briefcase sitting on the glass table between the older man's shrinking *bola* and the younger man's fidgeting cigarette lighter. When the men's gesticulations were not directed against each other, they were directed at the briefcase.

Lacey stretched her legs under the table. Soon it would be time to act. At any moment, the men might wind up their conversation and leave, taking the briefcase with them. And it was for the briefcase that Lacey had come. The briefcase was everything. Nip it, and a fifty-thousand-dollar commission was hers, plus first-class travel expenses. Let it slip, and it was youth hostels until she could book a three-leg return flight to New York—probably in the baggage compartment.

Casually, Lacey turned her gaze from her target to the only escape route—a zigzag gauntlet between seven tables, past Senhor Municipal Water Pump's expanding girth, out the glass door, and onto the street adjoining the Praca Camões. She gave the square a harder look as a yellow and white tram ambled by, laden with gaping tourists. Pedestrian traffic was thick and increasing as the workday ended, and people walked briskly along to join the Santo António festivities. Across the cobblestone street, past the trolleys, the plaza's white and black marble glinted in the late afternoon sun.

Lacey had inspected the square closely before entering the café, *Fodor's* in hand. The square's center formed an octagonal ring surrounding a layered octagonal pedestal supporting the cast bronze figure of Luís Vaz de Camões, Portugal's sixteenth-century poet laureate. His back was turned to Lacey now, but earlier she had seen that his right hand gripped a sword and his left hand his epic poem *Os Lusíadas*, which Lacey had tried to read in translation on the flight over and eventually given up in favor of a Brazilian science fiction movie poorly dubbed in English. Camões's sculptor had made no attempt to conceal the poet's maimed right eye, a gift from the Moors. Lacey had taken a long and critical stare at the eye socket sunken into bronzed shadow. Her uncle had lost an eye in a combine accident and, yep, that's about what it looked like.

Nothing material had changed about the escape route, which Lacey had been over ten times, so she returned her gaze to the restaurant. As her eyes passed over the glass storefront, she caught a glimpse of her own reflection. But it was not really hers. The blond whose eye she caught, that middle-aged Euro-chic tourist wearing too much makeup, was only her creation. If this attempt failed, there might be an opportunity to try again in different character.

One more time over the plan. Commotion: Topple remains of the *galão*. (Note to self: no need for much spillage, fine to take a few last swigs.) Distraction: Waiter will not come out quickly to clean up mess; start demanding loudly in accented English that he take care of it immediately; he will dawdle even more. Escalation: Draw men with briefcase into argument with waiter. Execution: Nip briefcase from table; slip out the door. Culmination: Run.

Now or never. Lacey exhaled slowly, took a deep breath, and tensed her muscles. She raised the *galão* for a last drink before she dashed the glass mug to the floor. Just then, the phone in her pocket jingled. Instinctively, she slipped it out and took a look. A text had appeared from Daisy Papparin.

Hi honey. What are you up to? Studying hard for the bar exam?

Lacey sighed and started to put the phone back into her pocket. Then she paused, sighed again, and gave the men with the briefcase a furtive glance. Their intense discussion continued unabated. Quickly, Lacey typed a response.

Hi Mom. Everything's fine. Studying hard for the bar exam. Gotta keep going now.

The phone was barely back in her pocket when it jingled again. Lacey looked hard at her pocket, then hard at the *galão*. Then she took an overly hasty swig and checked her phone again.

Study hard then!

A pregnant pause. Then, inevitably:

Maybe I'll come out to Boston to see you next weekend.

Out of the corner of her eye, Lacey noticed that the briefcase men seemed to be winding up. Mr. Stalin Moustache was gesturing to the waiter for the check and Mr. Gaudy Crucifix had stopped fiddling with his cigarette lighter. The briefcase still sat between them, unclaimed, but the window was about to close. Lacey fumbled the phone into position and typed:

Not so soon. Bar exam. Love.

She jammed the phone back into her pocket. Mr. Stalin Moustache handed the waiter a twenty Euro bill. The waiter surveyed it skeptically, as if certain it was counterfeit or carried the plague. Then he slouched off in the direction of the bar to fetch change. Now! Pretending to reach for her napkin, Lacey knocked the *galão* to the floor. It shattered on the terracotta tiles with a satisfying death shriek.

Momentarily, time went into slow motion. The dateless marketing student shot Lacey a conniving look, wondering if this might afford an opportunity to come riding to a damsel's rescue. The quarreling couple didn't even bother looking because they had grandchildren and this happened all of the time. The businessman from Porto gaped at Lacey's half-eaten *bola de Berlim*, tempted beyond reason to order one. Mr. Stalin Moustache, whose back had been turned to Lacey, nearly jumped out of his skin in surprise. Mr. Gaudy Crucifix glared at Lacey like a wounded aurochs. The waiter ducked behind the bar, pretending he hadn't heard anything.

And then, *deus ex machina*. The café's door swung open and a bearded young man wearing a black leather jacket and sunglasses walked in. He strode purposefully across the room as if headed for the bar. The moment he came within reach of the table where Mr. Gaudy Crucifix sat, he grabbed the briefcase, turned heel, and fled along Lacey's carefully planned escape route: zig-zag gauntlet between seven tables, past Senhor Municipal Water Pump's expanding girth, out the glass door, and onto the street adjoining the Praca Camões. Lacey's ticket home had vanished into the hands of another thief.

Lacey froze in place. She had considered many contingencies and this one had not made the list. Her Rube Goldberg scheme, refined in hours of planning, was suddenly out the window. The cheeky interloper had just walked in and taken the briefcase.

But no time for feelings of wounded pride. The action accelerated from slow motion to warp speed. Crucifix and Moustache were plunging out of the café, bellowing in rage. The other patrons were on their feet, chattering excitedly, except for the businessman who was trying to get the waiter's attention to order a *bola*. Lacey hesitated no more. Leaving a five Euro note on the table, she quietly slipped out the door after the pursuers, the shattered *galão* forgotten by all.

She recovered her wits in the seconds it took to exit the café. Fortunately, Crucifix and Moustache had been too slow out of the café to see the thief's direction once he vanished into the increasingly bustling Praca Camões. They had split up on the plaza and were stopping passersby, evidently to ask if anyone had seen the thief. For the moment, they seemed to have lost the scent.

Seconds more, and any chance Lacey might have to pick up the scent herself would vanish. She buzzed through her mental files. Though new to the city, she had done her homework thoroughly, walking the Chiado district for hours to plot her escape route. Eight different streets intersected the Praca Camões, and within a few meters they corresponded with dozens of other streets and alleys flowing into Chiado's byzantine quarters. Lacey's planned objective upon dashing from the café with the briefcase had been to make a sharp turn onto a busy street that could not be viewed directly from the square and melt away from pursuing eyes. That ruled out turning west toward the Bairro Alto along the main thoroughfares that continued in the plaza's line of sight, or east past the baroque church of The Lady of Incarnation and neo-classical Lady of Loreto and into the metro station. Turning south would have brought her to the confining riverfront within a few blocks. That left one clear choice—making a hard left from the plaza's east side to run north up the steep Rua da Misericórdia. Thieves might think alike. Trying hard to avoid Crucifix and Moustache's attention, Lacey scrambled toward the Rua da Misericórdia.

The street was crowded. Cars jockeyed with trollies and pedestrians trying to hold a place on the cobblestone sidewalks and avoid being bumped into the road. A row of five-story apartment buildings with brightly tiled facades and street-level shops and cafés lined the street. Glancing back down toward the Rua do Alcerim, Lacey caught a glimpse of the river's sparkling blueness, but none of the black leather jacket. She took off up the Rua da Misericórdia at a near sprint, dodging brusquely through the pedestrians and scanning up the street. Not a moment too soon she spied her quarry. A black leather jacket was just disappearing around the first right turn off the main street.

Lacey swerved across the street, narrowly dodging two black and green taxies heading in opposite directions. Their horns were still blaring as she rounded the corner onto the Largo da Trinidade, an alley that dead-ended momentarily into the Rua Nova da Trinidade. Lacey saw the black jacket turn right again and disappear from view. By the time she had dashed through the alley and reached the next street, the jacket had vanished. But Lacey had now seen enough to guess her quarry's mind. He was heading toward the Carmo Convent to hop the Santa Justa lift, the fastest way to drop from the old quarter to the Baixa, forty-five meters below.

Lacey sped down the Rua da Trinidade toward the Largo de Carmo, the quaint plaza that fronted the ruins of Lisbon's famed Carmelite convent. The streets were growing more crowded with early evening revelers, and the pungent aroma of roasting sardines drifted from little charcoal grills set outside houses and storefronts. Through the wafting smoke and thickening crowds, Lacey could see barely a few meters ahead. Twice she almost collided with pedestrians and once with a moped as she scrambled to reclaim a bead on Black Jacket. She arrived at the Largo de Carmo breathing hard, eyes stinging from the smoke, and sweating in the warm evening air. Black Jacket must be sweating even more underneath that thick leather, but where was he? Across the plaza, the convent's red gates stood resolutely shut underneath frowning Gothic arches. Behind the gates rose the arches of the convent's former roof propped on naked pillars of stone, the skeletal ribs left standing when the roof came crashing down on the congregation assembled for mass during the great earthquake of 1755.

The convent's doors were locked. Black Jacket could not enter the convent unless he had inside help. Lacey scurried on toward the covered skyway that fed into Santa Justa. The day before, she had ridden the Neo-Gothic iron elevator from Rossio Square, fixated on the views of the Castelo de São Jorge rising on the heights across the orange roofs of the Alfama. Now, the castle forgotten, she swept the skyway for any sign of the briefcase thief. A line of people formed to ride the lift snaked back halfway across the skyway. And there was her thief, jostling with irate tourists to cut the line. Cornered. But now she faced the problem of the dog chasing the fire truck—what to do if it succeeded. It would not be as simple as grabbing the briefcase as he had done from its owners. He was on alert.

Lacey joined the back of the line and surveyed the developing situation fifteen people in front of her. Providentially—or so her mother would have said—a bottleneck of burly blond Norwegians with folded arms, unwilling to be cut in on, had formed up ahead. A few extra moments to improvise a plan. Black Jacket made one more attempt at jumping the Norwegians in line. The Norwegians would not be moved. They stood their ground, shoulder-to-shoulder, remonstrating in impeccable English: "Hey man, what are you doing? Wait your turn!" Black Jacket muttered imprecations in Portuguese, then looked back anxiously over his shoulder. Lacey averted her gaze, but too late. Recognition flashed through his dark eyes. *The girl from the café.* He whirled about, left the line, and jostled back toward Lacey. She read menace on his scowling face, but, like the Norwegians, she stood her ground. Standing in the middle of the line, in the middle of a scene, she was protected. In any event, there was nowhere to go. Black Jacket swept by her, roughly clutching the briefcase, and snarled a word she did not know but could guess. Then he took off at a run again down the skyway back toward the Carmo Convent.

She was on his heels again. Now that he knew she was following him, it would be dangerous to get too close. For the moment, she must keep him in view and hope to see where he ended his escape. He was headed up the Calçada do Carmo, but not for long. Without warning, he veered off to the right between two buildings into a tight alleyway. Lacey ran after him and made the turn. The alley fell toward the Rossio square in a narrow canyon of cobblestone flights sandwiched between shops and apartment buildings. Brightly colored streamers and awnings fastened from building to building formed a fluttering ceiling unable to contain the greasy smoke of a thousand roasting sardines. Revelers crowded the alley, scrunched in outdoor chairs drinking beer at hole-in-the-wall cafés, dancing gaily to accordions, or flipping sardines on grills. There was no way to see Black Jacket through the crowds and smoke. If he decided to duck into a café and hide out, it would be game over. She could only hope that he had lost his head and kept running. In that case, he had nowhere to go but down.

Lacey plunged into the mass of festive humanity. Agile and slight of build despite the pastries, she slid down the slick cobblestone terraces, weaving through people and furniture like a slalom skier. Once she narrowly missed capsizing a low-lying grill by leaping over it at the last second, much to the amusement of its minder, who tried to offer her a glass of port. That set off a band of giggling girls in blue and white silk dresses, who chased her nearly to the bottom of the steps. Feeling nothing but the thrill of the chase, Lacey paid them no heed.

The steep descent ended suddenly. Lacey spilled out into a wide, flat alley running into the Rossio square. The smoke and humanity cleared just enough to reveal a black jacket dodging across the street into the expanse of baroque monuments and fountains that formed the heart of Lisbon. Her feet touched down on the square in moments and she found that the plaza's cobblestones, lapping in waves of dark and light, seemed to roll her forward toward her quarry. He was moving quickly, clutching the briefcase now in both hands, and casting anxious glances back as he ran. But she was gaining, and he appeared not to have seen her. Once he reached the far side of the plaza and joined the Byzantine streets of the Alfama, she would have cover again.

But before that could happen, Lacey heard urgent shouting over the din of the crowd. She glanced behind, in the direction of Santa Justa, and saw, on the far side of the square, a man gesturing wildly to two police officers toward Black Jacket. It was Crucifix. Leaving him panting for breath, the officers took off after the thief, wielding batons and calling out words that Lacey did not recognize, but clearly meant "stop" and had the effect of making Black Jacket do just the opposite. He clutched the briefcase in his right hand and took off at a sprint, the satchel banging violently against his right thigh.

Lacey stopped running and melted away into the throngs of revelers. Pursuing the chase in tandem with the police, with Crucifix and possibly Moustache wheezing up behind, was too risky. They might remember the Euro-chic lady who spilled coffee from the café and suspect she was in league with Black Jacket. The briefcase was gone. For today.

Since the chase had passed into the Alfama, Lacey would have to buy some time before heading back to her Airbnb apartment. She remembered a quiet café not far away in the Baixa where another *galão* might soothe her woes and give her time to think. Or, now that the job had ended in failure, maybe she could even up the caffeine dosage and order a *meia-de-leite*. Maybe even another *bola de Berlim*. It had been that kind of a day.

But neither coffee nor pastry brought the relief she hoped. She sat for a while in the back of the café, admiring the round perfection of the *bola* and the play of light in the sugar crystals clinging to its crisp brown surface, coffee untouched. *Black Jacket.* Who could he be? Who else besides her client knew about the briefcase or the rendezvous at the Praca Camões? And what to do now? Let her client know, of course, but he would either fire her on the spot or ask for her next plan. And that was something that she did not have. Not yet.

After half an hour, the cigarette smoke became unbearable. Smoking was prohibited inside the café, yet half the patrons were pulling on cigarettes, and no one seemed to mind. Growing up in rural Iowa, she had hardly ever seen someone smoke, much less inside a building. Lacey opened her mental file on infirmities of national character and added tobacco to excessive pork preparations.

The streets of the Alfama were throbbing with gaiety as she trudged up the hill. If Chiado rocked for Saint Anthony, the Alfama rolled. The oldest neighborhood in the city, its labyrinth of crooked streets had watched with equanimity the comings and goings of Christians and Moors, of armies and earthquakes. Tonight, inebriated tourists took turns leaping over bonfires between its whitewashed walls, the singed victors rewarded with briny little fish laced with spindly bones. Songs and laughter clattered through the medieval alleys, rising to reverberate among the flowerpots, bird cages, and drying laundry cramming the wrought-iron balconies. The Alfama had long been the neighborhood of the poor, but tonight it was rich in light and simple joy. For a moment, Lacey almost wished that she could release her cares and join the festivities, but the thought vanished before it cohered. Failure was an unfamiliar and unpleasant sensation. Amends must be made.

Lacey arrived at a four-story apartment building and unlocked the front gate. A brick patio adorned with potted geraniums and a rickety marble table with two folding wooden chairs ushered her into a ground-floor studio apartment. Upon arriving a week before, she had been amused that the ground level was denominated floor zero in the Portuguese custom. Floor zero seemed perfect for someone who didn't want to be known. The door opened into a spare, low-ceiling room with stark, white walls. There was a wicker chair, a bed, a kitchenette, a miniature bathroom, and nothing more. The advertisement guaranteed fast and reliable internet. The rest was icing.

A moment later, a blond wig and a Euro-chic blouse and jeans were strewn on the bed. Lacey sat in the wicker chair in a long T-shirt, phone in hand. She still had not come up with Plan B, but the call could no longer be avoided. It was midnight in New Jersey, but he had said to call as soon as it was over. He would be waiting. She rang.

"Do you have it?" It was a quiet male voice on the other end.

"No." She paused. "They were there, as you said they would be. With the briefcase. I was just about to take it when... when someone else showed up. A young guy with a beard, wearing a black leather jacket. He just walked in, grabbed the briefcase, and ran out. I shadowed him for a while until the police caught up. Then I called it off. I don't think they got him. No idea who he was." The last sentence was half part question.

There was a long silence. Lacey wondered what it would be like living in a youth hostel in Lisbon. That hadn't been in *Fodor's*.

Finally, he said: "Interesting. Very interesting." Another pause. "Anything else about the thief?"

"I got a close look at his face at Santa Justa. I'd recognize him again. I think he called me... something that rhymes with witch."

The man chuckled. "You're the only person in your field who won't even repeat swear words when quoting others. You're something else, Mouse."

She waited for him to go on, but it became apparent that he expected her to go next. Since Plan B still had not sprung to mind, all she could say was: "What next?"

"Ah, you mean are you fired?" He chuckled again, but not unkindly. "Not yet. This... this development has given me new directions to consider. You will get another chance. But the next round will be much more delicate than snatching a briefcase in a restaurant. This will require... what is it you always call it?"

"My trade secrets."

"Yes, yes. How ironic of me to forget, in this of all circumstances. Yes, your trade secrets. Now take down this address."

Hours later, in what should have been the dead of night, Lacey was still sitting up in bed, staring through the opaque glass window in the door leading out into the patio. It wasn't jetlag, which she had gotten over after three days, or even the raucous reverberations of revelry still echoing through the Alfama in honor of the patron saint of lost things. Lacey was awake because she had been given an impossible task, and it's hard to sleep when one is ecstatic.

Chapter 2

MADEMOISELLE GERTRUDE LECLERC FROM GENEVA

Leonor Fatima Esmeralda da Silva sat properly at the mahogany desk in the second-floor reception area of 255 Avenida da Liberdade. Through the window, she could just catch a glimpse of Sebastião José de Carvalho e Melo, the first Marquês de Pombal, standing astride a bronze lion and surveying the city he had famously rebuilt after the earthquake. Leonor shook her salt-and-pepper head grievously and made the sign of the cross over the small silver crucifix resting on the folds of her black sweater. It vexed Leonor's soul to pass underneath the Marquês' baleful shadow every day on the short walk from the metro station to the office. To be held in such honor after all he had done to the Society of Jesus! Over three centuries later, it was still a scandal.

It was nine-thirty on Wednesday morning, June 15, and there was little for Leonor to do at the reception desk. Donna Maria had asked her to look over a batch of invoices for silk rugs shipping from Mumbai, but that had taken all of fifteen minutes. Leonor could have walked back and asked one of the others if they needed help with anything, but the others seemed mostly interested in nursing lingering headaches from Saint Anthony's feast, two nights past. Leonor herself was a light drinker—only two glasses of Medeira and a Super Bock pale lager to wash down the sardines—so her own recovery was now complete. She drummed her fingers on the mahogany desk and rehearsed the familiar roster of venues in hell reserved for the Marquês.

At 9:35 the tedium broke when the elevator bell sounded a jaunty ding, and a woman stepped out onto the marble corridor. With an air of diffidence, Leonor observed the interloper's advance toward the glass doors etched with the words *Casa Fonseca*. Thirty, maybe thirty-two, with austere, brown hair cut at the shoulder, just a little mascara flanking an unfortunately large nose bridged by thick glasses, an unsmiling gray business suit, low heels, and a ponderous briefcase built for accountants, actuaries, and auditors in some grim Nordic factory. Clearly foreign, not a client, and not a friend.

"Can I help you?" asked Leonor in passable posh English, trying to avoid eye contact.

The new arrival said nothing but pushed a business card briskly across the mahogany. Leonor looked down and read: *Mademoiselle Gertrude LeClerc, Inspector First Class, Association of Importers and Exporters International, Geneva*. A Geneva street address was given. There was no more. Leonor waited patiently for an explanation, and when none was forthcoming, realized with mounting apprehension that she would have to make eye contact. The azure eyes she met bore down fiercely on her own.

"Yes, do you have an appointment with someone?" asked Leonor, knowing full well that the answer was *no*, since she kept the master calendar for the office.

Unexpectedly, Mademoiselle Gertrude LeClerc giggled, flashing a row of polished white teeth with overly pronounced canines, and said, with a heavy French accent: "But of course not! I am here to execute a dawn raid."

"Excuse me?"

"A dawn raid. Voila." Mademoiselle LeClerc produced a severe-looking stack of papers from her briefcase, flipped through them, and pulled out a sheet entitled "Powers of inspection—dawn raids."

Mademoiselle LeClerc gesticulated triumphantly at the paper. "You see here. It says the commission may enter any premises to examine books and records and interview members of the staff. Take it to your bosses, if you don't believe me." She slammed the paper down on the desk.

Leonor needed no further invitation to flee the front line and summon greater forces to repel the invader. Grabbing the business card and the paper, she scurried back into the corridor leading to the adjoining offices where Donna Maria and Inês presided. Both women were in their offices, pretending to answer emails. Upon Leonor's urgent summons, they slouched out to the corridor.

"*Nossa Senhora!*" exclaimed Leonor, clutching her salt-and-pepper mane and continuing in Portuguese. "It's an official from the European Commission, and she says that she will execute a dawn raid."

"*What* commission?" demanded Inês, a plump young woman with flashing dark eyes that seemed, iris for iris, an even match for Mademoiselle LeClerc's. She took the business card and paper from Leonor's hand, perused them, then snorted derisively.

"Can't you read, Tia? She's from some association in Geneva, not the European Commission. Switzerland isn't even in the European Union. I can't imagine what she said that's got you into this tizzy."

"She says it's a dawn raid," insisted Leonor, trying to snatch the paper back from Inês, who hid it behind her back.

A young man wearing a lavender sport shirt sauntered up from around the corner. "What's this racket?" he demanded. "It's making my head hurt."

"Your head's been hurting for two days because you drank too much with those floozies, Rui," retorted Donna Maria tartly, grabbing him by the ear with a mean twist. The boy laughed. "They were the nicest girls, *mamãe*. But what's this nonsense that Tia Leonor is saying?"

"It's a dawn raid," repeated Leonor emphatically. "They've come for our books and records."

"What poppycock!" Rui twirled his finger around his temple. "Where do you get these ideas, Tia? Anyway, what is a dawn raid?"

"Enough talking!" Donna Maria snapped. "Inês, your English is the best. You take care of this."

"Yes, *mamãe*. I'll take care of it. Come, Tia; show me to the front. And try to maintain some dignity."

Inês and her aunt now made their way to the reception area with Leonor clutching at her crucifix while Inês, whispering furiously, kept trying to slap the icon out of her aunt's hand. Mademoiselle LeClerc awaited their arrival behind the desk in the ramrod pose of a Prussian sentinel, her heavy bosom jutting like the battleship *Bismarck*.

Inês smiled professionally. "Good morning, Mademoiselle. There appears to be some confusion here. My aunt thinks that you are from the European Commission."

Mademoiselle LeClerc did not reciprocate the smile. "Certainly not! The Association of Importers and Exporters International is not—I repeat, not—the European Commission."

Leonor dropped the crucifix and sat down weakly at her desk, looking both confused and relieved. But Mademoiselle LeClerc had not finished. "It is not the European Commission, and it has never been the European Commission. But it does have the same inspection powers as the European Commission. This is what the Casa Fonseca agreed to in its Contract of Affiliation."

Inês raised her penciled eyebrows and purposefully locked the Swiss inspector in a stare. "What contract? What are you talking about?"

Mademoiselle LeClerc reached for her grim stack of papers, shuffled about for a moment, and then triumphantly produced a five-page document. "Voila again. Contract of Affiliation between the Association of Importers and Exporters International and the Casa Fonseca, dated May 10, 2014, signed by one Ricardo Nunes Fonseca. He is the boss, yes? Why don't you run along and fetch him?"

Leonor crossed herself twice and reached for the crucifix. Inês's face grew very white. She spoke slowly, in a low and dangerous voice. "I cannot fetch my father because he is dead. Does that please you, Mademoiselle Gertrude LeClerc from Geneva?"

Mademoiselle LeClerc showed no sign of remorse or dismay. "Then if he is gone, who is the boss now? I cannot wait all day to begin the dawn raid."

"No indeed," said Inês, some color returning to her face. "Especially since it is long past dawn." She shot Leonor a brief glance, but her aunt seemed to be lost in prayer. Then slowly, Inês took the contract and read it over carefully. Alas, there seemed to be little doubt about it. In 2014, her father had joined this trade association in Geneva. Exactly what the association did or why he had decided to join was far from clear. But that was certainly his signature, affixed just a few months before... Inês tried to stop the thought there. As Mademoiselle LeClerc claimed, the contract seemed to give the association the right to conduct unannounced inspections of members' books and records to ensure that they were complying with association policies.

The question was now how to get rid of this annoying person as quickly as possible. "Come, Mademoiselle LeClerc; let me show you to an empty office where you can make yourself comfortable." Inês gestured down the hallway. Mademoiselle LeClerc collected her papers and briefcase and marched stiffly after her unwilling hostess.

Ricardo's old office still sat dusty and unused next to Donna Maria's. Inês wondered whether it would be disrespectful to her father's memory to park this rude foreigner there, but no other office was available, so she unlocked the door and motioned for the unwelcome guest to go in. "Now where would you like to start, Mademoiselle LeClerc?"

"As per our protocols, the first stage is the interviews. I will start with the current head of the firm. Who is that?"

"My mother, Maria Louisa Fonseca."

"Very well. And while I am interrogating her, you can begin collecting all of the documents I will need to see. I've prepared a list."

Inês was handed a typed sheet of paper on the letterhead of The Association of Importers and Exporters International and gaped at the list of demands: bank records, tax filings, corporate registrations, supply contracts, bills of lading, commercial invoices, liens, securitization instruments, export packing lists, airway bills, certificates of origin, dangerous goods certificates, insurance policies; the list went on and on. "Mademoiselle, you will be here all day!" she exclaimed.

"Yes, and for several more days, I expect," she replied tartly.

"That's many dawns," said Inês, mostly under her breath.

Mademoiselle LeClerc took no notice. "But I'm sure that you have many of these records in the computer, so just supply me with the necessary passwords and authorizations. I can do the rest."

Inês looked momentarily ready to reinitiate hostilities, but then checked herself and asked: "I'll be back soon. While you are waiting, can I get you some coffee?"

"Yes, that would be proper. I take it with two sugars and some milk." For the first time, Mademoiselle LeClerc hesitated. "And do you happen to have any of those little custard tarts in pastry shells?"

Inês pursed her lips. "*Pastéis de nata*. Yes, I suppose that can be arranged."

"Thank you, Mademoiselle Fonseca!" exclaimed Mademoiselle LeClerc with unexpected enthusiasm. "Now be off. We have a long day ahead of us."

Inês was off, but not to fetch a pastry, a coffee, or her mother. Rounding the corner out of sight of the imperious Swiss, she burst into Rui's office. "Rui, Rui, get your head up off your desk! We need to look up this association now, on the computer. Maybe it's all a sham."

Rui groaned but took Mademoiselle LeClerc's business card. He typed stiffly at his keypad and then pointed to the screen. "There it is: the Association of Importers and Exporters International in Geneva. *Droga*, but they are an ugly bunch."

Inês peered into the monitor screen and sighed. On the homepage, underneath a banner with the association's name, was a picture of thirteen unsmiling men and women clad in unsmiling business suits, standing at the edge of Lake Geneva. On the far edge of the group, almost pushed into the water, stood none other than Mademoiselle LeClerc, holding the very same battle briefcase that she wielded for her assault on the Casa Fonseca.

Inês snapped her fingers. "I have an idea. Papai joined this confounded association. I don't know why, so let's unjoin it. Quick, Rui, go to that tab about membership and see how we resign."

Almost as if someone had anticipated great demand for resigning, it was all too easy to locate the instructions for terminating membership in the Association of Importers and Exporters International. Indeed, if Rui and Inês had not been in such a hurry to read the rules for unjoining, they might have been surprised to note that there were no rules *for joining*. But there it was, a big banner in English: *Rules for Termination of Membership*. Inês eagerly scrolled through the seven paragraphs of boilerplate specifying all of the odd reasons that the association could terminate a member—criminal syndicalism, conveyance of infectious diseases across state lines, acquiring a reputation for debauchery, acceptance of emoluments from foreign princes or potentates, consorting with warlocks—before coming at last to the solitary paragraph on voluntary resignation by a member. Her shoulders fell. It read: "Members may resign membership at any time, upon three months' written notice. Termination with less than three months' notice shall be available for a fee of 100,000 Francs. Failure to pay the termination fee in advance shall result in a penalty of an additional 100,000 Francs."

"How much is a Franc?" asked Rui.

Inês slapped him on top of the head and stalked out.

Fifteen minutes later, Donna Maria Louisa Fonseca entered the office of her late husband. She did not knock. She did not smile. She did not introduce herself. She sat across from Mademoiselle LeClerc in the stiff leather chair Ricardo had reserved for his business clients and folded her arms.

Mademoiselle LeClerc looked up, then returned to the *pastel de nata* that Rui had brought her, along with the coffee. He had tried to loiter and flirt, not because he found her attractive but to annoy Inês and rile his mother, but the inspector first class had dispatched him with a wave of the hand. Now, she finished her pastry, took a deep drink of coffee from a steamy glass mug, and turned to business.

"So, you are the head of the firm?" She asked it with a hint of incredulity.

"So I am." Donna Maria's English was better than her sister Leonor's—less stylized and more practiced—but her Luso accent was deeper than her daughter's and more evocative of transactional experience than fine grooming in the classroom.

"What happened to your husband?"

"Mademoiselle LeClerc, I do not see what that has to do with the business of the Association, whatever that may be."

"Very well, Madame Fonseca. I will say in my report that you did not wish to discuss your husband. That is noted. That is very noted. That is noted in italics. Now tell me about the financial condition of your business. Are you profitable?"

"Yes, we are doing passably well."

"We will see. Your accounting records will tell. Now let us review your import activities in the last six months. Textiles—are you doing good business in textiles?"

"Yes, some from China and India. And cotton from Mozambique."

"Furniture?"

"Yes, again, China and Vietnam."

"Do you travel much then?"

"Often."

"Computers?"

"No, those distribution channels have become too specialized."

"Toys?"

"Some. Mostly from a supplier in Malaysia."

Donna Maria relaxed as the interview settled into an easy back-and-forth cadence. Mademoiselle LeClerc seemed to be checking the boxes without taking much interest in the answers. Types of goods, sources, inventories, customs issues—the rhythm lulled into tedium. But, fifteen minutes in, an astute observer might have detected a subtle increase in the temperature when Mademoiselle LeClerc asked, without looking up, what business the Casa Fonseca did in pharmaceuticals. Donna Maria looked up sharply, seemed to catch herself, and then responded that the house did no business in pharmaceuticals because they were so bureaucratically regulated by the Serviço Nacional de Saúde. Mademoiselle LeClerc jotted down a perfunctory note and moved on to perfumes and spices.

After half an hour, Rui entered without knocking, carrying a carton of papers. "Your papers, *Senhorita*," he said in broken English, and then allowed the box to land on the desk with a percussive thud.

"*Malandreco!*" exclaimed his mother, reaching for his ear to exact punishment. But the young man had already escaped out the door.

"Ah, the first batch of documents," said Mademoiselle LeClerc, caressing the stack with evident pleasure. "Now we will see if you have been telling me everything, Madame Fonseca."

The matron of the Casa Fonseca snorted and rose brusquely to her feet. "You will find everything quite in order. Now, if you'll excuse me, I have a business to run."

For the next several hours, Mademoiselle LeClerc sat at the big desk of the late Ricardo Fonseca and sifted through stacks of paper. From time to time, Rui or one of the office boys would bring in more cartons. Mademoiselle LeClerc would nod curtly and return to her document review. Or so it would have seemed to a fly on the wall. On the other hand, a fly on the desk might have noticed something different—that Mademoiselle LeClerc was not reviewing the documents at all but ingeniously using them as a cover as she texted away on her phone. The texts she sent and received during those two hours included the following:

I'm in. No dirt yet. They haven't given me anything good, of course. Looking for the chance to dig.

To this she received the immediate reply: *Dig then.*

To a different virtual interlocutor, Mademoiselle LeClerc wrote: *Hi Mom. It's after five so I know you must be up. Still studying hard for the bar here. Are T and G leaving you alone? Don't let them take advantage of you.*

The reply came in fifteen minutes: *Hi sweetie. Don't overwork yourself! Remember to stop and smell the flowers. And don't worry about your brother and Glennis. You know how busy they are.*

Both the fly on the desk and the fly on the wall would have heard Mademoiselle LeClerc snort loudly as she banged back on her phone: *So they are still taking advantage of you. Don't take it, Mom. The kids are theirs, not yours.*

A minute later, the response came back in the form of a string of emojis. Mademoiselle LeClerc sniggered and wrote back: *Um, Mom, did you mean to say, "Little children are so tasty"?*

Mom replied at once: *Good gosh, is that what I said? I meant to say that your nieces and nephews are so sweet.*

At a quarter to one, Inês knocked on the door and then entered without waiting for an answer. Mademoiselle LeClerc looked up imperiously from underneath a heap of bills of lading as if certain her visitor was coming to confess grave transgressions to the Association of Importers and Exporters International's Rules of Member Conduct. But Inês had merely come to announce that the office was closing for lunch, that the entire staff was leaving, and that Mademoiselle LeClerc was invited to call again at two.

"No, no," said Mademoiselle LeClerc, gesturing at the bills of lading. "I'm far too busy for lunch. You do as you please. I'll stay here and work."

"The office will be closed and locked," said Inês pointedly.

"Then your papers will be all the more secure while I review them," rejoined Mademoiselle LeClerc.

In the end, Inês unhappily relented on the inspector staying to work over lunch but informed her that Rui would also be staying "in case anything else is required." She did not specify by whom anything else might be required.

At ten minutes after one, when the office had settled into a dull quiet punctuated only by the muffled sound of reggae coming from Rui's office, Mademoiselle LeClerc sallied forth and banged loudly on Rui's door. The young man, who had been slumped over his desk, jumped to his feet and scurried to his door with an apologetic leer.

"Monsieur Fonseca, would you be so kind as to fetch me a ham sandwich with cucumbers?" She thrust a ten Euro bill in his direction.

"What is this?" asked Rui, looking befuddled.

"It's money," she said acidly. "Take it and buy me a ham sandwich. With cucumbers. It must have cucumbers. Very fresh ones."

"But, but..." He looked around, as if trying to see whether anyone else had returned to the office. "But... I do not know where to find such a sandwich."

"I do." She held up her phone. "You see, it's on the menu of the Deleite do Marquês café, Rua Barata Salgueiro."

"But that's..."

"A ten-minute walk. So I expect to see you back in no more than twenty-five minutes. And the change should be three Euros thirty."

At that fatal moment, Rui's marginal English failed him, as he found himself lacking the idiomatic power to say, "But I promised my sister I would stay" or "But I must stay here to monitor you" or even that most primal of locutions, "No, I won't." Seeing victory evidently won on the uneven playing field of language, Mademoiselle LeClerc whirled about and marched back to her office. Rui remained at his desk for a moment, nursing his still-throbbing temples and wondering whether staying or going would result in a greater escalation of pain before finally relenting and leaving, ten Euro bill held limply in hand.

No sooner had the unfortunate Rui exited his family's place of business than Mademoiselle LeClerc embarked on a ruthless expedition. With the efficiency of a Swiss train conductor, she shuttled about the Casa Fonseca, methodically assaulting every nook and cranny capable of concealing the firm's secrets. Filing cabinets, drawers, and closets received full body cavity examinations, while a wooden umbrella from the reception area was commandeered into the service of tapping walls and prying at loose wall panels. Nimble fingers flipped through files, papers, binders, envelopes, and boxes underneath the mantle of a furrowed brow and aquiline eyes. If the flies on the wall and desk had followed Mademoiselle LeClerc in her search, they would have observed her several times react with interest to various artifacts—especially small boxes—pulled from desk drawers or cabinets, before discarding the objects after close examination. In fifteen minutes, she had rifled through every space, carefully leaving everything as she had found it.

It was for Inês's office that the inspector saved her most rigorous inspection. Entering, she immediately noticed that this office stood aloof from the baroque cosmopolitanism of the others. There was no porcelain vase or ivory statue, no patina of the Orient or of Africa, nothing alerting the visitor that this was an import-export house. It was a Portuguese room. Walls of simple white framed a solitary window peeking through red linen curtains toward the Praca Marquês de Pombal. A knotted pile wool rug with brightly colored bird and flower motifs graced the floor in front of the only piece of furniture, an antique desk of olive wood. One wall was covered with a floor-to-ceiling bookshelf stocked with books.

Mademoiselle LeClerc did not stop to peruse the titles because her eye was drawn to the opposite wall where three ceramic tile panels hung. She stepped closer for a better look. Each panel was composed of four square tiles presenting a continuous geometrical pattern of dark blue and green motifs against an orange background. Mademoiselle LeClerc ran a finger along one of the surfaces and found that the exquisite patterns were etched in bas-relief. In the window's dappled light, their chipped and worn arabesques reflected the antiquity of an older Portugal when Christians and Moors uneasily shared Iberia. Mademoiselle LeClerc lingered for a long moment at the tiles before turning to the desk.

Ten minutes later, she retreated empty-handed to her assigned office with an air of disappointment. A few minutes after that, the Casa Fonseca's staff trickled back into the office, still looking bleary and none too cheerful to see their visitor still at work in the late Ricardo's office. But she was not finished. At a quarter past two, it was Inês's turn to receive a summons for an interview, delivered by a rueful Rui who had already endured miserable tongue lashings from his mother and sister for abandoning his post to fulfill Mademoiselle LeClerc's craving for fresh cucumbers.

"Tell her it will have to be in my office," said Inês, filing her fingernails vigorously.

"I don't know if she will..."

"My office." Inês swiveled away from her brother, and that was the end of the discussion.

Surprisingly, Mademoiselle LeClerc obliged without complaint. Indeed, she seemed positively conversational.

"Such lovely tiles, Mademoiselle Fonseca," she said, gazing at the wall. "Do you import such antiques as well?"

Inês looked like she had swallowed a persimmon laced with chili pepper. "Those are *Portuguese* tiles, Mademoiselle. *Portuguese*. Sixteenth-century *azulejos*. You will not find anything like them elsewhere in the world."

"*A-zu-le-jos*." Mademoiselle LeClerc articulated each syllabus distinctly, as if charmed by the taste of a new food. Then, seeming suddenly self-conscious, she added: "Ah, so you are a collector."

"It runs in the family. Now, shall we get down to business?"

"Yes, of course. Tell me about your competitors."

"Which ones? We have many."

"Many, but perhaps not so many. Tell me about," Mademoiselle LeClerc looked down to a legal pad in her lap, "the Casa Têxtile Importação e Exportação. Did I say that correctly?"

Inês's eyes narrowed. "CATIE? Perhaps you would like to conduct a dawn raid on them next."

"Yes? Maybe I shall. And what do you think I would find?"

"Fools, lies, and skeletons."

"You know," said Mademoiselle LeClerc leaning forward, "I'm beginning to find you interesting." For a moment, her English did not sound very accented.

Inês looked on the verge of replying when Rui once again entered to announce that a client had arrived to see Inês. Surprisingly, Mademoiselle

LeClerc made no objection to terminating the interview so soon. As she left Inês's office, her eyes lingered thoughtfully over the *azulejos* on the wall.

The remainder of the afternoon produced no more drama at the Casa Fonseca. At 3:30, Mademoiselle LeClerc announced that she had concluded for the day and would resume her inspection the following morning. Leonor saw the Swiss inspector to the elevator and weakly tried to warn her about the moral risks of walking under the Marqueses' shadow on the way to the metro. Mademoiselle LeClerc shouldered her briefcase without comment and disappeared into the elevator.

A few minutes later, from a quiet café along the Avenida da Liberdade, the following text message sallied forth into the ethersphere: *Still no dirt. If anyone has it, it's Inês Fonseca. Daughter of the family. Wears the pants. Going back in tomorrow. One more place I want to check.*

Again, the reply came nearly instantaneously: *Do that, but watch yourself. Developments on this end. May have things to report tomorrow. Be ready to get out fast.*

The following morning, Mademoiselle LeClerc's appearance at the Casa Fonseca could hardly have been mistaken for a dawn raid. She stepped off the elevator at 10:30 and advanced at a sedulous pace unlikely to alarm even the perturbable Leonor. Neither Donna Maria, Inês, nor Rui came out to meet her. She closeted herself in the late Ricardo's erstwhile haunt and, to all appearances, busied herself at the computer reviewing files. No demands for further interviews were forthcoming.

At a quarter to one, Inês once again appeared to inform the inspector that everyone was leaving for lunch, including Rui. Mademoiselle LeClerc was welcome to stay, ahem, especially if that meant that she might finish her work sooner. Mademoiselle LeClerc expressed her pleasure to remain and continue her work but gave no indication of any intention to conclude her audit.

By a few minutes after one, the Casa Fonseca was as still as a convent at vespers. Like the day before, Mademoiselle LeClerc quietly left her office, this time carrying her briefcase. She did not look set to return. Around the corner and into Inês's office she swept with an air of familiarity and expectation. Straight to the *azulejos* she went, dropping her briefcase on the floor and setting quickly to work. The first tile panel slid off its hook. She lowered it gently to the floor and stepped forward to examine the space it had enclosed. There was nothing, apart from a nail hook and the tile's dull silhouette on the paint. Mademoiselle LeClerc ran her fingers along the silhouette. Then she placed her ear to the wall and tapped. The search yielded nothing; she removed the second tile from the wall and conducted the same search. Again, nothing. For the third tile set, she moved more quickly, as though aware of a ticking clock. This time, her search revealed a hairline crack in the plaster along the perimeter of the tile's enclosure. Taking a deep breath, Mademoiselle LeClerc pushed the panel. There was a quiet popping sound like the release of a latch, and a door the size of a dinner plate swung out from the wall.

With a triumphant smile, Mademoiselle LeClerc reached into the dark recess and withdrew its contents. Her smile faded as she surveyed the cache. It was evidently not what she had expected. There was a wad of official-looking documents typed in Portuguese on paper yellowed with age, and an equally worn postcard with a faded, handwritten scrawl. And there was a peculiar object—a chipped, three-by-three-inch tile fragment picturing the tips of human toes.

Just then, a vibration emitted from Mademoiselle LeClerc's pocket. She started, then swiftly pulled out a phone, unlocked the screen, and read a text message. It said: *We got our guy. Lab tech in Atlanta. Sample secured. Sent you on a wild goose chase. Will reimburse. Pull out immediately.*

Mademoiselle LeClerc shook her head in disgust, and then lost her balance and nearly dropped her phone. She caught the phone, slipped it back into her pocket, and began to replace the cache in its hiding place. Then, as if drawn by curiosity, she checked herself and withdrew the postcard and tile fragment again. She studied the postcard closely. It bore a stamp and a postmark dated 17-12-1975. The scrawled note was written in indecipherable Portuguese, except that it was addressed to Ricardo Fonseca at a Lisbon address and signed "Alfonso." The picture side contained the photograph of an elaborate panel of *azulejos* portraying a woman seated on a high-backed, gilded throne. She was dressed in a flowing gown of white with gold brocade, and a golden crown perched on her head over a white mantilla. Her deadened eyes lay under a muslin veil. It was apparent even in the miniature presentation of the postcard that something was dreadfully amiss about the woman. Her head flopped onto her right shoulder like a rag doll, with the gruesome implication of death and dismemberment.

The inspector tarried a long moment over the postcard. Then she closely compared the woman's feet in the picture to the tile fragment. Apparently satisfied with her inspection, Mademoiselle LeClerc replaced the postcard and fragment into the hidden recess, pushed the door closed, and rehung the third *azulejo* panel.

She turned to leave, then suddenly froze. Standing in the doorway, quiet as a church mouse, arms folded, and looking as though she had been there for a long time was none other than Inês. When she spoke, her voice was quiet and calm: "So inspector. I see you have made a very thorough search."

Mademoiselle LeClerc made a valiant effort to regain her composure. "Yes, yes, I must look everywhere. It's…"

Inês cut her off. "It's your job? No, I don't think so."

Mademoiselle LeClerc started to say something, but Inês again cut her off. "No, no more games. We both know that you are not Mademoiselle LeClerc from the Association of Importers and Exporters International in Geneva. There is no such Association." She paused, as if savoring the blanching of her antagonist's face. "You see, I have a cousin who studies in Geneva. I asked her to go by the address on your business card. It is a psychiatric clinic." Inês paused again and seemed almost to smirk. "I suppose that was your own little joke."

The faux Mademoiselle LeClerc responded in a voice that sounded decidedly younger and more American than the Swiss inspector. "I'm sorry to have bothered you. I will go now, and leave you alone."

Inês did not budge from the doorway. "But first I think you have some explaining to do to the police. Perhaps you would be so kind as to place your passport on my desk while I call them."

She said this, but did not reach for her phone. Perhaps sensing hesitation, perhaps acting strategically, or perhaps because she could not contain her curiosity, the other woman suddenly exclaimed: "You've gotta tell me about the postcard and tile fragment. It has nothing to do with my business here, but it will kill me not to know."

"You have some nerve to ask about that!" said Inês, but she seemed if anything less hostile than at any time since Mademoiselle LeClerk's appearance the previous day. "I will ask the questions first. Who are you, really?"

"My name is Lacey Papparin. I'm American. I'm... well, sort of like a private investigator, but it's not exactly like that. I was here on assignment for a client, but I just learned that sending me here was a wild goose chase. And that's God's honest truth."

She said the last bit with such vehement sincerity that Inês laughed out loud. "Well, Lacey Papparin, I like you better than Mademoiselle LeClerc. And, because of that, I will propose a deal. I will not call the police, and we will forget this business here. You are curious about the Crooked Queen, and I have a favor to ask of you. Let's go to coffee and discuss it."

When Lacey looked uncertain, Inês continued. "We will go to the Café de Pombal, which will ensure that my aunt is not lurking about. And besides, they have excellent *pastéis*."

And thus the deal was struck.

Chapter 3

WHAT HAPPENED AT THE REVOLUTION

A sultry breeze was blowing off the Tagus and rustling through the lavender jacaranda blossoms as Lacey and Inês strolled up the Avenida da Liberdade toward the Praca Marques do Pombal. The lunch crowd was dwindling along the boulevard's broad sidewalks, leaving the tourists to gawk through boutique windows at luxurious clothing and jewelry they could never afford. The two young women strolled together for a block, in silence. As they walked, Mademoiselle LeClerc underwent a dramatic metamorphosis entirely unremarked by the window-shopping tourists. The austere brown wig was first to go, liberating a sandy-colored and slightly disheveled bob. The prosthetic nose and glasses slid off and, when the mascara had been dabbed away, a demurely freckled and much younger face shone in the Lisbon sun. The unsmiling gray business suit no longer fit its wearer, particularly after the matronly bosom shrunk to waifish proportions through the excision of two wads of toilet paper.

After tossing the toilet paper wads into a garbage can, Lacey abruptly broke the silence. "Yeah, I'm sorry for all that."

Inês mulled the apology for a moment, then asked: "For all of what?"

"For wasting your time for two days."

"Oh, but you didn't waste much of my time, Lacey. I knew pretty soon that you weren't a Swiss inspector."

"Then why didn't you say or do something sooner?"

"Because the others don't know."

"But it's your family's business."

"Yes, it's *family business.*" She said it slowly and distinctly. Lacey took the hint and did not try to press for more.

"OK, but where did I slip up? Sorry for asking, but my mom always says that when we make mistakes we need to figure out how we screwed up right away."

Inês laughed. "You want me to help you become better at pretending you're someone you're not so you can trick other people? I don't think so. But let me tell you how I am, Lacey. The others were all looking at you one way, but I was looking for something else. In Portuguese, we have a saying, '*Quem vê cara não vê coração.*' It means—"

"No, wait!" exclaimed Lacey with violent enthusiasm. "Let me figure it out."

Inês shot her a curious glance, then smiled broadly. "OK, *está bem*. Tell me."

"Yeah, well, *quem vê*, *vê* again, and *não* are obviously Latin roots. Who... something. Who... sees. Who sees something does not see something else."

"Bravo."

"That leaves the two nouns—*cara* and *coração*. I only need to figure out one of them, and it will give me the other one."

"Are you sure, Mademoiselle?" Inês laughed.

"Yeah, it's about context. That's the way everything works. First rule of investigating: People are known by the company they keep. It's the same with words. There's even a maxim for that I learned in law school—*noscitur a sociis.*"

"Law school? Now you have me interested."

"But I haven't yet finished with *quem vê cara não vê coração*."

"Wow. Your pronunciation is excellent. Much better than your fake French accent."

"Thanks. OK, *coração*. *Cor*, Latin for heart. Oh, I get it. Who sees the face doesn't see the heart."

"*Bem feito!* Well done! You really figured out *cara* from its association with *coração?*"

"No, I cheated a bit. *Kára* is ancient Greek for head or face."

"Fantastic! I see you love to play with words and are good at it. My father was that way." Momentarily, she appeared troubled, but quickly she recovered. "But tell me: where did you learn Latin and Greek, Lacey?"

"Latin was from homeschooling. Mom, she was one for the classics. Greek was from Bible college back in Iowa. New Testament exegesis. Some Hebrew too."

"Bible college? Law school? And now some kind of faux detective? Really, you must start from the beginning."

Lacey sighed. "OK, deal, but I'll need a coffee and a pastry first."

"And here we are, the Café de Pombal."

They entered the near-deserted café. Inês led the way to a table near the back and announced: "Let me order the *pastéis*. We'll start with savory." She snapped her fingers in the direction of the waiter, who seemed to recognize her and came right over. "*Dois meias-de-leite, dois rissois de bacalhau, e dois empadas de frango.*" She nodded gravely at Lacey. "You will like this."

Lacey nodded expectantly.

Inês eased back in her chair and surveyed her American guest. "Well, we should not discuss business on empty stomachs, so first tell me about yourself, Lacey Papparin. How on earth did it come about that a young woman like you is playing detective so far from home?"

"Yeah, it's a long story," said Lacey, still uncomfortable.

"I have all afternoon. I told my mother that I would be away from the office."

"So... you planned to trap me and then bring me here?"

"Trap you? No, to catch you in the act. But look, here are our coffees and *pastéis*, so no more excuses now!"

Lacey took her *meio-de-leite*, added two sugars, and stirred the mug vigorously. Inês served her two pastries, a cod and potato fritter gushing with garlic and a flaky little pie stuffed with spiced chicken. Lacey sampled each pastry, then shrugged in resignation. "These are to die for, so I guess you have me now." She took a bigger bite of the fritter, drank deeply of her coffee, wiped the foam from her lips with a napkin, and then jumped into her tale.

"Here's how it is. I'm from a little farming town in Iowa. Do you know where that is?"

"In the middle of the States somewhere."

"In the middle of nowhere, except every four years when the reporters make it the center of American politics for about two weeks. Anyway, my dad died when I was little, leaving my mom with my brother and me and a little life insurance policy that got us through. Mom homeschooled us because… well, you'd have to know Mom." She finished the *empada de frango* and shot Inês an expectant look.

The other woman nodded. "*Sim*, I'll order some more *pasteis*. Keep going."

"OK, when I was seventeen I was off to Bible college still in Iowa, because that's the only thing we really knew. Some of the kids thought it was narrow and repressive, but I loved it. Took every class they offered in dead languages." She looked thoughtful for a moment. "Ya know, I've always been drawn to dead languages and dead people."

Inês grimaced. "Maybe that explains what you do?"

"Yeah, well, I do more work on living people than dead ones, although the dead ones behave themselves better."

"And then law school?"

"For about a week. I had been working as a paralegal for a law firm in DC. Well, I worked as a paralegal until the firm decided that they didn't like me… you know, going out and getting to the bottom of things. They were going to let me go, but a couple of the partners cut a deal where I worked in a dark hole in the basement of the building doing special projects. That's how I got my nickname." She immediately seemed to regret this last comment.

"Nickname?"

"It's silly."

"But now I must know!"

"OK, the Mouse. That's how pretty much everyone knows me today."

Inês laughed and tapped her spoon on the table. "The Mouse! But that's perfect. Unfortunately, in Portuguese our only word for mouse is *rato*, which really means rat. I can't think of you as a rat."

"Thanks. A mouse gets into anything and everything, and that's what I did. I mean, geez, I wasn't going to sit in that basement and stamp documents, not when there was dirt to dig. The partners I worked for knew it too, which is why they kept me on. I would bring them back the most useful stuff for their cases, and they pretended not to know how I did it. They used to joke that it was fine for me to be a *house* mouse but not a *field* mouse, but they never complained when I proved that the CEO of the other side's company was shredding documents or doing drugs or whatever."

"I'm not surprised that you only lasted one week in law school."

"Yeah, it wasn't my thing. My mom thought I should give it a try. Actually, to be honest, she still doesn't know that I dropped out after a week. That was three years ago. She thinks I graduated a few weeks ago and I'm now studying to take the Massachusetts bar."

"You lie to your mother?" There was something in Inês's tone that was neither quite hostile nor quite friendly.

"Yeah, it's a sin, I know it. But I don't think she would take it very well, knowing what I actually do."

"And now is a perfect time to tell me exactly what that is. But wait, they've brought the sweet pastries." She took the square China plate the waiter had left on the table and cut the three pastries into perfect halves with a butter knife. "This, we call a *pastel de feijão*. It's made with white beans, but don't worry—it's very sweet."

Lacey nibbled gingerly at the edge, then took a bigger bite and nodded with approval.

"Now this one is a *bolo de laranja*. Watch out or you'll get your fingers sticky. It's orange marmalade with a little bit of cake. And this one... this one is my favorite. We call it *mil folhas*, which means a thousand sheets of pastry. OK, the French have one like it, but the Portuguese claim the patent! Try it, and I dare you not to fall in love."

Lacey, whose face was already stuffed with bean cake and treacly orange marmalade, needed no second invitation. Apparently familiar with Inês's habits, the waiter brought two more *meias-de-leite*. Inês thanked him while Lacey, mouth too sticky for words, obliged with what passed for a courteous nod.

"Now tell me what happened after you dropped out of law school," said Inês, stiffening her posture. "And how did you come to our Casa Fonseca?"

Lacey took a deep drink of coffee and wiped her mouth again. "After law school," she said slowly, "I went out on my own. Kept an apartment near DC but was on the road most of the time working on special projects on contract. At first, it was mostly for the lawyers I had worked for at the firm. They were ready to take the risk of me working on my own, outside the firm, cash payment, because I dug up such good stuff and covered my tracks. Over time, I developed other clients—divorce lawyers, industrial spooks, private investigators that understood that I could get stuff they never could."

"Sounds like a dangerous business."

"Yeah, but only if you get caught, which I never did. Until today." Lacey gave Inês a glance, and the two women locked eyes for a moment.

"But why, Lacey?" asked Inês, dropping her eyes. "You are obviously a smart woman. If the law wasn't right for you, why didn't you try something else? Why sneak around like a spy?"

"I dunno. I never dreamed of being a detective or anything like that. Didn't even watch crime shows. One thing just led to another. It started when I was working for the law firm and they told me I was doing something called 'discovery.' But they weren't discovering anything at all, just stamping documents and looking for sound bites. They weren't even the prisoners in Plato's cave seeing shadows. They were like… I dunno, blind prisoners in the cave trying to hear the sound of shadows. I mean, imagine you're working on a product liability case where the plaintiff claims to be totally disabled and all the lawyers want to do is read medical reports, but if you just talked to the neighbors you'd learn that the plaintiff went to Russia and did nine Gs in a MiG." She paused and rubbed her chin. "Anyway, I make a living off it. But things were slow the last few months. That's when I took this job." She took another long sip of coffee. "I suppose I can tell you a little bit about it now. I think I owe it to you, and I also think you're going to make me."

"*Sim.*"

"It was for a pharmaceutical company in New Jersey. They make biologics. You know what that is?"

"I've heard of them. Cocktail drugs made out of complicated mixtures of components like vaccines and cells, right?"

"That's it. The next big thing in pharmaceuticals—very valuable, and very secret. My client got wind that someone on the inside was trying to steal biologic samples, smuggle them out of the country, and sell them to Chinese labs. But they didn't know who the thief was or where the samples would be sold. They got a tip that an Azerbaijani smuggler named Farid Hasanova—he's been involved in running biologics before—was meeting with a middleman in Lisbon for a transfer. Someone who worked for an import/export business with connections to the States."

"Us? Really?"

"No. Someone named Dinis Guimarães."

Inês let her fork fall with a clatter.

"I take it you know him," said Lacey.

"Know him? Yes. The Guimarães family owns the CATIE house."

"Fools, lies, and skeletons?"

"The very same."

"Well, they're involved in shady business, no doubt about that. Three days ago, I was snooping on the meeting between Farid and Dinis over at the Praça Camões. They had struck a deal for a briefcase that I thought was carrying the stolen samples when, weirdest thing, out of the blue a guy walks in, grabs the briefcase, and runs away with it, which of course is what I was planning to do."

Inês stared at Lacey intently. "This thief, what did he look like?"

"Youngish, bearded, leather jacket and sunglasses. Portuguese, I'm pretty sure."

Inês sighed. "That describes lots of people. So how did that lead you to us?"

"My employer had a thick file on CATIE. Seems it was easy to buy in the underground. Anyway, from that file they learned that your family and the Guimarãeses aren't on good terms."

Inês snorted.

"Yeah, I got that. My client thought that Casa Fonseca might have nipped the briefcase, either for profit or for vengeance. Either way, it wasn't good for the folks in New Jersey. They wanted their samples back and sent me in looking for them."

"But then?"

"That's the funny thing. Right before you, um, found me, I got a text from my client saying they had caught the thief and the sample never left the US. So this whole trip to Portugal was a wild goose chase."

"And, yet, when I, um, found you, you were still looking into my private papers."

"Look, I'm really sorry, Inês." Lacey leaned forward and took her by the wrists. "I know it's not nice to pry into other people's business. When I looked behind the tiles and found your hiding place, it was purely professional. But when I saw the postcard and tile chip... well, you asked me why I do what I do, and the real answer is I can't help it. Curiosity killed the cat, and I guess it will get me some day too."

Inês laughed and removed her wrists from Lacey's grip. "No harm has been done, and all is forgiven. And I will satisfy your curiosity and more in just a minute. But first I have a little bit more curiosity of my own. How did you do it all? The costume, the website, the picture, the documents, and, most of all, how did you know to look behind my *azulejos* for a hiding place?"

It was Lacey's turn to giggle. "Trade secrets, my dear."

"Trade secrets?"

"Trade secrets. Curiosity without trade secrets equals poverty. I still have to earn a living, and if I tell everyone how I do it, then I'll never get hired."

Inês made a pouty face. "That's not fair. If we are going to trust each other, you must tell me at least one thing."

"OK, one thing. The tiles. When I visited your office yesterday, I noticed them right away—they really catch the eye—but I didn't think to look behind them. But thinking it over last night, I realized they would be the perfect cover for a hidden cubicle because of the rule of paradox."

"Rule of paradox? Now you sound like a philosopher."

"No, no, it's a rule about hiding places. It goes like this: the less hidden, the more hidden."

"That just sounds like nonsense."

Lacey started bouncing in her chair. "No, no, no, it's so obviously true. If I go to your office looking for something, what will immediately grab my attention?"

"The *azulejos*."

"Right! They will grab my attention because they are beautiful, and ancient, and mysterious. And because they are those things, I will look at them for their own sake, and momentarily forget that I am looking for something else. And then I will catch myself and remember that I am looking not for these things, and that therefore I must move on. It worked even on me, and I've spent long hours contemplating the rule of paradox."

"I think you're making this up and just got lucky," laughed Inês. Lacey started to protest, but Inês cut her off with another laugh. "*Não, não*, I'm just joking. I can see that you're smart, even if I did outsmart you this time. In fact, it's because you're extraordinary that I would like to ask you for a favor."

"Ask away," said Lacey, "especially if it means telling me about the postcard and tile fragment."

"It does. And it requires me to tell you a long story, and that requires one more coffee. Before we begin, I suggest that we both use the ladies' room."

After Inês had taken her turn, Lacey loitered at the sink in the rose-colored powder room. It was not that she enjoyed looking at herself in the gilded mirror, even to ensure that the vestiges of Mademoiselle LeClerc had been extirpated. On the contrary, Lacey liked seeing herself in neither photographs nor mirrors. But now she needed a moment alone to breathe, to recharge, to recenter. The day's turn of events had jangled even her high-octane spirits. Jangled, but not lowered. If anything, she was feeling a greater rush of adrenaline than she had at any time since arriving in Lisbon. Lacey had always found it easy to be friendly but hard to make friends. Now, in the space of a strange hour, this Portuguese stranger had caught Lacey red-handed in the commission of a crime, elicited her life story, and invited Lacey into Inês's own intrigue. Lacey could read people and had read Inês like a book with many missing pages. Inês had called Lacey extraordinary, and, if she was right about that, it was because she herself was extraordinary too. Extraordinary, and in the midst of extraordinary affairs. It's *family business. Fools, lies, and skeletons.*

Two more *meias-de-leite* were waiting on the table when Lacey returned. Inês sat primly with her hands folded in her lap, her own coffee untouched. She waited for Lacey to take the first sip before touching her own. When they had dosed themselves with caffeine for the road ahead, Inês began.

"The story I am about to tell you is one that very few people know. You have already uncovered clues to pieces of it from your snooping, but it is an old story and a sad one. I will tell you the story and then ask you for a small favor."

"OK."

"It begins in 1971 in the City of Coimbra. Do you know where that is?"

"I believe it's north of Lisbon," answered Lacey. "There's a famous university."

"You have done your homework," said Inês, her face brightening. "Yes, it is a very old and famous university, from the thirteenth century. In 1971, two young men started attending the university and became roommates. One was Ricardo; he was from here, from Lisboa."

"Your father."

"*Sim*. The other was from a medieval town in the north called Guimarães. He came from an old, aristocratic family. In fact, his family name was Guimarães, the same as the town."

"We don't do that in America," said Lacey, biting her fingernail.

"We don't do *that* in Portugal," said Inês, looking hard at the fingernail. Lacey blushed and stopped.

"But where was I? My father and Alfonso Guimarães were roommates, and they became best friends. They studied business and dreamed of making their fortunes in the colonies. But those were hard times, if you know anything of my country's history. It was the dying days of the *Estado Novo*, the regime of António Salazar, Portugal's dictator for thirty-five years. Salazar himself became ill and stepped down in 1968, but his regime continued under other old men. It was a time of repression and fear, not a time for big dreams.

"But my father and Alfonso had a strange turn of fortune. One day, they were browsing at a flea market in Coimbra, looking for a picture or something interesting to hang in their room. They came across a shabby old montage of *azulejos* plastered to a board. The tiles made out the picture of a queen seated on a throne."

"The postcard and the tile chip!" exclaimed Lacey. She looked about eagerly as if expecting Inês to produce them. Inês shook her head.

"I put them back into their hiding place. They could be very important someday."

"But who is the queen? And why is her head falling off to one side?"

"She is Inês de Castro, wife of King Pedro I of Portugal from the fourteenth century. The story of Pedro and Inês is the most beautiful and saddest of all Portuguese stories. I do not have time to tell it to you now."

"But her head!" insisted Lacey.

"Severed by the order of Pedro's father. After his father's death, Pedro became king. Even though she had been dead for two years, he declared Inês his queen and made his courtiers bow down before her mutilated and decomposing body."

Lacey shivered with repulsion and fascination.

"My father and Alfonso of course recognized that the picture was of Inês. Coimbra was where she and Pedro used to have their secret trysts and where she was murdered. Her picture is all over Portuguese art."

"I think that Camões wrote about her too," added Lacey.

"But you are extraordinary!" exclaimed Inês, pounding her fist on the table. "First you speak Latin and Greek, now you quote Camões about Inês de Castro!" The waiter looked over and inclined his head toward the coffee maker. Inês shook her head and continued.

"They knew it was a portrait of Inês de Castro, but they did not guess at its antiquity or value. They were just two young men looking for something interesting to hang in their room. They each chipped in five hundred Escudos—that's about twenty Euros today—to buy the portrait. It hung in their room until they graduated from the university in 1975. Unfortunately, by that time they had begun to fall out. It was about politics. Since you seem to be a student of Portuguese history, maybe you can tell me what was happening then?"

Lacey almost bit a nail but caught herself. "There was a revolution. Twenty-fifth of April. That's all I remember."

"That's more than most young Portuguese these days. Yes, the twenty-fifth of April, 1974, *o vinte cinco de Abril*. The people threw off Salazar's regime. It was called the Carnation Revolution because people put flowers in the barrels of the tanks and the guns and no one fired a shot. But what started in peace quickly became anything but peaceful. For the rest of 1974 and 1975, the right and the left were at each other's throats. Our family was on the left. My father and his brothers even joined the communists when they tried to take power in November 1975. But Alfonso, oh no, his family was from the conservative north. They favored the return of the monarchy! As you can imagine, they argued. And because they were stubborn, they argued more. When they left Coimbra, they both headed to Lisbon but never spoke again."

"What happened to the portrait?"

"Of course you see where my story is going, curious girl! The portrait stayed behind in Coimbra because they couldn't agree on what to do with it. There is a palace in Coimbra called Quinta das Lágrimas, the estate of tears, because it was where Inês was murdered. It is a magical place, and haunted, but that is a story for another day. Today, it is a five-star hotel, but in 1975 it was still privately owned and used as a sort of shrine to Inês. Alfonso knew one of the stewards of the house, and he arranged for it to be kept there until he and my father could agree on what to do with it.

"As I said, both men came to Lisbon and got into business. After 1976, things became better politically and the economy grew. My father founded the Casa Fonseca, and Alfonso founded CATIE. They had shared so many ideas during their days in Coimbra, I suppose it was inevitable that they would both go into import/export. And, with Portugal losing its African colonies, there was an opportunity in those days for new trading houses looking in new directions, especially east. Both houses prospered. Naturally, they became bitter rivals. From the time I was a little girl, I came to hate CATIE. Whenever the name of Guimarães came up, my father would become silent and my mother and Tia Leonor would become agitated. I learned that we should not mention the family or the firm unless it was strictly essential in a business sense, and even then, only indirectly."

She paused and looked away from the table, out of the restaurant and toward the Praca de Pombal. Lacey tapped her foot quietly under the table, sensing that a moment needed to pass before the story could resume. At length, Inês brought her gaze back into the café and back to her new friend.

"Lacey, I know that things must have happened between my father and Alfonso that I have never been told. Politics and business are not enough to explain the hatred between our families. There is another event that I will tell you about now, but I think that is more effect than cause.

"About ten years ago, when the Quinta das Lágrimas was being renovated in preparation for its opening as a hotel, a curator discovered that the *azulejo* montage of Inês de Castro that had been sitting in storage was a sixteenth-century masterpiece. It had been lost during Napoleon's occupation of Portugal. That happened in 1807, but I'm sure you know that! Where it lay hidden for a century and a half, no one knows, but it is certain that it is a famous work by the Renaissance artist Grão Vasco. It was called *A Rainha Torta*. In English that means The Crooked Queen."

"Sweet!" Lacey started bouncing in her chair again. "That's gotta be worth some serious cash today."

"Surely, yes. It would have been easy enough to find out exactly how much by listing it at auction. But, oh no, my father and Alfonso would rather have died in hand-to-hand combat than do the sensible thing. They did agree on one matter, though. When they left Coimbra in 1975, they made an agreement that one of them could buy out the other's interest for two thousand Escudos. The problem is that they could not agree on which one was supposed to buy, and which one was supposed to sell. And so for many years, they were involved in a lawsuit over it. It dragged on and on and went nowhere."

"The postcard," Lacey interrupted. "That must have something to do with it."

"Of course it does, but don't interrupt me! There are other things that you must know first."

Lacey bit her lip.

"While the lawsuit dragged on, *A Rainha Torta* remained on display at the Quinta das Lágrimas. Then, one night, it disappeared. The police could find no trace of the thief. It had been secured in a locked room with a security system, and in the morning it was just gone without a trace. Naturally, each family blamed the other. The bad blood had never been worse.

"And my poor father. It seemed to take away his breath. He was a beaten man." She paused again and dabbed at the corner of her eyes with the napkin, not catching a tear that rolled down her cheek and onto her chin. Her voice cracked when she spoke again. "He was a beaten man, but I do not believe that he did it."

"Did what?"

"Killed himself. One afternoon, five years ago to this week, he left the office early and told my mother that he wanted to drive out to the sea to be alone. There is a place about half an hour out of the city called *Boca do Inferno*, the mouth of hell. There are high sea cliffs and an arch and chasm in the rocks where the Atlantic rushes up violently like a geyser. Several people saw my father leave his car and walk in the direction of the Boca. He was never seen again. A week later, his badly decomposed body washed up on the shores of Cascais."

"I'm so sorry," said Lacey, sounding for a moment more like Mademoiselle LeClerc and less like the Mouse.

"Of course Alfonso Guimarães had the audacity to tell a newspaper that it must have been suicide—that my father was sick of a guilty conscience for stealing the Crooked Queen. The police report called it a likely accident. Many people have died at the Boca over the years. But I—"

"You think it was murder," said Lacey quietly. She was not bouncing now.

Inês started. "How—"

"The postcard. Something that you would take such pains to hide..."

"Yes, yes, yes, the postcard." She stopped and again seized Lacey by the wrists, this time with such force that the American gasped. But Inês did not relinquish her grip. "You must swear to me, Lacey, that you will not tell this to anyone."

"Of course," said Lacey, gently trying to free her wrists. But Inês did not get the hint.

"Swear it!" demanded Inês again.

"Well," said Lacey cautiously. "My mother kinda taught me not to swear. Something about letting your yes be yes and your no—"

"Oh never mind then," said Inês, still not releasing her grip. "I have your yes, your *sim*, and even your poorly accented *oui*, and that will have to do. But, Lacey, you must really keep this to yourself." She took in a deep breath. "A few weeks after my father's death, I was going through the papers in his safe. It was a place that he always kept to himself, even from my mother. At the bottom of his papers I found the postcard. It was written by Alfonso to my father right before Christmas 1975. That was a very bad time. The month before, my father and his brothers had joined the Communists in a failed *coup d'etat*. It was put down in a day or two with no bloodshed, but tanks rolled through the streets and feelings ran high. Well, in the middle of all that Alfonso wrote my father the following words: 'Judas, we will settle it all at the mouth of hell. Bring me your thirty pieces of silver.'"

"And you think—"

"My father was right. They had a deal for my father to buy out Alfonso's share of the Crooked Queen. They were to meet at Boca de Inferno to exchange the money. And to say their last adieu at the mouth of hell. That would have been Alfonso's touch. He has the flair."

"But that meeting didn't happen in 1975."

"No. I don't know why. Maybe because they didn't know it was valuable yet. It would only have been a moral confrontation. But the meeting did happen five years ago, when the price tag had gone up. When I sorted through my father's safe, I found the chip from the foot of the queen. It must have broken off when my father and Alfonso were moving the montage. My father must have kept it as proof of his claim. I found the chip, but I did not find something else I was looking for. My father told me that he kept a pouch of gold coins worth tens of thousands of euros in the safe. He never trusted the banks. The coins were his safety net. But the coins were nowhere to be found."

"So you think that Alfonso stole the Crooked Queen and told your father he could only have it back at a price. Same deal as forty years earlier, down to the same place, only the price had gone way up. And when your father arrived at the mouth of... you know... Hades, Alfonso stole his money and pushed him to his death."

"*Sim. Sim.* That is what I think." Inês relinquished Lacey's wrists and put her head in her hands. Lacey sat silently for a minute, wondering whether she should opt for comforting or analysis. But she did not have to make the decision. Inês abruptly sat up straight, her dark eyes dry and fierce.

"Yes, that is what I think; that is what I know in my heart. It was murder, Lacey, murder."

Inês fixed her dark, keen, and inexorably penetrating eyes on Lacey's. The Mouse wiped her mouth slowly with her napkin, buying time, but did not yield her eyes. At length she asked, "What does your mother think of this?"

Inês snorted and dropped her eyes. "I have never raised this with her, nor with anyone else. There are things she did not know about my father. I am sure of it. Like the gold coins he hid in his safe. Like the postcard. Other things. I have never gone to the police. I have suspicions. No, I have convictions. But I have no proof. The Guimarãeses, they are a hard bunch. Hard, rich, cruel, and powerful."

"Not powerful enough to stop the theft of their briefcase in broad daylight," Lacey mused. "And now I really wonder what that was all about since it wasn't connected to you."

"Exactly!" Inês exclaimed, her mood suddenly brightening.

"Um, exactly what?"

"You wonder. You wonder at everything. And then you find out."

"Well... that's kinda what I do, yeah."

"So you will then?"

"Will what?"

Inês darted forward to seize Lacey by the wrists again, but the Mouse had learned her lesson and adroitly sprung her hands into her lap. Undeterred, Inês pursued the wrists to the lap with the ferocity of the Ancient Mariner. "Don't you see, Lacey? Everything happens for a reason. Yesterday, when I knew that you were not really a Swiss trade inspector, I realized that your coming was no coincidence. This is fate. I said before that you are an extraordinary young woman, and I have learned it all the more now over coffee. You must help me discover the truth about my father's death."

Lacey's freckled face lit up like fireworks with embarrassment, delight, and bewilderment. "Sure, yeah, of course, but wait... this was five years ago. Even if your father was... well, you know... the trail must be really cold."

"Yes, of course. But if you find the Crooked Queen, you will find who killed my father. I am sure of that."

"OK, OK." Lacey stopped and thought for a moment. "Listen, Inês, I do owe you one. I guess I'm getting paid for the pharma job, so I can afford to hang out here for a week or two. Besides, I'd like to see a bit more of Portugal. But I don't really know where to start."

"Oh, but I do," said Inês. "I want you to meet the Guimarãeses. There is the perfect opportunity coming up in three days' time. In fact, you will not only get to meet the Guimarãeses, but you will get to see them interact with my family. That is... what is the English expression? Rarer than hen's teeth?"

"I can't wait," said Lacey, sounding as if she could. "Now I have just one problem."

"What's that?"

"My mother. She'll be trying to visit me in Boston."

"Mothers," said Inês, "are always a problem."

Chapter 4

A TEMPEST IN THE CASTLE

Unlike the cities of the New World that could idle on horizontal prairies, the cities of the Old World featured high ground where the incumbents held the advantage behind rings of stone. In Lisbon, that place is a rocky hilltop overlooking the Tagus valley and the winding estuary below. The successive occupants of Iberia—the Celts, Phoenicians, Carthaginians, Romans, Suebi, Visigoths, Moors, and finally the Portuguese descendants of all the foregoing—recognized the imperative of fortifying the hill. Its bones as a fastness precede the birth of Christ. A citadel that has served for over two millennia is bound to have seen its share of heroes and villains. By popular acclaim, the hero of this particular hill is the crusader knight Martim Moniz who, in the year of our Lord 1147, wedged his body into a gate in the Moorish castle so that the valiant knights of Alfonso I could gain the keep and complete Portugal's *Reconquista* from the Saracens. Moniz perished in his glory but lent his name to the castle's gate, not to mention a modern metro station. Alas, remembrance in a castle gate and subway stop were the limits of the crusader's posthumous reward. Having purged the Moors through Moniz's sacrifice, the Christian kings of Portugal dedicated the hilltop castle to the megalomartyr Saint George, who also offered his body for the sake of Christendom but not jammed into a castle gate in Lisbon.

It was with less peril of mayhem, and less hope of glory, that Lacey toiled up the cobbled switchbacks of the Alfama toward the Castelo São Jorge at six o'clock on a sweltering June evening. Tonight, she went simply as Lacey Papparin, the Mouse. Mademoiselle LeClerc and the blond, middle-aged, Euro-chic tourist lay far behind.

The evening hinted at contradictions. The beating sun, now hidden by the white and pastel walls and orange roofs lining the narrow streets, now springing out of the shadows for vengeance, demanded comfortable attire. But the occasion required a higher sartorial standard. Lacey had prioritized occasion over weather and was now struggling up the streets in an ankle-length red and gold brocade dress and white low-pumps that threatened to catch in the cobblestones. Beads of perspiration sparkled on her freckled brow and she flicked back her mousy bangs to avoid them sticking to her forehead. The only consolation arrived when she turned a corner, found herself looking back down with a vista of the Baixa, and observed a few gray cumulous clouds forming to the west.

Lacey paused under the green awning of a tourist shop. From her pocket she withdrew a stub of shiny paper and reviewed the evening's bidding. The ticket read in Portuguese, Spanish, French, and English, although Lacey could only proficiently read the latter three: "The Lisbon Trade Association Portuguese Chambers of Commerce presents a gala dinner at Castelo São Jorge. Live music and open bar. Proceeds to benefit expansion of the Modern Art collection of Calouste Gulbenkian Museum. Admit 1."

The price paid for admission was not indicated. In giving Lacey the ticket the previous day, Inês had hinted that it had come dearly. "But remember, Mouse," she had said with a little smile that turned into a frown before she ended the sentence, "you will never have a better chance to observe the guilty all together at once."

Rounding a corner, Lacey emerged at the foot of the castle's outer wall. There was a light scent of pine sap and, at the end of the winding road, a decayed trunk of an olive tree ancient enough to recall Moniz's sacrifice, yet still sprouting gray-green twigs. Lacey peered up at the battlements soaring high over the Alfama, now topped by a Portuguese flag that seemed swollen by the humid breezes. Then, letting her eyes fall back to the foot of the wall, she noticed fossilized imprints of mussel shells and clams etched into the limestone, and she thought, as she often had, that it was often difficult to determine what was truly alive and truly dead.

An attendant collected tickets at the turnstile leading into the castle courtyard. Several couples were entering ahead of Lacey. The men wore skinny European suits and ties that Lacey thought were too short and narrow, and the women wore high heels and skirts cut above the knee. Lacey felt prudishly American, but it was too late to go back. Taking a deep breath, she approached the attendant and presented her ticket. He nodded curtly.

Passing the turnstile, Lacey entered a terraced and cobbled esplanade. To the left, it passed through olive and cork trees and past a bronze statue of Dom Alfonse Henriques, who conquered the castle from the Moors on the back of Moniz, and ended at a low wall, lined with cannons. Below the low wall, the rampart dropped away precipitously, affording viewers a sweeping panorama of the city's orange roofs and the Tagus estuary beyond. To the left, the courtyard wandered into several low, touristy buildings fronting the high walls and ten towers of the medieval citadel.

In the esplanade, the party was just beginning. A bandstand had been erected on the far side of the courtyard and the wail of a saxophone signaled ambiance. Long rows of tables covered with white cloths were arranged throughout the courtyard underneath crisscrossing strings of light. Most of the early male arrivers were clustered around the bar near the bandstand while their consorts waited for their drinks. Now, in addition to feeling prudishly dressed, Lacey began to feel self-conscious about coming stag.

She did not have long to nurse strained feelings. Almost immediately a familiar voice rang out: "Oh there you are, Lacey! Come and meet my family."

Inês, snugged into a short black dress, left a cluster of people seated next to a cannon along the low wall and came directly to meet Lacey. She was carrying two glasses of red wine and thrust one into Lacey's hands to deliver a ritual kiss on each of her cheeks, first right, then left. During their embrace Inês whispered fiercely: "Remember, Mouse. American classmate at the London School of Economics. Traveling to Lisbon on summer holiday from a master's program in Boston."

Lacey nodded agreeably, took a sip of the wine, and gasped.

Inês laughed and said in a louder voice, "It's Porto wine, very fortified. Most people have it for dessert, but my family believes in getting an early start. Especially on evenings like this." As she said the last part, her dark, bright eyes swept around the courtyard like a hawk. Then, turning back to Lacey, she added, unconvincingly, "You look fine, Mouse. Really."

Meeting the Fonseca family seemed vaguely redundant to Lacey, as she felt she already knew most of them, perhaps better than she wanted to. On the other hand, they did not recognize her at all, so it was a fresh start. Inês introduced Lacey as her "American friend from university at LSE," and they all took her with courteous nonchalance.

"It's a pleasure to meet you, Ms. Papparin," said Donna Maria, rising from the wall with stiff formality. "We remember hearing all about you from Inês during your days together at school in London." Lacey made a mental note: "Fabricates for social convenience."

"Thank you, Donna Maria," she replied with equal gravity. "I've long wanted to visit your beautiful country, and I'm honored to be able to join you tonight." Donna Maria seemed to make a mental note also.

Tia Leonor also tried to stand, but this was made difficult by the very full drinks she was holding in each hand. She abandoned the gesture and replaced it with an amiable nod. "*Meu deus*, but you look so much younger than Inês," she said, casting a critical eye at her niece. "Maybe you could give her some advice about how to take care of herself."

Inês seemed to be on the verge of offering her aunt physical chastisement when a more pressing need presented itself. Rui had rushed over to the bar and was hurrying back with two glasses. "Senhorita," he exclaimed, accosting his sister's friend from behind. "Must drink Scotch with me." He thrust a rattling, sloshing cup at Lacey, who giggled nervously and feinted to the left.

"Rui!" Inês grabbed him by the arm, causing him to spill scotch on his pants. She then proceeded with a furious excoriation in Portuguese that, from intonation alone, clearly translated into "don't you dare hit on my friend or I'll cut you where it hurts." Donna Maria handed Rui a napkin to mop his pants while Leonor crossed herself and surveyed her nephew with dark scowls. Rui sulked behind the cannon for a moment, and then disappeared to seek a better diversion.

Obligatory chit-chat ensued, and Lacey learned that Inês and Rui also had an older sister, Mafalda, who was married with children, did not work at the Casa Fonseca, and was tied up putting the children to bed.

"And do you have brothers or sisters, Lacey?" asked Donna Maria.

"Yeah, one brother," answered Lacey, feeling a bit more relaxed with the warmth of the port. "He lives near my mom in Iowa. And kinda takes advantage of her." Lacey had not meant to say the last part, but it had risen unbidden to her lips and slipped out. Instantly, she had their attention.

"Really?" asked Donna Maria, staring intensely at Lacey.

"Really?" asked Tia Leonor, reaching for her crucifix.

"Really?" asked Inês, seeming to have forgotten for the moment that Lacey was there on assignment.

"Really," Lacey answered with a sigh. She looked at the three pairs of expectant and unrelenting eyes and knew that she would not escape without explanation. "Well, my brother, who's older than me, is married to Glennis. And Glennis is what we could call a low-energy person. They have five children and Glennis is always dropping them at Mom's house and expecting that she will watch them for hours on end while Glennis says she is out shopping but is really at home taking a bath or a nap. And Mom's too sweet to say anything about it, so Glennis keeps doing it."

"And your father?" demanded Donna Maria.

"Oh, he passed away when I was little."

Donna Maria clucked her tongue disapprovingly, while Leonor crossed herself.

"*Que, mamãe?*" asked Inês incredulously. "You don't blame Lacey for losing her father."

"It seems rather unfortunate," answered Donna Maria darkly. "First her father dies, then her brother takes advantage of her poor mother."

Inês's indignant answer was interrupted by a piercing wail that overrode the syncopation of the jazz band with a sound like *hrrraaawwwhhh—eea-eea-eea-eea*. Lacey spun around to see a peacock strutting from the direction of the citadel. She had seen one before at a zoo near Iowa City, but that scrawny thing bore little resemblance to the magnificent array of verdant green and iridescent blue plumage now making its appearance at the soiree. The gala guests parted like the Red Sea to recognize the peacock's prerogative of passage. It made its way to the center of the courtyard, checked itself, looked around at its assembled courtiers, and then swooped into the low branches of a cork tree. There it roosted for the rest of the night, only occasionally startling the partygoers with one of its eerie cries.

"What a beautiful peacock," said Lacey to the Fonseca women, quite hoping that they had forgotten the unpleasant business about her family.

"Yes, and speaking of peacocks, look what we have now," said Inês, jutting her chin in the direction of the bar. The four women turned to take in a party of new arrivals making their way to the bar for drinks. Immediately, Leonor crossed herself vehemently while Donna Maria's face darkened like the storm clouds that were beginning to gather behind her back across the city.

"That's them," hissed Inês in a tone that made Lacey think she might be forgetting herself for a moment. But she quickly recovered and said, in a much more matter-of-fact voice: "Lacey, that is the Guimarães family I told you about. They run a casa that competes with ours. They are not our friends."

"I see," said Lacey.

"Now take careful notice, because these are not people you want to forget. The big bald man sweating in the gray suit that no longer fits him and wearing the green tie choking his neck, he is the *patrão*, the boss. He is Alfonso, a royal name that he thinks suits him." Alfonso had taken a martini and, at a distance, seemed to be berating the bartender about the olive.

"His wife—I don't need to describe her to you—she is Beatriz. We call her... how do you say it in English... we say *Medusa* in Portuguese?"

"Medusa," answered Lacey dryly. "I see why you would call her that, the way she wears her hair." Beatriz sported a coiffure of burnished curls that seemed to strike at her collar.

"No, we called her that when she went with a bouffant. Now look at the ox to his mother's right—the one without a tie and that ugly crucifix around his thick neck."

"*Meu Deus!*" exclaimed Leonor, reaching for her own crucifix as if to countermand the ox's incantations.

"Crucifix," muttered Lacey, the epithet springing unbidden to her lips as memories of the Café Luís de Camões came back.

"He is Dinis, the oldest son in the family. Do not get alone in a room with him." Inês paused, and her voice seemed more steely, or was it more bitter, when she spoke again. "And the last one there, the runt of the litter. They call him Pedrinho, which is a little boy's nickname, but listen to me, Mouse—he is the most dangerous."

Lacey gave Inês a curious glance. She had been thoroughly briefed on all of the members of the Guimarães family, including Dinis's younger brother, but Inês had not previously singled him out for vehemence. Lacey studied him carefully. He was much slighter than his bovine brother and fair of skin and hair for a Portuguese. His face was thin through the cheeks but square at the dimpled jaw, which gave the impression that his face was inverted. Dressed in a khaki suit with a white linen shirt open two buttons at the collar, he had taken a glass of white wine and wandered away from his family in the direction of the wall and the panoramic view of the city. As Lacey studied him, he turned his gaze suddenly in the direction of the Fonsecas and caught her eye, almost as if he had meant to trap her. Through wire-rimmed glasses, his keen gray eyes locked on hers.

Lacey resisted the urge to look away. She was here to meet the Guimarãeses, and this was one way to start. Pedrinho did not make her wait long. With a sedulous wink, he ambled over to the Fonseca party.

"*Boa noite*," he said, addressing Inês with a smile but setting his eyes on Lacey.

"Good evening," responded Inês archly. "We will use English. Let me introduce my friend Lacey Papparin from America. Maybe you remember her from LSE?"

Lacey looked curiously at Inês. Her new friend had not mentioned that the Guimarães boy had also attended college in London.

He shrugged, then smiled pleasantly at Lacey. "London, it's a big place. But what brings you to Lisbon, Ms. Papparin?" His English was excellent, on par with Inês's.

"I'm here on summer holiday," she answered, taking the hand he offered. His palm seemed too cool for the hot summer evening, and he held her hand just a moment longer than he should have.

"And have my esteemed colleagues shown you all of the famous sites? If not—"

"We don't need your sweet talk, Senhor Guimarães," interrupted Donna Maria. "Why don't you go join your family?"

"Oh, but I believe that they are about to join me," said Pedrinho with a little laugh. And, indeed, at that very moment the other three Guimarãeses converged on the little area of the esplanade that had not entertained more intense conflict since the crusaders had confronted the Moors.

"*Por que falas com estas vilões?*" demanded Beatriz, grabbing Pedrinho roughly by the arm.

"She asks why he is talking to us villains," explained Inês to Lacey, not bothering to lower her voice.

"Please, Mother, English," said Pedrinho with another laugh, pulling back from his mother's tug. "Our friends have an American guest. Whatever our differences with the Fonsecas, let's not be rude to a visitor in our country."

Beatriz snorted. "If she's with them she must be a *puta* too." Her English was obviously strong enough that she need not have substituted a Portuguese word.

Donna Maria and Leonor advanced on Beatriz making gurgling noises and had to be restrained by Rui, who had returned from his sulk and, having drunk both scotches and procured a third, seemed to be in a much better mood.

"*Desgraça!*" shouted Donna Maria.

"*Maldita seja você!*" wailed Leonor.

"She just called you a—" Inês began, but Lacey cut her off.

"Yeah, I got that. She called you one too."

Alfonso, who seemed much more perturbed by the olives in his martini than by his wife's fighting words, handed Pedrinho his glass and gestured toward the bar. The younger son dutifully walked off to satisfy his father's alimentary needs. Alfonso gave Lacey a once-over, shrugged, and asked, in a rough baritone: "So, have you heard about our families' little quarrel then?"

"A little bit," answered Lacey doubtfully. "Something about a work of art, maybe?"

"Not just any work of art!" roared the Guimarães patriarch, coming suddenly to life. "A masterpiece! The soul of Coimbra! To see it... to see it is to become a Portuguese."

"Is that why you thought it was a cheap piece of junk for years until an expert told you it was worth something?" asked Inês. The two families had now formed into juxtaposed semicircles surrounding Lacey, who began to fear that she would be caught in the middle when they came to blows. But Alfonso ignored Inês just like he had ignored his wife and continued to address Lacey.

"It is an *azulejo* tableau by the famous artist Grão Vasco called *A Rainha Torta*, the Crooked Queen, in English. Their... well, what shall I call him... father, husband... he and I bought it together at the university when we were young. We had an agreement that I could buy it from him—"

"*Mentiroso*! Liar!" exclaimed the three Fonseca women in near unison.

"Do not tell lies about dead men, Senhor Guimarães," said Leonor, brandishing her crucifix, "or may God strike you dead!"

Alfonso made a sound like *pshaw*, only in Portuguese. Addressing himself again to Lacey, he said: "You see what I have to put up with? Religious sentiments in leftists! It's a contradiction in terms." He paused for a moment, as if a new and enlightened idea had suddenly entered his mind. "But what do you make of it all? I'm a businessman. I have to be reasonable. Let me hear from someone neutral. What is your English expression—someone who doesn't have a bull in the fight?"

"A *dog* in the fight, father," said Pedrinho, who had returned with a martini more appropriately provisioned with olives. Alfonso took the drink and seemed to lose interest in his own enlightened question. But not Pedrinho. His eyes moved to Lacey and he stood watching her with an ambiguous little smile playing at the corners of his mouth.

Lacey knew that she was on—that now was the moment to glean the information Inês had wanted. Yet now that it came to it, she felt inadequate to the task. For all of the many successful charades she had performed under cover, in character, it felt very different to be playing detective as herself. Despite the dowdy dress, she was suddenly standing naked in Saint George's castle. Mademoiselle Gertrude LeClerc from Geneva took no prisoners. Lacey Papparin from Iowa was having trouble holding her drinking glass.

"So, what's your opinion of our catfight, Ms. Papparin?" pressed Pedrinho, still wearing the little smile that Lacey was coming to resent. Just like that, the two were now alone. Alfonso, with Beatriz and Dinis in tow, was chasing down a waiter carrying a tray of anchovies. Donna Maria and Leonor had headed for one of the elegantly set tables, apparently disgusted with their family rivals and hopeful of dinner. Lacey cast about for support from Inês, but her friend was nowhere to be seen.

"Well, I don't really know much about it," she said hesitantly. Then, straightening up a bit, she added, a bit too quickly: "But I did have one question."

"Yes?"

"The Crooked Queen. I understand it was stolen from the hotel in Coimbra."

"Yes, the Quinta das Lágrimas. It's a magical place. You must visit it sometime."

"Yeah, I've been told that. But back to the point, I've heard that the queen was in a locked room with a security system the night it was taken. Why are both of you guys accusing the other of the theft? Isn't it more likely that it was an inside job by someone at the hotel?"

He smiled again, but this time without ambiguity. "Ms. Papparin, you are trying to use your mind to solve an affair of the heart. If you want to understand anything about our families, you will have to take a different approach."

She started to ask him what he meant, but at that moment came the reverberating sound of a gong. The band trailed off; the crowd hushed. A sweaty, fat man in a black suit took a stage microphone and began to make a jovial speech in Portuguese. As people immediately began to make for the dinner tables, Lacey did not need to wait for the translation. Dinner was served at St. George's castle.

She turned back to Pedrinho to see if she might join him at the table, but he had vanished too. Lacey looked about the courtyard for where he might have gone, but there were hundreds of people milling around the dinner tables, and she could not make him out. Now alone again, she wondered what she should do. *Where was Inês?*

With nothing better to do, Lacey wandered to the table where she had seen Donna Maria and Leonor take a seat. It was on the far side of the courtyard near the low wall. Behind the wall, the panorama of the city and estuary was becoming increasingly choked with ominous black clouds. In the far reaches of the river, above a red suspension bridge and beneath the outstretched arms of a colossal monument of Jesus—the *Cristo Rey*—a flash of lightning outlined the sky. Already, though the sun was still high, the light was fading and the temperature was creeping lower. The evening might not end without further drama.

Donna Maria and Leonor were already eating while conversing in indignant Portuguese and pretended not to notice Lacey. Neither Rui nor Inês was with them, nor anywhere else to be seen. There were three or four vacant seats near the Fonseca women, and Lacey quietly took one of them. The women continued their conversation.

Before long, a waiter appeared with a platter of sizzling meat. "*Churrasco*," he said to Lacey, indicating that he could cut her whatever she wanted. Seeing that she was a foreigner, he added: "From Brazil." Lacey smiled and pointed to what appeared to be a side of beef. He sliced off three thick pieces with a long blade, then loaded her plate with samples from two other pieces of meat and a plump sausage as well. Another waiter came by with a platter of rice, garlicky black beans, and fried root vegetables. Lacey began to feel rather more pleased at being ignored.

While she ate, Lacey scanned for the Guimarães family. She located Alfonso and Beatriz at a table near the bar, speaking with one another and ignoring their neighbors. Dinis and Pedrinho were not with them. After she had eaten her fill and then some, Lacey stood up and walked over in the direction of the bar holding her drink glass, thinking that she might reengage the Guimarãeses in conversation. Before she arrived, something else caught her attention. On the far side of the bar, against the rough wall of a low stone building and mostly obscured by two cork trees, two men were involved in an altercation. Her radar up, Lacey changed direction to get a better view and found herself in an open space near the ticket turnstile.

To her surprise, it was Dinis Guimarães and Rui Fonseca. The ox-like Dinis had the much slighter and visibly inebriated Rui by the lapels and was shaking him like a rat. Dinis appeared to be demanding something of the wretched Rui, who seemed incapable of answering in any language.

Lacey wondered for a moment whether she should summon help, but Inês's brother seemed to be in no real danger greater than he had brought upon himself through intemperance. Dinis was bellowing and shaking but not punching or strangling. At last, he shoved a piece of paper into Rui's pocket and let him go. Rui slumped to the cobblestones with his back against the wall, seemingly ready for sleep.

Lacey turned back toward the bar, suddenly aware that it had gotten very dark as the clouds had rolled up from the Alfama and over the castle. A rumbling peal of thunder rolled through the battlements, and a collective gasp went up from the guests. The band waivered. A second rumble, even deeper, shook the castle's foundations down to its Celtic roots. Yelps went up from the crowd. The band stopped playing and frantically began packing away their instruments. A third rumble, a blinding crack of lightning, and then total darkness as all of the lights went out. Then, with the piercing shock of a volley of Crusader arrows, a torrent of raindrops fell on the assembly.

Pandemonium broke loose. Guests were jumping to their feet and scrambling for shelter, knocking over waiters and their trays of sizzling churrasco. Plates and glasses shattered, chairs and tables toppled. The cobblestone pavement, suddenly treacherous underfoot, sent people sprawling into the paths of others fleeing the scene. Intermittent flashes of lightning illuminated a battleground of fleeing infantry leaping over corpses in the courtyard.

Lacey wasted no time making for the exit. The night was clearly over and the best chance for shelter lay in the cafes just outside the castle walls. Gathering her soaked skirt to her knees, she joined the partygoers slipping and sliding over the cobblestones toward the turnstiles.

She was pushing through the dripping metal bars when a hand gripped her shoulder from behind. Turning with torrential rain driving at her eyes, Lacey barely made out the forlorn figure of Inês pushing through the crowd to reach her.

"Where were you?" asked Lacey, clearing the turnstile with Inês now at her back. Lacey heard something in response, but it was obliterated by a rolling boom of thunder. Inês took Lacey by the hand and pulled her away from the castle as fast as their feet would carry them over the slick street.

The Guimarães clan had escaped the castle before them. Up ahead, Alfonso lumbered along, cursing loudly with Beatriz clinging to his arm with one hand and pointing at her shoes with the other. She apparently meant for him to slow down, but he did not. Beatriz made an appeal to Dinis, who, charging forward with a lowered head like a *toro*, left his parents behind. Beatriz stumbled twice. Pedrinho appeared out of the chaos and reached for her free arm. But at that moment the Guimarãeses were overtaken by a stampede of fleeing revelers who lost control on the cobblestones and plowed into Alfonso and Beatriz. Both crumpled and went down with wild imprecations.

What happened next lasted only a moment, and Lacey missed most of it in the confusion of gyrating bodies washed with sheets of rain. But the convergence of a flash of lightning and a car's swerving beams gave her just a glimpse of a curious event. While the absurdly discomfited Beatriz held out her arms for assistance with wails of malediction, Leonor Fonseca slipped out of the shadows and grasped the prone woman's purse, which lay out of her view behind her back. Lacey distinctly saw Leonor unzip the purse, thrust her hand inside, then zip it closed and drop it to the ground before disappearing again, unnoticed by the purse's owner. Whatever she had taken Lacey could not make out.

"Come, come," urged Inês. Lacey could not tell if she had seen her aunt's larceny, but there was no shortage of reasons for fleeing the scene as fast as possible. The lightning and thunder were now waging open war on the castle's battlements, and streams of water were gushing down from the heights along the path of least resistance, which also happened to be the street leading down from the castle. The doorways of the cafes were already jammed with refugees from the soiree. Inês dragged Lacey down the street, twisted and turned through several narrow alleys, and came out on a wider road. Miraculously, a taxi was stopped at the door of a restaurant, discharging a passenger. Inês waved wildly to the driver who nodded curtly. She dragged Lacey into the car, opened the back door, and stuffed the American inside. Lacey scooted across the seat to make room for her friend, but Inês was already slamming the door.

"I'll call you tomorrow," she yelled as the door closed.

Perplexed, Lacey started to open the door to insist that Inês jump in, but the driver was impatiently asking in broken English where to go. Lacey told him, then settled back with a miserable squishing of water on the leatherette seat.

The taxi was just pulling out when Lacey was startled by a frantic rapping on her window. The driver slammed on the brakes, nearly sending Lacey's head into the passenger headrest. Inês's bedraggled face was pressed against the glass. Thinking her friend had changed her mind about a taxi ride, Lacey started to open the door, but Inês shook her head and indicated that she should lower her window a crack. When Lacey did, she pressed her lips into the hole and asked, "Lacey, Mouse, you never told me if you discovered any clues."

Lacey stared incredulously, but Inês clearly was not going to leave without an answer. "Clues, any clues?" she insisted.

"Oh yeah," answered Lacey. "Fools, lies, and skeletons. Let's talk in the morning."

And, with that, the taxi sped away from the Castelo São Jorge.

Chapter 5

THE MOUTH OF HELL

"Are you sure we're supposed to be here?" asked Lacey. Her tone suggested a small measure of concern and a larger one of guilty pleasure.

"I'm sure that we're *not* supposed to be here," answered Inês tartly. "We are supposed to be over there."

Lacey's eyes followed the sweep of Inês's arm across an expanse of jagged limestone, broken occasionally by a clump of grass, to a well-fenced visitor's platform on the edge of the cliff. Three Japanese tourists stood compliantly behind the fence taking pictures of the deep blue waves rolling into the hollow before exploding into white.

"*Boca do Inferno*," said Lacey slowly, delighting in each syllable. "Boca, from the Latin *bucca*, mouth. Inferno, from the Latin *infernus*, lower regions. Dante, *Inferno*, nine circles of... you know, Hades. Which one is this?"

"Watch yourself, Mousie." Inês took her firmly by the arm. "There's a reason we are supposed to be over there and not here. Many people have been taken by the ocean here."

"Like your father?"

Inês released Lacey's arm. Lacey bit her tongue, worried that she had crossed a line. But, when Inês answered, it was clear that she had been thinking philosophically. "No, the ocean didn't take him. Alfonso Guimarães did." She shrugged matter-of-factly. "Let's keep going."

It was two days since Mother Nature's revenge at the Castelo de São Jorge. The two women had not spoken on the day after, perhaps each expecting that the other would initiate a call. For her part, Lacey spent the day wandering the alleys of the Alfama, stopping three or four times for coffee and *pasteis* between her exploration of quaint shops hidden in the nooks and crannies. She had plans for a similar day in the Bairro Alto, but Inês texted at 7:00 a.m. the next morning to suggest a trip to "the scene of the crime." By 9:00 a.m. the two were zipping along the Marginal highway in Inês's diminutive red Fiat. A salty breeze was blowing off the Atlantic when they arrived in the resort town of Cascais. Inês parked in a tourist lot near the cliffs, and the two women began their trek toward the mouth of hell.

"Here, hold my hand, Mousie," said Inês strictly. Lacey allowed herself to be led like a child. They had come to the edge of the cliffs and could peer down forty meters or more into the churning waters. Beyond the land's abrupt terminus, the sea stretched out to the horizon, unbroken by any vessel. Mariners did not like to get close to these cliffs.

Inês gripped Lacey's hand more tightly as they came to a place where the cliff narrowed to an arch spanning a yawning chasm. "Cliffs and airplanes," murmured Inês through tight lips. "Both of them will kill you. I've never been on an airplane, you know, and never will. Always took the train to London. I guess that means I will never visit America. Cliffs, they're just as bad, but here we are." Far beneath their feet, the ocean surged into the ancient sea cave whose roof had long since been swallowed by Poseidon. When the roaring waters reached the back of the cave and found they could go no further, they exploded upward in a saline temper. Every few seconds, a plume of spray reached almost to the women's feet.

"The seas are calm today," said Inês. "You should see it in winter. We would be soaked by now. Or worse."

Lacey nodded. "And the day your dad disappeared. What was the weather like?"

Inês looked surprised and possibly annoyed. "The weather? Why does it matter? He was pushed."

"I was just thinking—" began Lacey, but suddenly stopped. Inês seemed to have moved on.

"You never told me what you learned at the Castelo."

Lacey looked down at her feet, feeling their way along the edge of the cliff and the hungry waves rolling into the cave below. "Well, I saw some of what you said I would see. Beatriz is, like, horrible, and Alfonso is full of himself—although I'm not sure yet that he's a murderer. Dinis is a brute, but I already knew that. Pedrinho, though…"

"Yes?"

"He gave me a different impression than I expected."

"What do you mean? That's very general."

Lacey, still holding Inês's hand, thought she felt her friend's pulse quicken. She answered cautiously: "Well, if I'm looking for fools, lies, and skeletons, he's certainly no fool, and neither truthful nor a liar, and that leaves skeletons. He has his skeletons, or maybe they're ghosts, but I don't think they all have to do with—"

At that moment, Lacey slipped on a patch of lichen and Inês grabbed her sharply with both hands. "*Cuidado, menina!*" she exclaimed. "I've lost enough people here. But what were you going to say? His ghosts don't have to do with my family?"

"Not exactly that. That his ghosts don't all have to do with the Crooked Queen."

"I see. Is that all you learned?"

Lacey laughed. "Oh no. Of course not! But the rest…" she trailed off.

"The rest?"

"I'm still working on the rest. My mother always told me not to serve a half-baked cake."

Inês shrugged. "Let me know when it's out of the oven. Now come and see this."

They had come down from the edge of the cliff to a small, white plaque mounted on the face of the limestone. At the top of the plaque, engraved in large letters, appeared the words:

Não Posso Viver Sem Ti. A outra 'Boca De Infierno' apanhar-me-á não será tão quente como a tua.

Inês let go of Lacey's hand and said, "OK."

In their short acquaintance, the two had become so habituated to Lacey's affinity for divining Portuguese that Inês did not have to explain what she meant.

"OK, yeah," said Lacey, rubbing her palms with enthusiasm (or perhaps to restore the circulation). "The first part is easy. 'Can't live without you.' The rest... something about the mouth of, *ahem*, hell and 'like yours.' Someone comparing this place to someone's mouth. I think... 'the other mouth of hell that will catch me won't be as hot as yours.'"

Inês, who was becoming blasé about the American's unselfconscious genius, gave a half smile. "Right again. I won't make you translate the explanation below, partly because it would just encourage you to show off more and partly because it doesn't tell the whole story of this suicide note."

"Suicide note?"

"Yes, but not really. He was a Brit named Aleister Crowley and a real *esquisito*—a weirdo. He was famous as a magician and astrologer, founded a religion with himself as the prophet, and spied on Berlin communists for the British. In 1930, he came to Lisbon to meet the poet Fernando Pessoa. During his visit, he leaped to his death right here at the Boca, leaving behind this suicide note for whatever man or woman—there were plenty of both—happened to be his lover at the time."

Lacey shivered, a bit too enthusiastically.

"Yes, it caused quite a sensation in all of the papers. British cult leader jumps to his death at the mouth of hell; leaves behind a note for his lover."

"But it wasn't true. He faked it."

"You read ahead."

"No, you said 'not really.' Which means either it was murder rather than suicide, or he faked his own death. I'm guessing he was bluffing."

"I still think you read ahead, but that's right. Three weeks later, he suddenly shows up in Berlin for the opening of his art exhibition. It was all—"

"A publicity stunt."

"Yes, and it worked brilliantly. See, he has a plaque."

Lacey nodded and looked around. "So that's it for the mouth of you know what?"

"Yes, that's it. Did you expect something else?"

"I didn't expect anything."

"Did you learn anything?"

"Oh yes, this was useful."

"And..."

"And I'll tell you when the cake's out of the oven."

Inês laughed and released Lacey's hand. "You and your trade secrets! At least tell me if you know your next step."

"I do. Drop me off at my place, and I'll get right on it."

They drove back to the city chatting freely about other things. Inês did not have a boyfriend. Neither did Lacey. Each assumed the other was too religious to ask about a girlfriend. No, Lacey had not seen any of Europe. Where would she most like to visit? Paris, of course. And so on.

It was lunchtime when the Fiat pulled up near the Airbnb and Lacey took leave of her friend, promising to call the next day. She entered her garden apartment and flicked off her shoes into the corner. The only apparent lunch options sitting on the counter were a pale orange and two-day-old *pasteis de nata*. She reached instinctively for one of the *pasteis*, then checked herself, felt her still slender but perhaps slightly expanding waistline, and then reached ruefully for the orange. "Come to me, my little pretty," she muttered, taking the unloved citrus to the wicker chair next to the bed.

While Lacey ate the orange, wondering whether it earned her the right to eat the *pasteis*, she checked her messages and saw that her mother had called. Reluctantly, she called back.

Her mother answered on the first ring. "Oh, hi, sweetie. You haven't called in two days. Bar that bad?"

Lacey swallowed hard, hoping that the sound wouldn't carry across the Atlantic. "Uh, yeah, Mom. You know. All these crazy rules to learn. No interest is good unless it must vest not more than twenty-one years after some life in being at the creation of the interest—that kind of thing. Driving me nuts."

"Well, sweetie, I looked into airline tickets, and they're pretty cheap right now. I could come out and take care of you a bit. Cook, clean, that sort of thing. Wouldn't get in your way at all, sweetie."

"Uh, that's super nice of you, Mom, but I really just need to stay in the zone by myself right now. I'll come home after the bar exam. Promise."

"OK, honey, whatever you say." She sounded disappointed.

"Hey, Mom."

"Uh-huh."

"Maybe you should drive down to Aunt Sallie's for a few days."

"Why do you say that?"

"Well, Mom, it's just that... you know... Glennis..."

"What? Oh, sweetie, you think I just want to come out and see you to get away from your nephews and nieces?"

"I just thought—"

"Don't give it another thought. You know I don't mind Glennis... as much as you do."

"Right, Mom. I'll keep at it, and you keep at it."

They said goodbye. Lacey allowed her eyes to wander to the *pasteis*, then forced them back to her phone. In a moment, she was poring over a map of Lisbon, the wheels of her mind inexorably rolling over streets, plazas, churches, and anything else that might matter down the line.

Lacey remained rooted to her chair and phone until three o'clock, when she snapped out of her trance and went out again. It was a long, hot walk up the Avenida da Liberdade toward the Casa Fonseca offices. She had hopped the metro often enough to know that she could have shortened her trip by rail but welcomed the exercise and moist air to gather her thoughts. The pieces were still many and mostly unconnected, but shapes were starting to form. This afternoon might yield more definition for some of them.

At ten to four, Lacey set up vigil across the broad avenue from the Casa Fonseca. Traffic was bustling as the workday waned, and she barely felt the need to conceal herself as she flitted behind a pungent eucalyptus tree. At precisely 4:01—just enough time to dash down the stairs and away from responsibility—Rui burst through the door and began to hurry up the street in the direction of Praça do Marques de Pombal. Lacey donned a red Benfica baseball cap and a pair of absurdly dark sunglasses and set to follow at a distance.

As Lacey had suspected, Rui descended into the metro at Marques de Pombal and toward the blue line southeast. Lacey came equipped with a weekly metro pass and easily followed him into a crowded car. Rui plopped down in a seat reserved for the disabled and checked his phone. Balancing herself with the aid of a hand strap, Lacey kept him under surveillance from opposite the car.

After three stops, Rui hopped out at Terreiro do Paço with Lacey in veiled pursuit. The metro station exited next to the Praça do Comércio, an immense plaza enclosed on three sides by yellow, neo-classical buildings and fronting the harbor to the south. On the north side of the plaza, the triumphal Rua Augusta Arch commemorated Lisbon's rebuilding after the 1755 earthquake and beckoned tourists into the city. But Rui wasn't going back into the city. He took off at a moderate pace to the west along the estuary, in the direction of the 25th of April bridge.

Lacey followed at a distance. The Praça do Comércio was teaming with tourists and locals, giving her cover at least for the moment. In the center of the plaza, underneath a soaring statute of Dom José I the Reformer crushing Jesuits and other snakes, a banner proclaimed that a sporting goods store was holding a Cristiano Ronaldo look-alike contest. A gaggle of boys and young men holding soccer balls assembled for inspection. Mothers, sisters, and girlfriends formed a ring around the contestants, giggling and pointing.

Rui continued along the water's edge, skirting the trendy cafes of the Cais do Sodre and coming shortly to the commercial docks of the Port of Lisbon. Here the foot traffic became lighter, and Lacey had to fall back to avoid being seen. She watched from a growing distance as Rui wound his way through freight containers and dock machinery, moving forward whenever necessary to keep him in sight. At last, he reached his apparent destination on the far side of the wharf. Near the water's edge, a protected area populated with intermodal containers had been segregated by a chain-link fence capped with barbed wire. A heavy-set security officer sat in a folding chair at the gate.

Someone was waiting for Rui outside the gate. Lacey immediately recognized the bovine figure of Dinis Guimarães. From a distance, she saw Rui and Dinis exchange words in a businesslike manner, then present identification to the guard and slip into the protected area. They disappeared from sight into the maze of containers.

"Gotcha," she muttered triumphantly to herself but of course realized that she was overstating her triumph. There was still the small matter of getting past the security guard. Trying to keep out of his eyesight, Lacey maneuvered around to see if there was any other way in. There wasn't. Storming the gate it would have to be.

"Well," Lacey murmured to herself, "I could start by asking."

A moment later, the young American walked casually up to the guard, her face lit in a friendly smile. "Hi there," she said forthrightly. "Speak English?"

The guard glanced up from his phone and gave her an unfriendly look-over. "Yes, why?"

"Oh good. I need to get in there to meet my boyfriend." Lacey gestured encouragingly in the direction Rui and Dinis had disappeared.

The guard shook his head. "No, go in."

Lacey screwed up her face. "But he's waiting for me in there. He'll be angry if I don't come."

The guard looked annoyed. "Call him," he said, gesticulating toward his phone.

Lacey shrugged, took out her own phone, pretended to punch a number, waited a moment, then shook her head. "No good. He didn't answer."

"Then he no want you," said the guard, signaling brusquely that the interview was over.

So far, nothing unexpected. The likelihood of the guard letting her in for the asking had always been low, but the encounter had not been wasted. Lacey had collected quick mental notes: surly with a temper, not too fast on his feet, and most importantly, holding a clipboard. Time for Plan B.

Lacey nodded agreeably and walked away across the wharf. As soon as she was out of sight, she broke into a fast jog, retracing her steps toward the Praça do Comércio. Five minutes later, she was back in the sprawling plaza. Under Dom José I's baleful eye, the Ronald look-alike contest was just breaking up. Lacey looked around and identified a promising candidate: a tall young man wearing a Real Madrid jersey and carrying a soccer ball. He was walking away from the crowd with drooping shoulders and a sulky look.

"Excuse me," said Lacey. "Speak English?"

"Yes," he answered, looking at her curiously.

"Wow!" said Lacey. "You look just like him."

"Really, like Ronaldo?" the young man asked hopefully.

"Of course you do. Just like him." In truth, although Lacey was no great fan of the beautiful game, even she could recognize Ronaldo's iconic mug, and the one before her was off by many degrees.

"Well, I get fourth place," he said ruefully.

"That's not bad," said Lacey encouragingly.

"*Sim*, but only top three get prize. I... I get fourth."

"Oh, that's too bad. What was the prize for third place?"

"Fifty euro."

"Well," Lacey reached into her pocket and fished out two twenties and a ten, "I know of a way that you can still make fifty euros being Ronaldo."

A moment later, Lacey and the faux Pride of Portugal were jogging back toward the wharf. Lacey was beginning to sweat freely in the beating late-afternoon sun when they arrived at the gate. The guard looked up from his phone with an expression of mixed exasperation and curiosity.

"Hi again," said Lacey cheerfully. "Look who I just met. It's Cristiano Ronaldo!"

"That's not Cristiano Ronaldo!" exclaimed the guard with a snort. "Why you say this *merda*?"

"Sure it is. He's in Lisbon on holiday."

The guard stormed to his feet. "He look nothing like Ronaldo. Where's his..."

The guard pointed furiously at the imposter's upper lip.

"Oh, his mole? That's why he's in Lisbon. He had that removed. Plastic surgery."

"*Ta bem, espertinho*," he said threateningly to the imposter. Then, wheeling on Lacey, he demanded: "If he's really Ronaldo, show what he can do with ball."

"OK," said Lacey with equanimity. "Cristiano, show him your stuff."

The young man, who had been looking uncertain during this interlude, dropped his ball onto his foot and began juggling. The first three touches went smoothly, but the fourth shanked wildly off the side of his left foot. Lacey caught the ball, gripped it between her elbows, and clapped wildly.

"He no even dribble!" roared the guard, getting very red in the face.

"What, can you do better?" Before the guard could protest, she grabbed the clipboard from his hand, handed it to the fake Ronaldo, and handed the guard the ball. He stared at her in disbelief, then roared something in Portuguese and booted the ball high into the air. It sailed with ethereal majesty over rows of containers and landed inaudibly in the river, far out of sight.

"Well done!" said Lacey, clapping again.

But neither of the men was listening. As soon as the ball left the guard's foot, the fake Ronaldo took off at a run with the clipboard. Spitting with surprise and rage, the guard took off after him. Lacey watched as her hired hand gained ground on his pursuer—she had estimated that correctly—then she ducked inside the gate.

There was no time to lose. The guard was sure to return as soon as he retrieved the clipboard, which Lacey had directed be dropped just outside the dock. That would give her two or three minutes.

No one else was in sight in the enclosure. Lacey quietly passed rows of containers, listening for the sound of voices or cargo being moved. Soon, she heard a muffled conversation around the next corner. Quiet as a mouse, she crept to the edge of a rusted container and peered slightly around it. It was enough to see what she wanted.

Around the corner, a corridor opened into the mouth of another container, this one with its doors opened wide. By the light of a lamp, she could see three men gathered inside. Rui and Dinis were inspecting the cargo while a Middle Eastern–looking man loitered against the wall, his arms crossed.

"Persian," Lacey whispered to herself. This time, she was not surmising based solely on physical characteristics and dress. There was also a clue from the nature of the cargo. It was a stack five feet tall of exquisite Oriental carpets. Rui and Dinis were lifting them one by one, inspecting them inch by inch, turning them over, and then stacking them in a new pile.

Lacey was by no way a connoisseur of rugs, but even from a distance she could tell that these were first-rate. Intricately woven birds, beasts, flowers, and plants adorned silky backgrounds of red, black, and tan. The two or three Lacey was able to see glinted with the gentle patina of age. These were antiques, she guessed. So this is what the Fonseca and Guimarães boys were up to. Importing oriental carpets. But why together? And why the secrecy?

There was no time to ponder these questions. Lacey's internal clock told her that she had already overstayed. Soundlessly, she slipped back toward the entrance. The guard was just returning to the gate, breathing hard, his face scarlet with exertion and anger, his white knuckles gripping the clipboard. Seeing Lacey, he lumbered forward to catch her at the gate. They had roughly equal distances to reach the gate, which gave her the advantage. Spry as an elf, Lacey darted out of the gate just as the guard was arriving, sprang lightly past him, never looked back, and closed her ears to the imprecations hurled through the air, needing no translation.

As Lacey sprinted helter-skelter away from the dock and back into the Baixa, she thanked herself for having chosen the orange over the pastries.

Chapter 6

THE GRAVEDIGGER'S SCENE

For the rest of the evening, cozily alone with a bottle of port (to which she had taken quite a fancy), Lacey debated whether to tell Inês. Already, she had not mentioned Leonor's pilfering of Beatriz's handbag, since it did not have anything obvious to do with the Crooked Queen or Ricardo Fonseca's death. The same could be said for Dinis and Rui's furtive commercial operations. But Lacey was beginning to suspect that many interesting things she might discover would have nothing to do with her charge directly, even while everything to do with it indirectly. If Inês had been a client, Lacey would have felt ethically required to disclose her observations, but Inês was not exactly a client. She had held the power to get Lacey into trouble but chose not to wield it, and then had asked a favor as a friend. She had obviously not told Lacey everything there was to know about some things, even while bringing Lacey deep into her confidences about others. Perhaps there were things Inês wanted Lacey to find out, without ever having to speak about them.

At ten o'clock, just as Lacey was drifting into sublime relaxation, her phone rang. It was Inês. Since Lacey had not yet reached any decision on what to say about Rui and Dinis, she decided to say nothing for the time being. Fortunately, Inês did not ask her about her afternoon's sleuthing. She had something else on her mind.

"Hello, Mousie," she said a bit hesitantly. "I'm sorry to bother you this late, but something just came up."

"No problem. I'm awake, sort of."

"Listen, as I told you this week is the fifth anniversary of my father's death. The day is actually tomorrow. My mother is going to hold a visitation in his memory at her home tomorrow afternoon. I thought it was going to be just for family, but Mother insisted I invite you too. But really, you don't have to come."

"Oh, sure, I'll come," said Lacey quickly, sounding much more awake.

Inês seemed to hesitate again. "OK, but you should know it could be a little... strange."

"How so?"

"Well, it is a tradition with some old Portuguese families that a widow sits with her husband's bones on certain anniversaries. She'll be... well, dusting them off and holding them in her arms for three hours tomorrow afternoon while the family and a few close friends come by to comfort her."

"Really!" said Lacey, with far too much fascination.

"Really. If you come, you will see."

At five o'clock the following afternoon, Lacey hopped off the green line in the Parque das Nações north of the city on the Tejo's left bank. It was a short walk through the neighborhood of gleaming corporate headquarters and modern apartments to the building where Donna Maria had moved following her husband's untimely death. Lacey buzzed apartment 9B—the penthouse—for admittance. A man's voice she did not recognize came over the intercom: "*Sim, quem esta?*" Hoping she had not mistaken the address, Lacey answered: "Lacey Papparin, a friend of Inês." Immediately, the door buzzed open.

Lacey entered a pristine lobby of white and black marble, passed a row of bronze mailboxes, and found her way to the elevator. She rode alone to the ninth floor and exited into a long landing separating the two penthouse apartments. At the far end of the landing, a glass block wall looked out over the sparkling river and the Vasco da Gama bridge, Europe's longest. Judging from her apartment, Donna Maria had done well in the import/export business.

The door to apartment 9B was ajar, but Lacey decided it was best to knock gently. An older man dressed in a dark suit answered and beckoned her to enter. Either he did not speak English or had nothing to say to Lacey because he simply stood back and allowed her to pass him.

In contrast to the bright sunlight in the lobby, the apartment's interior was funereal. The foyer had a window that must have afforded a beautiful view of the river on less somber occasions, but it was covered in a black sheet. A single candle flickered dimly in the corner, and the faint aroma of incense lingered in the air. It was very quiet.

Lacey began walking uncertainly down the hallway leading out of the foyer. The candle was the only source of light for the moment. Fortunately, Inês appeared out of a doorway and hurried over to her friend.

"Hi Mousie," she said in a whisper. "I see Uncle Jose let you in. Thank you for coming. I'm sure it will mean a lot to my mother."

"Sure. Does she always keep it this dark?"

"No, no, it's just for today. We'll have you back over some time so you can see the views. Come, let's go into the living room where everyone's gathered."

They passed into a grand room with four marble columns and a row of windows, all draped in black. Around the perimeter, a circle of candles cast eerie light onto the backs of the twenty or so people seated in a circle of chairs. Their shadows flickered like wights on a low-pile carpet filling the center of the room. In the middle of the circle, seated on a severe mahogany chair, Donna Maria held her vigil. A black shawl covered her bent head. On her lap, a pile of bones and a leering skull kept her company.

Inês ushered Lacey to a vacant chair and sat down beside her. For some time, no one spoke. No one moved. Then a woman dressed in black rose made her way over to Donna Maria, knelt beside her chair, and took the widow's hand. Noiselessly, the two women caressed the bones one by one. Finally, they came to the skull. Donna Maria lifted it to the woman's lips for a kiss. The woman bowed to Donna Maria, then resumed her place.

For the next hour, this pattern repeated over and over again. At some understood interval, a mourner would leave his or her chair, kneel before Donna Maria's chair, caress the bones, kiss the skull, and then return to the silent vigil. Rui dutifully took his turn, adding the flourish of embracing his mother on both cheeks after pecking his father's skull. Lacey noticed that he wiped his lips as he took his seat. Leonor also presented herself, only she appeared to break down into a fit of convulsive weeping amid the bones on her sister's lap. Finally, Uncle Jose and another relative pulled her off and escorted her back to her seat, where she sat, clutching her crucifix. Her piteous sniffles were the only sound to be heard until they subsided after several anguished minutes.

At about the hour mark, Lacey began to debate when it would be her turn. It seemed presumptuous to go before Inês, and she had not seen her friend perform the odd ritual, but maybe she had gone before Lacey arrived. Eventually, it seemed that most people in the room had taken their turn, and there came a long lull. Lacey took a deep breath, rose, and approached the throne. Close up, Donna Maria's face shown pale in the distant flicker of the candles, barely more alive than the skull she cradled. Lacey knelt at the widow's feet as she had seen the others do. Without moving her eyes from the skull, Donna Maria took Lacey's right hand and ran it slowly over a bone. *The femur*, thought Lacey. *And now something that feels like a vertebra—gross. Now how funny, the humerus. And now, the skull. Show time.*

As Donna Maria lifted the skull of her dearly departed husband to the lips of a stranger, Lacey made her move. Rather than kissing the cranial remains of Ricardo Fonseca, she took the skull in her hands and pried it gently from Donna Maria's fingers. The widow let out a little gasp, but by the time she realized what was happening, Lacey had seized the skull and stepped two yards clear of her stupefied hostess. A louder gasp ran like a tremor through the audience as, one by one, they apprehended through the dim candlelight what Lacey had done. Clenching the skull tightly in her right hand, Lacey raised her left index finger to her lips and made a vehement "Shhhh!"

Instantly, the room fell more deadly still than before.

Lacey threaded her way through the ring of chairs right next to Inês without meeting her friend's eye and seized a candle in her left hand. Then, whirling about theatrically, she returned to the center of the room to face Donna Maria who, for the moment, seemed transfixed in her chair. Holding the skull aloft in her right hand and the candle in her left, the Mouse bowed low to the widow.

"Here's a skull now," she began in a rough masculine voice. "This skull has lain in the earth three and twenty years."

Then, whirling away from Donna Maria and as if back toward the original speaker, she demanded in a haughty voice: "Whose was it?"

The first voice answered: "A whoreson mad fellow's it was: whose do you think it was?"

Not a soul in the room stirred.

"Nay, I know not," the haughty speaker answered.

"A pestilence on him for a mad rogue! A' poured a flagon of Rhenish on my head once. This same skull, sir, was," here Lacey took a long pause, held the candle close to the skull, and peered deeply into its black crevices, "Yorick's skull, the king's jester."

"This?"

"E'en that."

Lacey strode back to the stricken Donna Maria. "Let me see. Alas, poor Yorick! I knew him, Horatio: a fellow of infinite jest, of most excellent fancy."

And, with that, she knelt again before the widow, deposited the skull into her pallid hands, curtsied ceremoniously, and walked purposefully out of the room. As she passed through the dark hallway she heard footsteps pounding after her, but she did not stop until she emerged into the luminous marble of the landing. Blinking as her eyes adjusted to the light, she stopped before the elevator and waited for Inês to catch up.

Her friend—if she still was that—burst out of the apartment and descended on Lacey, her red face flushed in tears. "What are you doing?" she demanded in a furious whisper, apparently forgetting that she had left the apartment.

"Hamlet," Lacey answered with equanimity. "Memorized it all in eleventh grade."

"*Why are you showing disrespect to my father's memory?*" Inês's whisper was now a muffled scream.

"I'm not."

"Don't you understand—"

Lacey cut her off. "Chill out, girl. Whoever's skull that was, it wasn't your father's."

Chapter 7

ISTO E FADO

"Are you sure about this?" demanded Inês, her face now much less red, but her dark eyebrows still furrowed. Three hours had passed since Lacey's stunning assertion in the penthouse landing. They were sitting in a café near the river a few blocks from Donna Maria's apartment. Lacey had offered no further explanation at the apartment, nor had Inês asked for one. After staring wide-eyed at Lacey for two full minutes, Inês had simply whispered that they should not speak about the matter any further until they were alone and suggested that they meet at the café once she was able to get away from her mother's side.

Lacey, having succumbed to the temptation of a *meia-de-leite* and a bola, discreetly wiped sugar crystals from the corner of her mouth and slid a manila folder across the table. "See for yourself."

"What's this?" asked Inês. She opened the folder and looked uncomprehendingly at its content.

"Dental records. Your father's. Fillings on left upper bicuspid and lower right and left second molars and crowns on lower right first molar and bicuspid. Our friend in your mother's lap had a very different profile, including evidence that two gold crowns had been removed to prevent casual identification."

Inês slammed the folder shut. "How did you do this? And you will not use the excuse of trade secrets this time!"

"I just walked in and took them. All of your family's medical records are in the bottom drawer of the credenza in the file room at Casa Fonseca. I came across them when I was, um, exploring. This morning, I dropped into the office. Leonor let me right in, thinking I had come to see you. Well, I just took what I needed and left."

"But how? How did you think of looking at my father's medical records?"

"It was the obvious thing to do once I heard about your mother's little ceremony thing. The obvious way to check if it was really your father."

"But that's what I mean. What made you think it might not be him?"

"Oh, that." Lacey paused and looked longingly at the bola, wondering if she might be permitted another bite before answering. Inês hadn't ordered anything, and it seemed rude under the circumstances to keep eating. She refrained. "Well," she said slowly, "now we're getting back into the fools, lies, and skeletons. I'm sorry to say this, Inês, but I think they might not all be with the other family."

She had rehearsed this line for the last several hours, but it didn't sound quite as benign coming out now as she had anticipated. Still, Inês seemed neither surprised nor offended. She shot Lacey a sharp look, gave the dental records another cursory glance, and then clicked her fingers for the waiter. She did not say anything until a coffee had arrived in the company of a little bread roll covered in coconut, egg glaze, and sugar.

"Well, Mousie," she said at last. "I was wondering how long it would take until you figured that out. Yes, our family has its issues too."

"What family doesn't?" asked Lacey lightly. And then she added, because she really couldn't help herself. "I'm sorry, but what's the name of that pastry? I didn't catch it."

Inês laughed, and a swell of relief seemed to pass over the table. "*Pão de Deus*."

"Bread of God. I'll have to try one. It does look divine. But now here's the thing about your father. Ever since you told me about his disappearance with the money from the safe, being seen by people leaving his car near the cliffs, and the discovery of his badly decomposed body, I had my doubts. Yesterday, at Boca do Inferno, when you told me the story of Aleister Crowley it suddenly clicked. A man famously fakes his death at the very place your father disappeared. Surely he knew that story too."

"But the coroner identified his body by the remains of clothing and his wedding ring and even his dental records."

"Which is not that hard to do with a little…"

"Backsheesh." Inês shrugged her shoulders in surrender.

"Backsheesh? Hmmm. Give me a sec. That's not Portuguese."

"No, but it's one of the many words we Portuguese have borrowed from the Moors. It means a tip, a bribe."

"Exactly. You see my point. If your father wanted to disappear—or someone else wanted him to disappear—how hard would it be to find the body of some poor lost soul, dress it up in your father's things, and bribe the coroner not to notice the discrepancies?"

"But then my father may still be alive." She took in a deep breath. "Then where is he?"

"The only way to start answering that question is by asking the antecedent one—why would he want to disappear?"

Inês gave Lacey a hard look. "I don't know, and I'm not sure I want to know."

"The Crooked Queen."

"You mean…" She paused uncertainly. "You mean that my father was the one who took it and then disappeared to cover things up?"

"That's one hypothesis. Do you have another?"

"No, but I don't like that one."

"So let's just keep it as a hypothesis. Look, we don't know that your father is still alive. He could have disappeared five years ago and died since."

Impulsively, Inês took Lacey's hands. "Thank you, Mouse. You have already done a great deal more for me than I had any right to ask. I have already imposed too much on your time. If you need to return to

America now, I can't ask you to stay on. But if you can stay a few more days, let the hunt now be for my father, not the *azulejos*."

It was Lacey's turn to laugh. "Are you kidding me? Things are just getting interesting. I can stay another week or two, as long as I can keep my mom at bay."

"Excellent!" Inês clapped her hands. "So what's next?"

"I think," said Lacey slowly, "that I need some time with your aunt?"

"Tia Leonor?" Inês seemed surprised.

"The very same. Do you think that she will talk to me after today?"

"Oh yes! Believe it or not, she was very taken by your performance of Hamlet. My mother didn't think much of it, but Tia seemed to think it was some sort of aristocratic English tribute. I think she would be very happy to have coffee with you."

"Port, yeah, there needs to be port," said Lacey emphatically.

And so it was decided that there would be dinner with port. The following morning, Inês called to report that Leonor would be delighted to sup with Lacey that same evening. They were to meet at eight at the Tasca do Fogo in the Baixa. "It's one of our family favorites. The food is only OK, but they have excellent *fado*," reported Inês with satisfaction.

"*Fado*? Fate?"

"Fate, yes. It's why you and I are together right now. But *fado* is about more than fate. You will learn all about it tonight, believe me. And maybe much more too, after a few glasses of the port."

The tiny restaurant was located off a cobblestone alley between residential buildings not far from the Praca Camões, where Lacey's Portuguese adventure had begun. Lacey arrived at three minutes to eight and found Leonor already waiting underneath a green awning outside the door. Leonor smiled warmly at Lacey's arrival and embraced her on both cheeks. "It's so nice of you to have supper with your friend's aunt," she said, then added with disapproval: "Most young ladies your age have thoughts only for the boys."

Lacey laughed. "We have boys back in America too, but I really want to learn all about Portugal while I'm here."

Leonor managed to nod with approval while making a contradictory *tsk* sound. "I wish I had thought of that when I was your age." Her hand reached involuntarily for her crucifix.

The maître d', who doubled as a waiter, seated them at a plainly set table near a small riser adjacent to the bar. "That's where the singers will be," said Leonor. "But not for an hour. More people will come," she added, indicating the nearly deserted restaurant. It was a cozy room divided in the middle by a rounded arch. Lamps mounted on the orange walls and candles on the tables provided the only light.

"Let me order for you," said Leonor as the waiter approached. "*João, Bacalhau à Gomes de Sá para a menina e para mim também. E uma garrafa de Ramos-Pinto.*"

The wine arrived first. "You know that port should be drunk at the end of the meal," said Leonor, nonetheless imbibing with vigor. "But our family—"

"Yes, I've heard that your family does things a bit differently."

"Yes. So many things."

"Like what?"

"Like business. Who runs a business like we do?"

"What do you mean?"

"It's a family business mixed with *family business*."

"I've heard that before too, but what does it mean?" asked Lacey, looking Leonor squarely in her black eyes.

But the chance for Leonor to say more pre-port evaporated as the waiter approached carrying two red clay pots and Leonor looked expectantly for Lacey's reaction. Shrugging off the lost opportunity for elaboration on the intrigues of the Casa Fonseca, Lacey peered optimistically into the pot. It was what her midwestern mother would have called a casserole, although that seemed far too vulgar a way to describe this simmering delicacy. There were thinly sliced potatoes mixed with onions and shallots, hefty chunks of garlic, and flakes of succulent cod, topped with lightly boiled egg quarters, Kalamata olives, and generous sprigs of flatleaf parsley. Lacey took a bite.

"*Deliciosa!*" she pronounced in her best Latinate accent.

Leonor smiled beatifically and reached for her port. "I see that my niece has been teaching you some Portuguese. *Que bem*! But now tell me all about yourself."

Lacey judged that a little investment in her personal backstory might pay dividends later in the evening, so she launched into a narrative not entirely dissimilar to the truth. There was childhood in Iowa, lots of corn, her father's death, and homeschooling. Her mother might have been surprised to hear about the university in London, her participation in an exorcism involving a transvestite Romanian warlock, and her ambition to become a Carmelite nun ministering to orphans in Africa. Leonor, however, was most impressed.

"*Quão abençoada*! How blessed!"

"Now tell me about yourself, Senora Fonseca."

"Oh, I'm not a Fonseca," said Leonor, with a mouth full of *Bacalhau à Gomes de Sá*.

"Of course, how silly of me. It was your sister who married into the Fonseca family."

"Yes, although I met Ricardo first."

"Is that right?"

"Oh yes. We were both students at the university in Coimbra. I still remember the first time I saw him in an economics class—so sure of himself, so funny, so handsome. I made a mistake introducing him to my sister! But I suppose it could never have worked out between us," she added wistfully. "He always thought me too religious, and I did not think myself religious enough! Anyway, I'm happy about that. I think he grew to love his *azulejos* more than anything else."

"You mean the Crooked Queen—the one that was stolen?"

"Not just that one. He became a great collector in Lisbon. It was his passion."

"That's funny," mused Lacey. "I didn't see *azulejos* at the Casa Fonseca, except in Inês's office."

Leonor made an indeterminate guttural noise. "Maria took them all down after he died. Maybe she thought he loved the *azulejos* more than her."

Lacey backtracked: "So you never married?"

"No, no. I'm the... what do you say in English? The old servant?"

"Old maid. But don't say that. You never know who will walk through the door next!"

Leonor shook her head darkly. "*Não, não.* That chance passed long ago." She stopped eating and peered bitterly into the dregs of her port. Lacey quickly poured her another glass.

"Tell me, how did you come to Lisbon?"

"I followed Maria and Ricardo, of course," answered Leonor, dabbing again at her *bacalhau*. "It was 1975, the year of the revolution. What a time!" She seemed more cheerful again.

"What was it like? They don't have revolutions in Iowa." Lacey was finding herself genuinely interested.

"Oh, it was a crazy time. People were so scared, but also excited. It had been dark for so long; at least that's how Maria and Ricardo felt. You know, I felt a little bit differently about it because of the church and everything, but I wasn't supposed to have my own opinions." An edge of bitterness returned, but then Leonor remembered something that brightened her mood again. "Let me put it to you this way because this is one thing that I clearly remember. Growing up, I only ever remember people dressing in dark clothes. No one said why, but it was because of the PIDE."

"The PIDE?"

"Salazar's secret police. They were everywhere, always. Everyone always had to watch what they said and did because you never knew who was a *bufo*—a spy. If the PIDE didn't like you, you might disappear for a week or a month or forever. No one wanted to be noticed; no one wanted to stand out. So people dressed in black and gray. But that changed with the revolution. Suddenly, the streets were full of color. The stores ran out of bright clothing. It was like a rainbow had melted into the city."

"That sounds wonderful."

"Whatever your politics, it was wonderful for a time. But such things quickly run their course. After 1975, Portugal was still a little better than a Third World country. Imagine this, Lacey. Portugal is smaller than your state of Iowa, but once our navigators ruled the seven seas. A country of a million souls controlled Brazil and large pieces of Africa and Asia. Gold, spices, and slaves poured in from our colonies. But all our power decayed over the years, and we became the heel of Europe. I remember the day we drove to Lisbon and our car had to stop four times because of sheep in the road."

"But it seems like a very modern country now," said Lacey, feeling the need to protest in the role of the cultured visitor.

"Yes, yes, there has been much progress. Here is an example. Just outside of Lisbon, there used to be windmills. For many years, Maria and I would drive out to one of them on the weekend to grind fresh flour for baking. Today, there are also windmills outside of Lisbon, but these are the modern kind for making electricity."

"I hope you still have some of the old kind too. I would love to visit one."

"You are a nice girl." Leonor took Lacey's hands and squeezed them in a manner reminiscent of Inês. Lacey saw a chance to shift the conversation but also wondered about dessert. Following Leonor's lead, she had sopped her clay pot clean with some excellent crusty bread. The bottle of port had been drained with the balance of trade decidedly in Leonor's favor. Seeming to read Lacey's mind, Leonor ordered another bottle of port and two servings of caramelized flan pudding.

Lacey was just about to ask another question when three musicians arrived and made their way to the riser. A heavyset woman wearing a dark shawl sat on a barstool and waited patiently while two men at her flanks unpacked a guitar and a mandolin. The restaurant, which had filled to about half capacity over the past hour, hushed to a dull murmur of whispers and the occasional clinking of forks or glasses. A waiter dimmed the lamps. Then, without fanfare, the trio launched into their first song.

Only the woman sang, and she never made eye contact with her accompanists or the audience. The men plucked and strummed their instruments with downcast eyes. The music was unadorned and deeply melancholic, casting shadows of lament to darken the soul. Lacey understood many of the mournful words, but the ones she didn't understand stung the more. There was heartbreak, unrequited love, and the dying embers of dissipated life. Occasionally, there was a hint of dawning, or of melancholy longing on the verge of joy, but that was only a tease, or a dim candle to accentuate the darkness. The *fado* laid bare the heart of a great nation in its twilight.

The fadistas sang for about half an hour, then retired to a table in the corner for a break. "So," asked Leonor expectantly, "do you like it?"

"No!" Lacey answered, surprising herself with the vehemence of her admission. Leonor looked hurt. "Wait, I mean, of course it's very beautiful, and I'll remember it for the rest of my life. But how can you say that you *like* something when it fills you with so much—"

"*Saudade*," filled in Leonor.

"What's that mean—wait, wait, don't tell me. Hmmm." Lacey drummed her fingers on the table. Even though she had drunk far less wine than Leonor, the combination of the *fado* and the port had left her feeling more moody than intellectual. "*Saudade, saudade, saudade*. I'm missing the roots. Maybe something related to *solitas*—solitude?"

Leonor smiled. "That's a good guess, but if you are going to learn Portuguese this way, you will have to remember that ours is a country of many layers. *Solitas*, maybe, but also *sawda* from Arabic, which means black like bile. So maybe a kind of black solitude."

"You see why I couldn't say I like it? It's very sad."

"Sad, yes, but never bitter."

Lacey noticed that it had been many minutes since Leonor had clutched her crucifix. On a sudden impulse, she decided to bring up a subject that Inês had raised but never fully addressed. "You Portuguese seem to have many sad stories, Tia Leonor. Like Pedro and Inês, the Crooked Queen."

"Oh yes, but that is a sad story." She shook her head mournfully and reached for her port.

"Tell me the story, won't you? It seems so... so connected to your family."

Leonor gave Lacey a sharp look, and for a moment it seemed that her hand would stray back to her crucifix. Lacey took the older woman's hands and said, almost in a whisper: "Tell me."

"OK," said Leonor. "But it's a long story, and our fadistas will return soon. But at least I can start now. Where to begin? Inês de Castro was a young woman from Galicia, which is in Spain, just north of Portugal. By the way, that is where St. James is buried, and I went there once on a pilgrimage, but we will not speak of that." She looked away for a moment, as if distracted, then resumed. "Anyway, her father was a Galician nobleman and her mother was a Portuguese noblewoman, but they weren't married, so poor Inês was called a bastard. As was the custom in such cases, she became a lady-in-waiting to a relative of higher standing, her cousin Constança of Castile. When Constança moved to Lisbon to marry Pedro, Prince of Portugal, Inês went with her."

"And so the trouble began," said Lacey dryly.

"Was it trouble? Well, it was a sin, that's for sure. Pedro never loved Constança. I don't imagine that she loved him too much either, but maybe she tried. Anyway, Pedro and Inês fell in love, and she became his mistress."

"That's a sin, all right," Lacey agreed.

Leonor continued. "Yes, a sin. And they both paid the price. At first, it was not considered anything important. Many nobles kept mistresses in those days. Pedro had a son with Constança. That was good for politics. But the boy was weak and sick. Pedro had many children with Inês, and they were strong and became popular at court. Inês's brothers became friends and counselors of Pedro. Pedro's father was King Alfonso IV, a hard man. He could have forgiven his son a lover, but not one who might threaten his rule. Alfonso was afraid of the growing Castilian influence over his son. He began to watch Inês carefully.

"Poor Constança; she did whatever she could to win back her husband. She made Inês godmother to one of her children, which made relations between Pedro and Inês technically incest. But that didn't stop them—they were fated to love, and to suffer for it. Constança got her revenge by dying in childbirth in 1345. Pedro must have thought he had received good fortune. He announced that he would marry Inês. But Alfonso would not permit it—she was a bastard. Eventually, Alfonso banished Inês from the court and ordered her held at the Monastery of Santa Clara-a-Velha in Coimbra."

"Coimbra, it all comes back to Coimbra, doesn't it?" asked Lacey.

If Leonor sensed any deeper meaning in the question, she didn't let it show. "Yes, Coimbra. That is where Pedro and Inês wrote the greatest love story of Portugal. You see, Pedro could not meet Inês openly, but there was a royal palace next to the monastery, on the left bank of the Mondego River. There were woods and gardens between the palace and monastery, and a stream that flowed through the rocks, separating the palace from the monastery. When they could not meet openly, Pedro would send messages to Inês on little wooden boats that sailed through an irrigation channel in the rocks. Some say that there are secret tunnels under the rocks and that at times they would come together. And there is also the most famous fountain in Portugal, the Fonte das Lágrimas—the Fountain of Tears."

"I believe there's a hotel nearby that everyone wants me to visit," added Lacey.

"Ah, yes, the Quinta das Lágrimas. Of course, in those days, there was no hotel, only tears. You see, putting Inês into the convent wasn't enough for Alfonso. He knew that his son's heart was still with her. And so he sent three assassins to Coimbra. Their names will always be remembered in Portugal: Pêro Coelho, Álvaro Gonçalves, and Diogo Lopes Pacheco. They came to Inês at the Fonte das Lágrimas and cut off her head, right in front of her little child." Leonor, visibly affected by her own story, dabbed her napkin at her eyes. "In front of her little child. The rock of the fountain is still stained red by her blood. You can see it at the Quinta, where the ghost of Inês still moves about at night, searching for her lost lover."

"Can't wait," said Lacey, with no hint of irony.

"After that, Pedro's heart was broken, broken. But he could not yet take his revenge, because his father was still the king. Alfonso died two years later, and Pedro became King Pedro I. Claiming that he had secretly married Inês, he declared her the queen of Portugal. Pedro had men dig up her body and place it on a throne, dressed in royal robes and a crown. All of the nobles had to come and kiss her cold, dead hand, giving her in death the honor that she could not enjoy in life. Pedro sat there watching all of them kissing her rotting flesh, looking with murderous anger for any who might show a sign of disgust."

"The Crooked Queen," whispered Lacey. "Her head..."

"Yes, her poor head, her poor body after two years underground. You saw what happened to Ricardo's body after five years..."

"Maybe," said Lacey vaguely.

"But did she deserve it for what she did to Constança? I've wondered that for many years." Leonor's voice dropped, and her fingers wandered to the crucifix. She seemed on the verge of saying something difficult, but at that moment the fadistas ambled back onto the riser.

"Let me finish the story quickly," she said, "and it's the part of the story you shouldn't think about too much. After becoming king, Pedro pursued the assassins across his kingdom and beyond. Pacheco was never captured and died in France, but Pêro Coelho and Álvaro Gonçalves were caught in Castille and brought to Santarém. While Pedro feasted, he ordered his men to tear out the two assassins' hearts, one from the front and one from the back. He said that they should no longer have hearts because they had broken his."

Lacey shivered despite herself.

"Pedro and Inês," Leonor said with a sigh. "Their bodies now lie in marble coffins facing each other in the Monastery of Alcobaça. When they rise from the dead, the first thing they see will be each other. Carved on their tombs is a promise from Pedro that they will be together *até ao fim do mundo*."

"Until the end of the world," said Lacey quietly, not even conscious that she was translating again.

"Their love lives on. Their story lives on in the hearts of all Portuguese. Especially in our family. Inês. They gave her the name." Leonor straightened herself self-consciously. "What am I saying? I am drunk."

"I am too," lied Lacey. "Say more."

But she did not say more. The languid plucking of a guitar, followed shortly by the vocalist's woebegone lamentations, announced that the *fado* break was over. Leonor turned back toward the musicians. Lacey slumped in her chair. Patience. Patience now more than ever. *She wants to say more. She's just getting up the courage.*

Another half hour passed in the company of sorrow. Leonor sat with her eyes closed, her pale and aging face expressionless in the candle's dancing shadows. She did not clap for the songs, nor drink any more port, even though half a bottle remained. Lacey studied her covertly, making a comprehensive mental file of anything that could prove relevant. Dark, drab clothing of a widow, bespeaking something pre-revolutionary in her own telling. Was that a fact, or a statement? Long fingernails faintly painted pink, subtly out of keeping with her clothing, as if the one protest to her spinsterhood. Her purse—expensive. However she might resent her sister's family, they paid her respectably for her work at the Casa Fonseca. Or was the purse a gift—and from whom? And what of the crucifix? Dinis Guimarães wore one too—so did many Portuguese. But was there anything in this particular crucifix and her relationship to it? When did she grope for it? When morals were threatened? No, when *Leonor* was threatened. What did that mean?

The fadistas wrapped up their second act and retired again to their table. Still thinking of her next move, Lacey excused herself to the ladies' room. As she was returning, she saw someone familiar seated at a table out of sight of her own table. It was Rui. He was seated with a young lady, apparently on a date. Lacey tried to duck out of his view, but it was too late. He caught her eye, and quickly rose and walked over to her. His demeanor was considerably less friendly than at the castle.

"What you do here?" he asked roughly.

"I'm having supper with your aunt," Lacey answered, gesticulating in the direction of their table. She instantly wished that she had made up some other story.

"Oh, eat with Tia," he said with a sneer. "Come, say hello." He took Lacey by the arm and walked with her to her table. Leonor's face darkened when she saw her nephew.

"*Boa noite, Tia*," he said sarcastically.

"*Vá embora*—go away," she said, forcefully indicating that he should leave.

Rui laughed, rumpled Lacey's hair, and left.

"What was that all about?" asked Lacey innocently, not even bothering to fix her hair. But it was clear that Leonor was upset and the evening was over. Leonor summoned the waiter for the bill, brushed off Lacey's entreaties to contribute her fair share, and announced that she was retiring for the evening. "I'm sorry, Lacey. You should not see our family like this. Thank you for tonight. You are a lovely young lady."

Lacey followed her out of the restaurant. There was one more question that she had to ask. "Tia Leonor, please, before you go, one last question."

Leonor paused in the cobblestone alley. "*Sim?*"

"That night in the castle, when we were all running away from the thunderstorm, and Beatriz Guimarães slipped and fell. I saw you take something from her purse."

Leonor stared at her very hard, then said quickly: "No, you are mistaken." Then she hurried off toward the Praca Camões.

Chapter 8

TO MEND A BROKEN TILE

Lacey slept lightly that night and didn't get up until nearly nine o'clock the following morning. But she kept busy during her somnolent hours, working the pieces slowly and methodically. At first, she imagined them pieces of a jigsaw puzzle, and grew frustrated in her drowsiness that so many were still missing. Little by little, her latent mind came to realize that she was working not with puzzle pieces but with tiles. Tiles, but there was a better word for it. *Azulejos*. That was it. The *azulejos* must fit together to form a mosaic, a montage. They must make a picture. But a picture of what? A picture of a queen. A crooked queen. Why was she crooked? Because she was dead. Or was that the whole picture?

She awoke without the satisfaction of an answer and went through the motions of setting out microwaved coffee, kiwi, and a day-old *papo seco* roll whose stale sins were hidden by a pat of salty, amber-colored butter. At half past nine, Inês called.

"What happened last night?" she asked, with only a hint of accusation. "Tia Leonor is in a sulky mood this morning."

Lacey was still not ready to discuss the Beatriz incident with her friend. "Everything was fine until Rui showed up," she said, feeling satisfied that this, at least, was the truth.

"Ai, those two! They have never gotten along. She asks for it, and he gives it. I didn't know he was going to the Tasca last night or I never would have sent you there."

"That's OK. It was useful."

"Yes?"

"Your father—I didn't know he collected *azulejos*."

Inês seemed to hesitate before responding. "Well, he did—a lot—especially in the later years, before the theft. My mother didn't like it for some reason. When he died, she sold most of them to a dealer in the Bairro Alto. They were worth quite a bit."

"But you kept three panels for your office."

"Yes, Father had given them to me."

"This dealer you mentioned. I want to talk to him."

"If you want to learn about *azulejos*, there's a whole museum."

"I don't want to learn about *azulejos*. I want to find your dad."

"OK, Mousie," said Inês with a little laugh. "You're the detective. Or whatever you are. I have meetings until the midafternoon. Let's meet at São Pedro de Alcântara at three-thirty. It's not far from there."

Despite having disclaimed any interest, Lacey spent the morning scouring the internet for information about *azulejos*. She was one of those people who can become absorbed in almost anything with a past and a future, and before long found herself transfixed at this window into the Portuguese soul. Though the firing of clay squares is an old idea, Lacey learned, the *azulejo* art form came to the Portuguese through the Mudejar Moors, who remained in Iberia following the Christian reconquest. It did not escape her attention—how could it?—that *azulejo* derives from the Arabic *azzelij,* meaning a flat or smooth stone, and that the earliest surviving examples from the fifteenth century display the geometric and floral patterns characteristic of Islamic art. Like so much of Portuguese culture, the birth of the *azulejo* reflected the intercourse of the Gothic and the Moorish, the Christian and the Muslim. Lacey could have made sense of those words intellectually before, but over the course of the morning they became pictures and patterns indelibly etched in her memory and understanding as her eyes moved sedulously across the centuries.

She reached back to the late fifteenth century, when the Christian kings were ruthlessly driving out the last of the Iberian Moors even while memorializing their Muslim brothers in the extravagant *alitacados*, arabesques, and parallel-piped *azulejos* of the Sala dos Arabs in the Sintra palace. (She made a mental note to visit.) Over time, the *azulejo* evolved away from its Mudejar roots into vibrant Gothic classicism of the Manueline period, when tile tableaus began to depict scenes from the Bible. Lacey lingered over a sixteenth-century tableau from a pool pavilion in Setubal depicting the heroic Susanna harassed by two lecherous elders. Being a Protestant, she didn't know the story from the apocryphal Additions to Daniel, but lapped it up with fascination and, in the end, with satisfaction, as young Daniel got the lechers executed for their sins.

Lacey watched with nostalgia as the didactic simplicity of the Manueline era gave way to the baroque exposition of the seventeenth century. Now *azulejos* consumed entire chapels, interspersing Madonnas, cherubs, and passions with falcons and birds of paradise. She followed anxiously as the polychromatic freedom of earlier years reduced to canonical blue and white presentation in the early eighteenth century and breathed a sigh of relief when an explosion of color and organic forms returned under rococo influence following the midcentury earthquake. Here, also, she remembered Leonor's words about Portugal as a faded colonial power as she browsed depictions of native inhabitants and trees from Africa, Asia, and the Americas in the Palácio Nacional de Queluz. Being an archaic sort, she wasn't bothered much to learn of the decline of the *azulejo* form in the nineteenth century in correspondence with Portugal's political and economic waning, nor was she that interested to learn of its modernistic revival in the twentieth century. Maybe she would have been more interested if it wasn't already almost two o'clock, with the morning's meager breakfast long since dissipated.

Dreamily—and feeling that her night had been rather continuous with her day—Lacey shut off her laptop with images of tiled gardens, palatial porticos, and Gothic churches swimming through her head. She had almost forgotten why she had spent the morning on this expedition—a voracious interest in the interesting can be a detective's Achilles heel—but now remembered that she must meet Inês on business. Exactly what her business was, or had become, she was not entirely certain, but she now felt bound to reach some resolution for, or with, Inês. Having received the promised wire of funds from her pharmaceutical client, she extended the Airbnb for another week and placed her airline ticket on an indefinite hold.

Lacey's mother had been silent for a couple of days, so there seemed to be no immediate threat of her showing up in Boston. A little time remained to play things out.

Lacey wandered on foot from the Alfama to the Baixa, then hopped the Santa Justa lift up to the Largo do Carmo. The skeletal Carmelite convent seemed friendlier than when she had rushed by it in pursuit of Black Jacket during the sardine haze of St. Anthony's feast but still gave her the willies. Black Jacket. There was an open question. If he hadn't nipped the biologics, what had he nipped? And why, or for whom? Dinis might know, but Dinis wasn't exactly accessible.

Lacey retraced the steps of her chase and emerged onto the Rua da Misericórdia just below the Igreja de São Roque, the former Portuguese headquarters of the Jesuits. Continuing past the church, she found herself on a ridiculously narrow sidewalk between the sheer church wall and the busy street. There was barely room for a single person to walk without slipping off the cobblestones into the street, and whenever pedestrians met going in opposite directions, one was forced to dart out into the street and pray that he could regain the sidewalk before a trolley or car zipped by. *Great place to bump off your cheating spouse or something*, she thought, because that was the way her morally decaying mind had come to work.

Emerging past the church into the heights of the Bairro Alto, she came to the rendezvous point, the Miradouro de São Pedro de Alcântara, a landscaped terrace with a stunning view of the castle and city. It was still a few minutes before 3:30, and there was no sight of Inês. Lacey wandered through the geometric gardens flanked by pedestals of the Greek and Roman gods and took in the orange roofs of the city and the distant, sparkling river. A gaggle of shrieking children played in the grass and gravel walkways, dodging the occasional street vendor on the lookout for tourists. Lacey made a mental note to return sometime so she could sit quietly on a bench with a *meia-de-leite* and some previously undiscovered species of pastry.

"*Ola, menina*," said Inês, coming up behind Lacey. "It's a splendid place, isn't it?"

"Yeah. I was just thinking about—"

"Coming here with a cup of coffee and a pastel," interrupted Inês.

Lacey looked first stunned and then crestfallen. "Have I become that transparent? First you catch me in the act of plundering your office; now you can read my mind. I must be losing it."

Inês laughed. "No, I wish I could read your wonderful mind, because I'm quite unsure what's in it most of the time. But you do give a few things away, Mousie, and your passion for our delicacies is one of them."

Lacey managed to laugh as well. "Well, give me a few more days, and I may start feeling the same way about *azulejos* too. They're growing on me."

"Really? I thought you said that you didn't want to learn about them."

"Yeah, well, that was before I looked. Once a girl looks..."

"Then let's go look some more."

It was a short jaunt up the Rua dom Pedro to Lunar Antique Tiles. The storefront was hidden among a row of mid-tier clothing stores, bicycle shops, pharmacies, and apartment entrances. It was the sort of place that one would never see unless looking for it, even then might easily miss it, and might well decide not to enter even if one found it.

The windows were protected inside by a heavy metal lattice, as though the proprietor were more interested in keeping people out than inviting them in. Through the barred front door, Lacey could barely make out a rough and, curiously, untiled cement floor and a dim clutter of oddments.

Inês tried the front door. Though a sign indicated they had arrived during normal business hours, it was locked. Inês rang the bell, and a moment later a short, older lady who might have been a housekeeper or a bookkeeper, but surely not a tile dealer, answered. She seemed to have been expecting Inês and opened the door with a welcoming gesture. The visitors waited in a front room jammed with worn pottery, urns, ceramics, candelabras, and tiles. Lacey felt mild disappointment. After her evening's reverie and morning's research, she had somehow expected to be ushered into a boudoir of kings, some tabernacle of ancient mystery and dramatic revelation. Instead, the store gave the impression of antiquity of the shabby and dusty kind, of age without elegance.

"*Boa tarde*, Senhorita Fonseca," said a thin, balding man dressed in an oxford shirt and pressed trousers.

This, undoubtedly, is a tile dealer, thought Lacey. Inês introduced her friend to Miguel Pereira, explaining that she was a college friend in Portugal on holiday and was interested in learning about *azulejos*. Not to buy, explained Inês. Her friend was traveling through Europe on a limited budget.

"Of course," said Miguel in impeccable English, as if he also had been expecting the visit. "It will be my pleasure to show you a few pieces. Come this way, please."

They passed through a narrow hallway lined with somber paintings of Portugal's naval history and into a room divided by a wooden staircase going up and a half-story set of stairs descending to a lower level.

"Down here is where I keep my most interesting pieces," explained Miguel as they descended through an increasing aura of dust into a barely lit sub-floor. If the upper level felt like a cluttered closet, the lower level felt like a mason's tomb. There were stacks of old tiles, many of them faded, chipped, or broken, lying all about the cramped room.

"These are organized by century," explained the proprietor, picking up a piece close to the landing and handing it to Lacey, who thought that "organized" might be an overstatement. "The piece you are holding is from the early twentieth century. I bought a lot of these from an apartment building that was being renovated. The style is Art Nouveau, very popular on storefronts before the first war. The tourists love it, but I find it foreign and not Portuguese at all."

Lacey studied the smooth ceramic depicting a brightly colored bird resting atop a vine-encircled flower. Miguel watched her closely for a moment, then asked strictly: "Do you see what I mean?"

"Of course," answered Lacey, returning the tile as if washing her hands of the plague.

"You do?" asked Inês. "I think it's quite beautiful."

"Hummingbird," said Lacey.

"I beg your pardon?" asked a confused-sounding Inês.

"Hummingbird. A species native to the Americas. Faunal appropriation, totally not Portuguese." She did not add that *azulejos* depicting exotic birds and animals from the colonies had been among her favorites.

Miguel nodded gravely. "Let's move back in time. Take this one." He handed Lacey a plaque of four square tiles mounted in plaster with a wood backing. The organic pattern of yellow and blue came together in the center of the plaque to form something in the shape of a throwing star. "What do you make of this one?"

It occurred to Lacey that this was turning into more of an interrogation than a browsing session, but she didn't skip a beat. "Of course, the plaster and wood backing is very recent—probably something that you did here." Miguel nodded. "The tiles themselves I'm going to put in the middle of the eighteenth century."

Inês, who seemed to have realized it wouldn't pay to doubt Lacey's guesses, protested: "You skipped the nineteenth century, Miguel."

"No, he didn't," retorted Lacey. "The nineteenth century skipped itself." She moved closer to Miguel, effectively cutting Inês out of the discussion. Then, not waiting to be served the next course, she began rummaging through stacks of tiles. "I'm skipping these boring blue and white ones from the early eighteenth century—they're just copied from the Dutch… but here's an interesting one." She fished out a small, individual piece. It was chipped and badly worn but still clearly showed the form of a rat crouching amid green plants.

"Wait, I know that one!" said Inês suddenly. "It was from my father's collection. Or at least one very like it."

"*Sim*," agreed Miguel. "You remember that your mother asked me to sell them after your father's death. I sold almost all of them to another dealer, but this one got left behind."

"So," said Lacey to Inês. "Tell us about it."

"Oh, I don't know," answered Inês with some irritation. "My father was the expert, not me."

"Seventeenth century," Lacey announced without superiority or condescension, but only that equanimity born of being right. "This would have been part of a pictorial bestiary, maybe in a garden or around a bath."

"Yes, a villa garden fountain in Coimbra." Miguel did not seem at all bothered that she had taken over. "There were many other pieces—dogs, boars, roosters, deer, all kinds of fantastic beasts like hydras, fauns, satyrs, nymphs. It would have been exquisite in its time."

"Coimbra," Lacey repeated. She seemed on the verge of asking something, then checked herself and asked a different question. "Why didn't you put them back together into the original tableau? I expect that would have been much more valuable than the individual pieces."

"Yes, but the fountain had been very neglected and many of the pieces were broken. To mend a broken tile—that is very difficult. It takes a master. But Portugal is full of well-preserved *azulejos* still in place in churches and palaces and gardens, so I can sell the small pieces to the collectors."

"And now we've come to the beginning of time, which means the end of your collection," said Lacey, holding up another four-square on plaster and wood. "This one I will handle with special care, because I can see it's very old. Late sixteenth century, Senhor Pereira?"

"I see that you are more than familiar with *azulejos* already," said the proprietor, giving Inês a shrewd glance sideways. "Tell me what *you* see."

"I see," said Lacey slowly, caressing the geometric relief patterns, "I see the hand of the Moors, who cost Camões his eye. I see blue for cobalt, green for copper, brown for manganese, yellow for iron, and white for tin. And I see the marks of authenticity, that tell me that you are one of the few dealers in Portugal that is selling genuine Mudejar tiles and not trying to dupe gullible tourists with cheap imitations from Tunisia."

"Really!" exclaimed Inês, who had been trying for a while to get back into the conversation and now brusquely elbowed her way back in, at some risk of causing Lacey to drop five hundred years of history. "How can you know that, Mousie—apart from the obvious fact that I would not bring you to a counterfeiter?"

"Yeah, well, there are three signs," answered Lacey with confidence. "First, see these runs in the colors? Imperfections that later craftsmen would not have tolerated. But for the first Portuguese craftsmen, the applied glazes inevitably ran in the kilns. These blemishes are the beauty marks of genuine Mudejar tiles.

"Second, see these little indentations in the shape of a triangle?" Inês peered closely and nodded, while Miguel watched coolly from a distance. "In order to keep the running of the glazes from going from beauty mark to scar, the Mudejar craftsmen baked them face-up in the kiln, with ceramic tripods separating the pieces. Another blemish, another mark of truth.

"And finally..." She handed the *azulejo* to Miguel. "Well, this has nothing to do with this tile, but, good heavens, look at this place! We're standing in a dungeon knee-deep in dust. The lighting's terrible, the doors are locked, the windows are barred, the organization is slip-shod, no one offered us coffee, and there isn't even an American Express sign anywhere. No, this is the real deal."

Inês looked horrified—although not as much as after Lacey's Hamlet performance—but Miguel allowed a hint of a grin to play at the corners of his mouth. "Thank you for your visit," he said. "Inês told me that you were an extraordinary young woman, and I can see what she meant."

Lacey blushed. "No, stop it. I just started reading this morning on the internet and got interested."

"I can't allow you to leave without taking an *azulejo*," he answered.

"No, no, as Inês said, I'm on a budget."

"But you cannot leave Portugal without an *azulejo*, Ms. Papparin, not after that performance. It will be my gift to you. Here, take this one. I believe that your nickname is Mouse, yes?"

He handed her the tile with the rat.

"Well, thank you, Mr. Pereira," she said, sounding suddenly shy. "That is very kind of you. I will keep it safe. I think my mom will get a kick out of this, although she obviously doesn't know about my nickname." She kicked herself for saying that last bit, but Miguel didn't follow up.

The visitors thanked Miguel for his time and left the shop. Inês said that she would catch the metro at Baixa-Chiado, and two women began down the street.

"I'm surprised that you didn't ask about my father," said Inês when they were well clear of the shop.

"Is that what you told him I would ask?" answered Lacey, with a bit of an edge in her voice. "But, actually, I did ask, and I guess you didn't hear me."

Inês sighed deeply. "Oh, Mousie. I wish you would tell me more directly what you're up to. I'm not good at riddles."

"And I wish the same," said Lacey. She could not bear to look at Inês when she said this, but her companion's silence suggested that she had hit a mark.

They walked along in silence past São Pedro de Alcântara. Below the overlook, the city shimmered in the summer heat, not different than it had for hundreds of years. Looking to the distant river, Lacey wondered if anyone had been standing at that very spot on All Saints Day in 1755 to witness the tsunami ripping up the Tagus to swallow ships and sailors, before rolling into the city to gorge itself on people fleeing on horseback and trapped in the rubble of their homes. Intermittent thoughts of the earthquake had made her uneasy since she had passed the remnants of the Carmelite convent during her chase of Black Jacket. Seeing the convent again that afternoon had re-upped her creeping sense of a goose walking over her grave, of an undefined danger lurking underneath the cobblestones or behind the tiled walls of the Bairro Alto. It was an irrational fear, she realized. Then again, she countered herself with a twitch; instincts are not always rational.

Lacey realized that she was falling behind Inês and hurried to catch up. The two women continued in single file along the narrow sidewalk skirting São Roque's western wall. As they came to the plaza in front of the Jesuit church, Lacey suddenly broke their silence: "Darn! I left my hat at the shop. You go on without me."

"It's not far," Inês answered. "I can wait for you here."

"OK. I'll be right back."

Lacey half jogged back up the street, playing chicken with pedestrians coming in the opposite direction along the narrow sidewalk. She scurried past São Pedro de Alcântara, consciously averting her eyes from the panorama of the city. A moment later, she was back at the door of Lunar Antique Tiles. She rang the bell, received admittance, and soon reemerged wearing her red Benfica hat. A few moments later, she was scurrying along the narrow sidewalk adjacent to the church for the fourth time that afternoon.

It had struck her as an uncanny place each time she had passed that way, but this time her spine was tingling. The traffic had picked up in the late afternoon and a steady stream of cars, motorbikes, and trolleys whizzed by inches from the sidewalk. Since pedestrians generally kept to the right, the person coming down was always adjacent to the street, and Lacey found herself constantly dodging in and out of traffic to accommodate pedestrians coming from the opposite direction hugging the church's wall. When she was about halfway past the church, a cold sweat broke on her forehead. Something was not right; she was sure of it. Looking up ahead, she could see Inês waiting patiently at the corner of the church. She felt an almost irresistible urge to jump onto the street and make a mad dash for her friend. Trying to hold herself together, Lacey scanned the few oncoming pedestrians left between her and the end of the sidewalk. Just a pair of older British tourists obliviously reading a map, a school girl carrying her books, a businessman talking too loudly on his phone and—

Too late; it all came together. The next person in file loomed up suddenly before her. In a dreadful instant, she recognized a profile, a beard, a pair of dark sunglasses, a black jacket. His shrouded eyes were on her, his hulking body bore down with deadly intent. Lacey tried to whirl about but crashed into a fat boy behind her who pushed her back into the path of Black Jacket. His shoulder and hip swung into her viciously, and she bowled into the street and into the path of an oncoming taxi.

In the slow motion of the next seconds, Lacey heard several distinct sounds. There was a squealing of tires, a blaring of horns, excited shouts from the sidewalk, and, above it all, the ear-piercing screams of Inês. Lacey expected to hear the crunching of her own bones as well, but perhaps, some six thousand, seven hundred kilometers away in Iowa, Daisy Papparin was praying for her daughter. To her surprise, Lacey found that she had nicked the bumper of a car, rolled over three times, and landed back on the sidewalk quite intact.

Inês was on her almost as quickly as Black Jacket had been, and Lacey found herself smothered in her friend's teary grip with sobbing inquiries about whether she was hurt.

"No, I'm fine," she answered quickly. "Let's get out of here." A gawking crowd was awkwardly—and hazardously—forming along the narrow sidewalk. Black Jacket was nowhere to be seen.

"Thank God!" said Inês, her tears abating. "I thought you were going to be hit. We must find the police."

"No," Lacey said sharply. "Quickly, into the church."

Inês did not argue. Fleeing the crowd as if they were the wrongdoers, the two women passed through the doors of the Igreja de São Roque. As they entered the baroque building and caught a glimpse of the gilded reliquary altars housing martyrs' bones, Lacey had a vague recollection that this church was one of the few buildings left unscathed by the earthquake. Somehow, that calmed her nerves. The two women stepped into an empty chapel off to the right, where ornate gilt woodwork covered every surface of the walls and ceiling.

"That was Black Jacket," hissed Lacey, not wishing to break the deep silence of the church. "The guy who stole the briefcase."

"Why?" demanded Inês. "Why did he try..." She could not finish the thought.

"I don't know yet, and I swear I'm not hiding anything from you."

"You're in a church, Mousie. You had better be telling the truth."

Lacey glanced about. High above in the center of the gilt wood, St. Anne held aloft her daughter, the baby mother of God, and imparted to her sound doctrine. *Perhaps Daisy Papparin should have done better with me*, thought Lacey.

"Listen, Inês. I'm not hiding anything from you. I swear by... well, you know that I don't swear. I haven't told you everything that I've seen or suspected because I can't work that way. It's not just trade secrets. It's..." She wasn't sure exactly what it was. Just instinct, maybe. The same instinct that might just have given her a second's forewarning and saved her life.

Inês put her hands on her hips. "But you must report this to the police. That man is dangerous. He may try to hurt you again."

"No. If I go to the police, I may never find your father. But I promise to be careful. I have one more appointment here in Lisbon tomorrow, and then I will leave the city for a while."

"Where will you go?"

"I'm not sure yet, but I'll call you in a day or two. Now you go on home. I'm going to stay here for a while."

"What for? So he doesn't follow you?"

"No. To see what I can learn from St. Anne."

Inês was not at all happy about any of this, but she soon saw that Lacey's mind was quite fixed. After poking and prodding at Lacey for five minutes to make certain that she wasn't suffering any latent injuries, Inês gave her friend a hug and kiss and disappeared back into the world.

Lacey lingered for many hours in the Chapel of Our Lady of Doctrine. If previously she had been a field mouse, she now became a perfect church mouse. Sunken stock-still in a recess of the chapel, she became virtually invisible to passersby. With her eyes alternately fixed on the iconic St. Anne and closed in meditation, she slipped into a well of deep tranquility.

What little daylight crept into the church through its high windows had long since faded when the mouse finally stirred. What made her move was not any desire to leave her well but a sensation in the pocket of her jeans that had been growing uncomfortable over the past quarter hour. She couldn't immediately remember what it was and had to stand to retrieve the object from her pocket. She was dismayed to see that it was the tile of the crouching rat that Miguel had given her, broken in two by her fall. *I promised to keep it safe, and here I've already broken it.*

But then a thought came to her, and she laughed, making the first noise she had in many hours. *To mend a broken tile. Yes, to mend a broken tile.*

As she walked back to the Alfama, she felt no fear, but she did stay in the shadows.

Chapter 9

THE COMMITTEE TO SELECT PROMISING SCHOLARS

Beatriz Guimarães approached the gate of the American embassy sporting a blue power suit cut at the knee, a white blouse, and a red Hermès scarf. It bothered her that there were little golden anchors here and there on the scarf, but that was the only red scarf she had in her closet and the invitation had come on such short notice that she had not had time to organize a proper shopping spree. She would have to hope that the Americans would forgive the anchors. Or maybe they would think it an encomium to the US Navy's Second Fleet, whose vessels occasionally put in at Lisbon. Beatriz had been invited to a party on a US destroyer docked in Lisbon once and had been mortally disappointed to have to leave early when Alfonso had gotten seasick and retched off the poop deck.

But here was an opportunity for redemption. If there was one thing that Beatriz understood, it was power. Actually, there were two things—power and money—but they were so connected in her mind that she filed them together. In her youth, she had studied for a year in Manhattan and come away with the definite impression that Americans had power and therefore money, or maybe it was the other way around, but the direction of causality seemed unimportant. What was important was that Beatriz

Guimarães's status in the great hierarchy of the universe depended on the success of the Casa Têxtile Importação e Exportação, which in turn depended on the firm's relationship with people of power and money, of which Americans seemed to have an endless supply.

It was not that she held Americans in undifferentiated high regard. New York had been full of annoying people, particularly taxi drivers, shopkeepers, and university bureaucrats who spoke rudely—when they were comprehensible at all—and didn't seem to understand social hierarchy. And then there had been that American girl who had shown up at the Castelo party in the company of the Fonseca scum. Beatriz had immediately seen that she was the wrong kind of American—not from the coasts where most of the rich and powerful people were, unless they were from Texas, but from the vast paleolithic interior, where people drove pickup trucks and married their cousins. The American tramp would have been the kind to dislike on her own merits, but the association with the Fonsecas put the matter over the top.

As Beatriz handed her *Bilhete de Identidade* to the guard at the gate, she wondered, with unconscious modesty, why exactly she had been asked to help out in this particular way. To be sure, she was well known in Luso-American social circles as the wife of an important businessman with stateside dealings, and it was further known that she had studied in New York and that her English was respectable, but this was not exactly the sort of task for which she thought herself comparatively advantaged. They could have asked her to host a soirée for the ambassador, or a luncheon for women in business—which she was, at least by marriage. This job, on the other hand, sounded like the kind of thing to be asked of effete university intellectuals with shabby clothes and shabbier politics. Still, Americans smelled of money, and now she was in their house.

A receptionist at the front desk took Beatriz's name and business and summoned an embassy attaché. The attaché, a middle-aged woman who was probably Portuguese but with an American passport, greeted Beatriz cordially, thanked her on behalf of the Fulbright Committee to Select Promising Scholars, and walked her down a shiny corridor to a conference room. The attaché opened the door without knocking and escorted her guest inside. There, Beatriz froze like a petrified victim of her namesake, Medusa. Seated on the far side of a long wooden table, the only person in the room, was that American girl from the Castelo party.

"You!" said Beatriz, the words escaping involuntarily from her lips.

"Yes, it's me!" said Lacey brightly, leaping to her feet and rushing over to pump Beatriz's hand with vigor. "Last time we met, you called me a *puta*, and I still haven't figured out what that means!" Lacey laughed uproariously and slapped Beatriz on the back. The attaché, who seemed to think it was all an off-color joke, laughed too. "I see you've met," she giggled. Seething from head to toe but bereft of any choice in the matter in the presence of an embassy employee, Beatriz had to join in the laugh too.

The attaché indicated a stack of manila files on the table and started to give instructions. "Wait," said Beatriz, sounding imperious despite herself. "Shouldn't we wait for the other members of the committee?"

"Oh no, it's just the two of you today," said the attaché cheerfully. "Hard to find people willing to do this job," she added with a wink.

This bit was entirely true and accounted for the ease with which Lacey had orchestrated the setup. Pulling off something like this might have seemed like magic to Beatriz—which is why she didn't suspect a setup—but it was ordinary science to Lacey. It had started with a single chain of words that Lacey had once read somewhere, and never forgotten, because she didn't forget anything: Fulbright Committee to Select Promising Scholars. To this chain she added the recollection that the Fulbright program was meant to be a two-way street, with Americans going abroad and foreigners coming to America, and now calculating at a speed approaching that of light, surmised that someone, somewhere must pick promising young Portuguese as Fulbright scholars, and that somewhere must be Lisbon, because there would have to be interviews of these Promising Scholars, and Lisbon was where they were. In short order, Lacey also calculated that the Fulbright program, belonging to the US government, this activity must reside in the seat of the American government in Lisbon—the embassy. And, finally in the chain of progression—although this all occurred within a few microseconds within Lacey's extraordinarily fecund brain—she calculated that, of course, the embassy must always be in short supply of qualified people to read through the application dossiers, because who on earth would want that thankless job? Having exposed the delicious possibility in a chain reaction of rarified recognitions, there was the simple matter of making it happen, which merely involved a call to a lawyer in DC who owed Lacey a favor for exposing the CEO of an adverse party as having faked his MBA, that lawyer calling his best friend from Harvard, who served as associate general counsel in the State Department, that person calling someone in the Bureau of Educational and Cultural Affairs, and that bureaucrat letting Lisbon know of two highly qualified people who would love to serve on the Committee to Select Promising Scholars, so long as it happened this week. QED.

The attaché now finished the instructions on reviewing the files—basically, just select the three or four most promising out of the stack of twenty-seven for forwarding on to Washington—thanked the two guests for their service, and took her leave. As soon as the door gave its magnetic click, Beatriz sprang from her chair like a jack-in-the-box and confronted Lacey with an outstretched index finger tipped with a blood-red fingernail. "You!" she repeated, as though the personal pronoun held inherent potency to wound when hurled from her curled lips. "What are you doing here?"

"Well, Sugar Belle," Lacey said with a drawl. "I was planning on reading some files, but now that you're here, what'ya say we call it a party?"

"I will not be mocked!" spluttered Beatriz, with unpleasant memories of insubordinate New Yorkers of the lower classes flooding back to mind. "You will be sorry for that. I am friends with the ambassador himself."

Lacey's smirk widened. "I bet you're making that up."

"How dare you!"

"OK then, what's his name?"

"I will not take this!" exclaimed Beatriz, marching toward the door. By the time her hand was on the handle, she realized that this was a miscalculation. The goal must be to get the girl to leave and for herself to stay. "*Bem*," she said, whirling back around. "It's Nichols."

"You call your friend the ambassador by his last name?"

"Of course not, you stupid girl. I call him..." she paused, seeming to realize with growing panic that she was not entirely certain of his first name. "I call him Norman," she exclaimed triumphantly, after a moment.

"That's funny," said Lacey. "My uncle calls him Norm." She had been planning to say "my father," but, at the last second, remembered that the Fonsecas knew her father was dead. No sense taking the chance that the Guimarães family had heard that too.

"Oh, your uncle, eh? So tell me *his* name."

Game, set, match, and Beatriz—who, although a shrew, was not an idiot—realized it at once. The ambassador's name was instantly verifiable; Lacey's uncle might have *any* name.

"Patrick O'Malley," said Lacey winsomely, "and he lives in Chicago." *Good luck checking on your phone for Patrick O'Malleys in Chicago, Medusa.*

Beatriz walked slowly back to the table, each click of her heels foreshadowing a nail in the impertinent American's coffin. Without looking at Lacey, she took the file at the top of the stack and began reading.

Lacey gave her about thirty seconds, and then said: "Now that one's interesting. Ze Tomas Silva Maria da Olivera from Braga. Father is a store clerk at Carrefour; mother died of pancreatic cancer when he was six. Ze basically raised himself and was the first in his family to graduate from university, at Catolica, where he had perfect grades. He wants to study international relations at Georgetown in order to enter the diplomatic corps."

Beatriz snorted. "These kids from poor families always think they can tell some story to make us feel sorry for them. That doesn't make them any smarter." As she ended this thought, an uncomfortable realization seemed to come over her. "But how did you know all that?"

Lacey leaned back in her plush leather chair. "I got here an hour ago to read the files. Like to get a good head start, ya know."

"But how..." Beatriz trailed off.

"How did riffraff like me remember all of these details from the file? Well, my dear, that's for me to know and you to find out."

"It doesn't matter," scoffed Beatriz, tossing the file onto the table. "I'm starting the *no* file." She took the second file and began reading. After a moment she said: "Now this one is better. Good family, I've heard of them."

"Ah yes, Matilde Maria Teixeira. A precocious little girl from the beginning. First in everything. First to walk. First to read. First violin. First in her class. First to have a baby—although I do think that seventeen's a little young, don't you?"

"What, where does it say that?" demanded Beatriz, scanning the file with dagger eyes.

"Of course it doesn't *say* that! But surely you noticed the year's gap in the résumé."

Of course Beatriz *hadn't* noticed, but she recovered quickly: "She could have been sick."

"Aw, you're a bit of a softie after all, Beatriz. But, no, if she had been sick, that would have been in her personal statement. There's only one other thing it could have been—a year in prison—but we want to give people the benefit of the doubt, don't we, Beatriz?"

Beatriz tossed the file to join Ze Tomas Silva Maria da Olivera's. "Don't bother with the next one," advised Lacey. "He can't put together two words in English." Beatriz, who was beginning to feel like a marionette but saw no way to stop it, did as she was told, tossing the next file into the *no* stack and moving on down the pile.

The room fell quiet. For half an hour, Beatriz read through twenty-three more files, sorting twenty into the *no* stack and leaving three as *yeses*. Lacey watched her work in silence until the stack was down to one last file.

"I'll admit to being up in the air about the last one," said Lacey, breaking the silence. Beatriz shot Lacey a quick glance and sat listening without opening the file. Lacey continued. "She seems very religious—not the sort of worldly person I imagined for a Fulbright Scholarship. Also, she's Portuguese but lives in Santiago de Compostela in Galicia. What do you think about that?"

Beatriz scowled. "About her being religious or living in Spain?"

"Both! I understand that people go on pilgrimages to the Cathedral of Santiago de Compostela to venerate St. James. Leonor told me that she did that once."

For the first time, Beatriz's expression appeared more shrewd than angry. "Did she? And what did she tell you about this... this pilgrimage?"

"That's the funny thing. She wouldn't tell me anything about it."

Beatriz pushed back the files in front of her and leaned toward Lacey, with a triumphant gleam in her narrow, savage eyes. "Why do you suppose she won't tell you about it? What do you suppose she is hiding?"

"I have no idea."

"Oh, but I do. Yes, I do." Beatriz's voice became dangerously quiet. "Yes, I know many things about your dear friends, the Fonsecas. Things that the world doesn't know. Things that should *never* come out."

"But you obviously want to tell me."

"Why should I tell you anything, you piece of trash?"

"OK," said Lacey with a little shrug. "Read the file then."

Beatriz slammed closed the manila folder Lacey was trying to open for her. "Not so fast," she hissed. "You think you're so clever, you little tramp. Maybe you're working for *them*. Well, know this. It will never help. My club is still bigger! Go back to America to make babies with your cousins before you get hurt!"

With that, Beatriz grabbed her purse and stormed out of the room.

Lacey remained in the conference room for another ten minutes to make sure Medusa didn't return. Before leaving, she took two actions on behalf of the Committee to Select Promising Scholars. The last file, which Beatriz had never read, in fact did not belong to a religious girl from Galicia but to a chain-smoking boy from Lisbon who was lying about his grades and was sometimes cruel to his cat—Lacey was almost sure about the last bit, although it could have been his dog. That file made its way unceremoniously to the bottom of the *no* stack. Lacey also moved Ze Tomas Silva Maria da Olivera's file to the top of the *yes* stack. She then left the room. A moment later, Lacey was back and plopped down in her chair again. She searched through the *no* stack, retrieved a file, and for five minutes sat drumming her fingers on it without reviewing its content. Finally, having reached a decision, she moved Matilde Maria Teixeira to the *yes* stack and left the room for good. *They have daycare at Duke*, she thought to herself as she walked down the embassy corridor.

She passed under the embassy building's jutting eaves and walked toward the gate, feeling growing urgency to make good on her promise to Inês to leave Lisbon as soon as possible. Her bag was packed and ready to go at the Airbnb, and she had checked the train schedules for that evening. She would hop the blue line on the metro to retrieve her bags, and arrive at the Oriente train station within an hour.

Lacey passed through the gate and onto the Avenida das Forças Armadas. Just outside the gate, she was arrested by a familiar voice. "Is that you, Ms. Papparin?"

She turned and saw Pedrinho Guimarães leaning against the embassy's white stucco wall not far from the guard gate. Her initial instinct was to run, but she quickly saw the foolishness of that move. If he meant her immediate harm, he had chosen a poor spot to commit a crime. Lacey walked over to him, trying to look casual, but feeling oddly exposed as she had at the castle.

"Yes, Mr. Guimarães; it's me. But you can call me Lacey. We don't do formality anymore in America."

He laughed. "That's true! But there's formality still in London where you studied, isn't that right?" He peered at her intently through his wire-rimmed classes.

"Yes, the Brits can be a little stuffy," she replied, answering the safer half of the question. "But what are you doing here? I was just with your mother."

"I know, and that's why I'm here. To meet her."

Lacey looked around anxiously. "Is she still here? I thought she left fifteen minutes ago."

Pedrinho laughed again. "Oh no, don't worry; she took the Mercedes home. I decided to stay."

"Why?"

"To see you." His gray eyes tried to lock on hers, but she glanced quickly away as if distracted by something.

"Why? Was there something you wanted to see me about?"

"Nothing in particular. It's just that..." he hesitated, and for the first time Lacey saw the slightest crack form in his armor. "It's just that I know how my mother can be. She wasn't always that way, you know. At one time, before I was born, she was actually very religious. I suppose she still is very religious in her practices, but I've heard that she used to be religious in her soul."

For a moment, Lacey forgot her apprehension as a thought crossed her mind. "That's interesting. Has she ever talked about taking pilgrimages?"

"Oh yes. Growing up, we visited every shrine and looked at every martyr's bones in Iberia. I didn't mind it so much, but my brother, he hated it! I think he wears that enormous cross as an excuse never to have to go to church again."

"Just out of curiosity, is there any shrine that your mother avoided visiting?" She wasn't sure if she might be walking into a trap, but something in his manner told her that their respective feelings of vulnerability had equalized.

"No," he answered slowly, as if thinking about it still. "But wait, yes, I do remember my father making a suggestion several times, and my mother saying absolutely no, we were not going to visit that place. Now what was it?"

"The tomb of St. James in Galicia?" asked Lacey, now taking the offensive to look Pedrinho in the eyes.

"Yes, that's it! But how did you know?"

"Just trying to use my mind to solve an affair of the heart."

He laughed for the third time, and a shield of bonhomie seemed to swing back into place. "Well, you must have your... what do you call them—trade secrets?"

Lacey froze. That was not a phrase she had used with Pedrinho, nor that he was likely to have made up on his own. The apprehension she had felt before being attacked at São Roque and that had begun to swell again as she left the embassy now billowed up inside her. "Goodbye, Mr. Guimarães," she said quickly, and hurried off down the avenue.

The familiar sight of a black sedan with a green roof appeared on the street. Lacey hailed the taxi with an urgent gesture. It was still slowing when she opened the door and jumped into the back seat. "Estação Oriente, *por favor*," she said hurriedly, as the cab sped off into traffic. It was a shame to leave her bag at the Airbnb, but she had her passport, computer, and the broken rat tile in the satchel at her side. Clothing and toiletries she could buy in the morning. She would not stay in Lisbon a minute longer.

Chapter 10

FLESH ON DRY BONES

The Alfa Pendular high-speed train sliced an exorable track through the rolling olive hills to the north of Lisbon. Lacey sat in a comfortable seat by the window with her nose pressed unhygienically against the glass. The train's little jostles rattled her nose as the former capital of the empire disappeared in a summer haze and medieval country opened and closed in a blur of dappled evening light.

Lacey's feelings of apprehension faded but did not disappear entirely as the train left Lisbon behind. It was not her first time working society's rough margins in the company of rogues and cutthroats, but there were things she still did not understand about this case. Lacey could accept being shoved into the path of an oncoming automobile as the cost of doing business, but she was not at peace with knowing she was still peering through a glass dimly. It was her prerogative, her security, to see what others couldn't see. When that sight eluded her, as it had with Pedrinho Guimarães, confidence eluded her too.

Impulsively, Lacey reached for her phone and texted: *Hi Mom. Just checking in.* It was late back home and her mother would surely be asleep by now. To her surprise Daisy texted back almost immediately.

Hi sweetie. How's the bar studying? You eating and exercising?

Feeling vulnerable and vaguely homesick, Lacey briefly considered telling her mother the truth that she had dropped out of law school, had never studied for the bar, and had nearly been killed in a foreign city the previous day. But that wouldn't do. Home was for sweetness and light and the scent of freshly baked biscuits, not for the harsh realities of the world. Better to maintain her mother's feckless daughter-in-law as her biggest problem than to pull back the curtain on the often seedy and dangerous world that Lacey inhabited through choice. She texted: *All good Mom. Why you up so late?*

It took Daisy longer to answer this query than the initial text. When she did answer, she did not say what Lacey expected—up with a migraine, or worrying about your brother's job—but instead, *Oh nothing really. Get some rest, sweetie.* Reflecting that it was her mother who needed the rest, Lacey put away her phone with a sigh and resumed her post at the window.

The city now lay far behind and a rural Portugal of quaint towns, crumbled walls, and dusky olive groves rushed by. It was a short hour and a half to Coimbra on the fleet Pendular, and the sun had not yet sunk below the horizon when the train pulled into the station.

Disembarking, Lacey caught sight of a broad, winding river flanked by a hill layered with white and pink buildings topped with the obligatory orange-tiled rooves. At the heights, the eighteenth-century university clocktower presided over the city. Lacey had read that locals called it *a cabra*—goat—and that it still regulated university rhythms. It made her at ease to be stepping back to when tintinnabulation rather than text alerts set the pace of life. More at ease, but also invigorated, for there was tricky work to be done in Coimbra.

Unburdened by luggage, Lacey set off on foot from the train station toward the Baixa, the lower quarter of the old city that had catered to the lower classes when kings and their court roosted at the city's peak. It was too late to do any shopping, so she headed straight for her lodging. Most of the hotels in the city had looked disappointingly modern when Lacey had made her reservation the day before. She would not—*not*—regress to a medieval university town only to be cloistered in a soulless cube of steel and glass. After fifteen minutes of winding through narrow streets she came to a shabby building in a row of stores and apartments. The sign above the door read *Pensao do Cabra*. Feeling instantly at ease with a boarding home of either the university clock tower or a genuine goat, she entered.

The clerk was an owlish young woman with a pinched beak and overly large eyes lurking behind a pair of glasses two sizes too small for her wan face. She was reading Sartre with an expression that looked simultaneously surprised and bored. Lacey presented her credit card and passport and received in return a brass key attached to a ponderous wooden fob on which was etched the number 233. The clerk attempted to duck back into Sartre, but Lacey caught her eye.

"Are you at the university?" asked Lacey.

"Yes," the clerk answered in impeccable English. "Everyone here is, except for the boys trying to pick up the university girls because they think it will make them smarter and the girls trying to pick up the university boys because they think it will make them richer."

Lacey laughed. "That's well said!"

"I thought of it while reading Sartre," replied the clerk, giving the book a dour expression.

"Say, where would you go to meet some of these university students? I'm visiting from the States and want to hang out a bit."

"Well, that depends on what kind of student you want to hang out with. There are many types, you know. There are the philosophers who smoke French cigarettes and get lung cancer. There are the business types who only talk about the stock market. There are the political ones who plan how they will hang the business types during the next revolution. And there are the literary types who drink wine while quoting José Saramago. It's really up to you."

"I'd like to meet the artistic types."

"But you must be more specific. Do you mean the classicists who keep asking to paint your naked portrait, the romantics who run around naked in the countryside, the modernists who are circulating a petition to remake *a Cabra* out of steel and glass, or the post-modernists who want to dam the river until it floods the Baixa and call it art?"

"Oh, I don't know. Maybe the types who care about Portuguese culture?"

By way of answer, the clerk took a notepad from behind the register, scribbled something, and handed a note to Lacey. "You'll find them there," she said and returned to reading Sartre with an air of finality.

Lacey checked into her room, a tight and dingy affair that nonetheless smelled clean and fronted a quaint alley of hanging flowers and drying laundry. Having nothing to unpack, she freshened up, then sallied forth to meet the intellectual denizens of Coimbra. Dusk was laying a cool blanket on the radiant cobblestones when Lacey stepped into the street. She had committed the directions to memory and walked with purpose, occasionally casting a glance over her shoulder. She guessed that danger lay behind in Lisbon, but she had not survived thus far through guesses alone.

The entrance to *O Sapo Risonho*—The Laughing Frog—was tucked in an archway deep in the Baixa. The reek of cigarette smoke greeted Lacey's nostrils as she pushed open the door and stepped down a flight of stairs into a dungeon-like room. It was a weeknight in a university town, but there was hardly an empty seat around the fifteen or so crowded tables. A roar three notches up from dull amplified the smoke to give Lacey an instant headache. She picked her way to the bar, found a safe opening between two backs turned away for conversation, and sidled in. After a few minutes, a bartender arrived, looked her over appraisingly, then jerked his head to the side, demanding an order. Lacey ordered a *Sagres* beer. It arrived, and she pretended to drink while studying the scene, well aware that the minute glass was counting down, because a young woman cannot sit alone at the bar drinking a beer for long in a university town.

Lacey quickly determined that the Sartre-reading clerk had known her business. This was, indeed, the place for the artistic types who cared about Portuguese culture, although there was plenty of chaff as well. Take, for example, the three young men in the corner drinking beer and laughing at each other's *bon mots*. Only one of the three—the one with the inexplicable, long-sleeve paisley shirt—was plausibly enrolled in school, and even he was in serious danger of expulsion for plagiarism. The other two, his hometown friends, were posing as students in the hopes of getting a date with college girls, not because they valued the life of the mind but the life of the body.

The old coot with the ponytail was clearly not a student, but at first Lacey wasn't quite sure whether he was an art professor or a genuine artist. The five moonstruck students at his table grasped at every pearl of great price that dropped from his lips, but it wasn't until he began to make sketches on a napkin that Lacey pegged him as a mere professor. A genuine *artiste* would not have spilled his genius on such a vulgar medium.

And so it went, with much greater alacrity than told here, for table after table. Under the Ockham's razor of Lacey's eye, the bar's denizens were reduced to their simplest selves—the freshman ingénue from Braga searching for the meaning of life in canvas, the fat boy from a fishing family who would revolutionize modern sculpture if he could conquer his asthma, the retrograde girl from the Algarve who thought that the human spirit died with Michelangelo, and many more stories of souls written in the half closure of an eyelid, the wrinkles of an old Bob Marley T-shirt, or the careless twisting of a faux pearl necklace.

The minute glass was dripping its last granules when Lacey locked on her target: a pod of three university students—no doubt about that—a young man and two young women. They were seated at a rectangular table with six or seven people they didn't know and were keeping to themselves. They were drinking enjoyably, but not belligerently, and seemed to be having trouble hearing each other above the din—a favorable fact, given Lacey's plan. She paid for her untouched beer, being sure to leave a generous tip, picked up her drink, and walked purposefully over to the threesome's table.

"*Boa noite*," she said, putting her beer down on the table as if staking a claim. "Can I join you?"

Three mildly surprised, but not hostile, pairs of eyes flashed up to hers. The man and one of the women looked at each other in uncertainty, but the other woman, the one with the dragon tattoo on her bare shoulder, answered without hesitation in excellent English. "Of course. But you will have to find a chair."

Lacey had planned for this and knew exactly the location of the closest vacant stool. She had seized it and returned before the threesome had a chance to confab about the stranger. "I'm Lacey," she said, squeezing in between dragon girl and her male companion. And she pumped three hands with Yankee bravado.

The young man introduced himself as Diogo, dragon girl as Francisca, and the second woman as Catia. "You're American?" asked Francisca.

"Yep, yep, getting my masters in art history at Tufts—that's near Boston. Just traveling through Europe on my summer holiday. Hoping to meet new people and learn more about European art."

"Ah, then you've come to good place," said Diogo agreeably. His English wasn't as strong as Francisca's. "Coimbra, much art."

"But I hope not *new* art, *modern* art," said Lacey with a wrinkled nose. "I can't stand anything made after 1900."

Francisca and Diogo looked sympathetic; Catia like she was having trouble hearing what Lacey was saying. "Yes, that's what we think too," said Francisca. "We are university students too, and we all study art. Catia, she will become... how do you say it... a curator for a museum."

Lacey nodded encouragingly.

"And Diogo, well he doesn't have a job yet but he wants to be a school teacher, teaching children about the history of Portuguese art. But maybe he will have to teach math too."

Diogo grimaced.

Lacey reckoned the probability that Diogo would teach math at 97 percent, and that he would teach art at 7 percent.

"And what about you?" Lacey interrupted, knowing that Francisca was going there next anyway.

"Me? I will work for the Gulbenkian Museum in Lisboa, doing acquisitions. Have you heard of the Gulbenkian?"

"Oh yes! It's a very famous museum. In fact," and here Lacey lowered her voice confidentially so that Francisca and Diogo leaned in and Catia virtually climbed onto Diogo's back (which seemed to please Diogo), "it was because of something that I learned through the Gulbenkian that I decided to come to Coimbra. I have a bit of a mystery to solve, you see."

"A mystery!" said Francisca expectantly. In the dull background, Catia could barely be heard to ask: "What means a mystery?" No one bothered to answer her.

"Yes, yes, a mystery. And an *art mystery* at that."

Francisca and Diogo leaned in further. "I can't hear nothing," moaned Catia.

"I'm so sorry, Catia," said Lacey, lowering her voice even further. "Listen, I would love to tell you all about it—in fact, maybe you could help me solve the mystery—but maybe this isn't the place to talk about it. Is there somewhere else we could go to speak more privately?"

"*Sim, sim*," said Francisca. "Come back with us to our *república*."

"Your what?"

"*República*. Republic. Our house."

"Your house is a republic?"

"Come, we will tell you about it as we walk. It's not far."

The foursome left O Sapo Risonho and walked through Coimbra's darkened streets. Diogo and Catia walked a bit too close for comfort—well, the comfort of others, that is—while Francisca kept up a lively narrative. "The repúblicas are community houses where students live. The tradition is very old, going back to the fourteenth century. Many of the houses seem that old too—everything is always falling apart!"

Francisca and Lacey laughed at the joke. Catia and Diogo giggled at each other.

"Anyway," continued Francisca, "they're good places for poor students because the university pays for them and lets us live there in... how do you say it... communism?"

"Oh, that wouldn't sound good back in Iowa! How about *community?*"

"*Sim, sim*, community. Although we do have communists too!"

They laughed again. Diogo and Catia were falling behind and seemed to be in danger of falling in love. Francisca and Lacey left them to their fate and pressed on through narrow cobblestone alleyways lined with umbrellas, tables, chairs, and flower pots.

"Well, the repúblicas are supposed to be political places, which is why Salazar tried to stamp them out. He couldn't, of course. It's hard for one man to put out a tradition that has lasted six hundred years. But what Salazar couldn't do, Steve Jobs did instead!"

"Steve Jobs?"

"You know, Apple, iPhone. The repúblicas used to be places where students came together to dream, to talk, to sing, to laugh, to make love, to conspire against the old people. They would drink wine and hold elections for presidents and ministers whose powers were to clean toilets and wash dishes. But now everyone sits around the house making love to their phones. It would make Salazar happy."

"Salazar liked to make love to a phone?"

Francisca and Lacey broke into laughter again. Speaking of making love, Diogo and Catia were nowhere to be seen.

"Here we are," announced Francisca. They had arrived at a shabby double wooden door of a two-story building. Graffiti-style painting depicting various features of the human body—ears, eyes, nose, hands, feet—surrounded by hieroglyphs covered the walls. On each panel of the door was painted a skull and crossbones and in a continuous line underneath the words, *O povo unido jamais será vencido.*

Lacey stopped before the door and said: "Let me figure this out. *O povo.* The people. *Unido*, well, that's easy—united. *Jamais* is the same in French. Comes from the Latin *iam magis* and means *never. Será* I recognize from *que será, será,* and I suppose *que não será, não será,* because *vencido* is like Julius Caesar said, *veni vidi vici,* and it means to conquer or be conquered, and so the whole phrase means 'the people united will never be defeated.'"

Once she began to roll in elocution she could not stop, so that by the time she came to the end, she was very much out of breath. Francisca stood watching her with an apparent mixture of apprehension, awe, and concern that the strange American might faint.

"You are right, of course," she said after a moment's hesitation. "It's a revolutionary phrase. In the *repúblicas* there is always supposed to be revolution. Please, come in."

They stepped into a dim vestibule tiled in a harlequin pattern. On the worn banister of a long, straight staircase leading to the second floor sat a wicker basket. Francisca took a phone from her pocket and dropped it into the basket and motioned that Lacey should do the same. "House rules," she explained. "We are taking steps to restore the revolution. *O povo unido...*"

Francisca led the way along a hallway into a dark common area furnished with tattered and ill-matched furniture. The room was vacant. The two women sat in rickety chairs bathed in the flickering light of a table lamp. With each flicker of light, Lacey could make out tendrils of dust snaking through the stuffy air.

"Now tell me about this mystery involving the Gulbenkian," said Francisca with anticipation. "We don't get many mysteries here in Coimbra."

"Oh, I'm sure you do," answered Lacey. "Mysteries are everywhere. They're in the faces of people on the bus, in songs on the radio, in the silence after the rain."

"What are you, a poet?"

"No, a detective."

"*Really?*"

"Yeah, sort of. Well, something like that."

"You're not an art student?"

"No. I'm sorry that I didn't tell you quite the truth. I have to be careful."

"But now this is even more interesting than before! Tell me everything."

"I just told you that I have to be careful."

Francisca reached over and turned off the lamp. A moment of awkward silence ensued.

"Um, you know that won't help, right?" asked Lacey when it seemed like Francisca was waiting for her to continue.

Francisca clicked the lamp back on, looking disappointed and embarrassed. "I suppose you're right. I was thinking like an artist, not a detective."

"It's OK. The case I'm working on does involve art, and I can tell you a bit about it."

"You have to if you want my help."

"Now you're thinking like a detective. So here's the deal. I'm looking for a dealer in *azulejos* here in Coimbra. I know his name, and I have a piece that might be of interest to him, but he doesn't seem to exist. There's not a trace of him on the internet, and you know, the internet knows everything."

"Steve Jobs."

"No, Steve Jobs didn't create the internet. That was someone called Al Gore. But it doesn't matter. In order not to show up on the internet today—or, I should say, the internet that I know how to exploit—you have to try really hard and be really good at it."

"Maybe you have the wrong name."

"It could be an alias—that's a fake name someone uses when they want to stay in disguise. The person who gave it to me was an *azulejo* dealer in Lisbon. He said that this dealer is known by this name among other *azulejo* dealers."

"Then we must go upstairs," said Francisca, jumping suddenly to her feet. "He's sleeping there."

"The *azulejo* dealer is sleeping upstairs?" asked Lacey with surprise.

"No, Guilherme is sleeping upstairs, and if anyone can help, it will be Guilherme." She paused, then added: "If he will ever wake up."

Francisca led the way up the long flight of stairs to the second floor and down another long hallway strewn with collegiate detritus—dirty laundry, textbooks, beer bottles. As they walked silently down the hall, Lacey surveyed the decorations plastered on the walls: dog-eared rock concert posters; political pamphlets with red carnations or hammers and sickles; semi-erotic black and white photographs; Soviet kitsch. Suddenly, she stopped abruptly before a framed black and white photograph of four young people—two women and two men—at the beach. The women wore two-piece calico bathing suits with high-waisted bottoms and modest tops. Both were slim and pretty. Conversely, the men wore short trunks presaging the noxious Speedo. One was trim and muscular; the other already portly. Lacey peered into the picture with rapt attention.

"You know them?" asked Francisca curiously.

"Oh no," answered Lacey quickly. "It's just so interesting to see pictures like this of people our parents' age when they were young. See how women's bathing suits have gotten skimpy as women have been more liberated, while men's trunks have dropped down to the knees. Weird, isn't it?"

"Yes, I see what you mean," answered Francisca, as if she didn't. Lacey laughed and signaled that they could move on.

Toward the end of the hallway, they came to a closed door with a poster depicting the iconic Rooster of Barcelos weeping tears of gold filament. At least it appeared to be gold filament. Lacey wasn't perfectly sure whether it mightn't have been the shredded innards of a cellphone.

Francisca pushed open the door without knocking. The room inside was perfectly dark, but Francisca seemed familiar enough with its furnishings to push her way inside without turning on a light. Lacey followed. The hallway light barely revealed the edge of a bed and, on it, a prone figure swaddled in a blanket far too heavy for the season. From somewhere under the covers, a rumbling snore rattled the shutters.

"Ten o'clock and he's already been out for an hour," snorted Francisca. "And he'll still be sleeping when I've had breakfast and a bath tomorrow morning. *Guilherme, preguiçoso, acordar!* You have company." She shook the sleeping figure rudely.

There was a noise somewhere between a groan and a full-fledged appeal to Amnesty International, and Guilherme rolled away.

"*Acordar*, wake up, wake up," jeered Francisca, tugging at the covers.

That, at least, prompted a sentient response. "*Pare com isso, menina, estou nu sob as cobertas!*" exclaimed a muffled voice.

Francisca made a sound between a giggle and retch and stopped pulling on the covers. "He says…"

"Yeah, he says he's not wearing his nickers," said Lacey. And she added, involuntarily: "Ick."

"*Sim*, we don't want to see *that*," added Francisca, not sounding the least bit ambivalent in the matter.

Now the bereft Guilherme made a half effort to sit up, wrapped protectively in his blanket. He stared out with globe-like, unblinking eyes at his housemate and the strange girl so rudely disturbing his tranquility and threatening his virtue.

"Guilherme," said Francisca. "This is Lacey. She's American, but not *that* type of American."

"Oh good," said Guilherme, as though it were perfectly understood what the disqualifying type of American was.

Francisca continued. "Lacey is looking for an *azulejo* dealer here in Coimbra. He is part of some mystery. She has a name, but there is no record of him."

"Yes," said Guilherme slowly. "What is the name?"

"Cisterno Vazio," answered Lacey.

"That's a strange name," said Francisca.

Guilherme seemed unsurprised by the name. He peered balefully at his tormenters. "If I tell you where to find him, you leave me alone?"

The two young women nodded emphatically.

"Twenty-five Rua da Matemática." And, with that, he rolled back into his covers and was rocking the shades with his snores before his unwelcome guests closed the door behind them.

Lacey committed the address to memory. The evening had been a success; she had what she had come for. It was tempting to bid Francisca good evening and retire to the Pensao do Cabra after a long but profitable day, but her new Portuguese friend had done her a favor and seemed eager for conviviality. Lacey allowed herself to be led back into the dusty haze of the living room and sat pondering the strangely unfolding case while Francisca made herbal tea. They sat drinking tea and talking until well past midnight, when the denizens of the *republica* began to drift or stagger or slink back in and find their beds, or each other's. In the meanwhile, Lacey and Francisca spoke of Coimbra, and the university, and of Portugal old and new. It was a moment of fleeting friendship, and it grew in Lacey's mind for many weeks to come. She had had no friends since, college really—only accomplices, clients, and antagonists—and now, in the space of a few short days on assignment in the Old, Old World, she had formed an odd and unsettled friendship with Inês and now with Francisca. Turning down a fourth cup of tea and with pleading the need for an early start on the morrow, Lacey found herself offering her phone number and promising to stay in touch.

Despite the late night, Lacey rose earlier than usual the following morning. She was showered and ready to go by the time breakfast opened at 6:30 in the lobby. The Sartre clerk was still on duty and still reading Sartre over a mug of coffee. She did not look up as Lacey helped herself to a steaming *popo seco* roll and a dollop of orange marmalade.

Lacey arrived at Rua da Matemática well before eight, a good hour before the shop's opening time. Over a facade of glass walls and doors, an arched plaster recess announced the Passeio Lusitano, Regional Gift Shop, in marine blue lettering against a white background. Behind the glass menagerie of tourist items—mandolins, flutes, pottery, dishes, jewelry, handbags, dolls, linens, rugs, wine bottles, and cork roosters—invited window shoppers to enter and browse. There were no *azulejos* on display, which explained why Lacey had previously been unable to find the shop.

There was a little café cattycorner to Passeio Lusitano, and *popo seco* roll with orange marmalade notwithstanding, Lacey felt no compunction about taking an outdoor seat under a blue awning and ordering what hobbits call "second breakfast" and Lacey called "a good start." She ordered a *meia-de-leite* and two *pasteis de natas* and sat enjoying them with a hawk's eye on the Passeio's glass doors. At 8:45, a fat man wearing a Panama hat and linen shirt already ringed with sweat marks arrived, unlocked the doors, stepped inside, and relocked the door behind him. Too young, fat, and conspicuous to be her quarry. Five minutes later a young woman arrived, knocked on the door, and received admittance. Then, promptly at nine, the linen-shirt man opened the door to the public. Business hours had begun without any sighting of Cisterno Vazio.

Lacey did not enter the shop at once. At 9:05, a German couple on holiday—they had quarreled about money the night before and made up by agreeing to go shopping first thing in the morning, Lacey surmised—walked through the glass doors holding hands. Three minutes later, an American family (that needed no surmising) with three children too young for Passeio Lusitano entered after the Germans. Lacey was hot on their heels. Distraction, cover, time.

Both of the clerks were preoccupied with customers as Lacey entered the shop. The female clerk was showing the Germans a vase, and the linen-shirt man was showing the American mom a set of fans while keeping his body between her rampant children and the pottery collection. Oblivious or indifferent to the behavior of his offspring, the dad fiddled presumptuously with a mandolin while humming a Broadway tune in broken Spanish. The situation was perfect. Lacey moved progressively toward the back of the store, browsing noncommittally. After reaching the cashier desk at the rear, she looped back along another aisle to come up behind the Germans. She caught the clerk's eye and asked: *"Azulejos?"*

"I'm sorry. I'll be with you in a moment," the clerk answered pleasantly. "We have some *azulejos* downstairs in the *porão*, the cellar. Go on down if you like." She gestured toward the back of the store, "But watch your head."

Lacey knew what she meant. At the back of the store, she had seen an alcove leading to a back door facing a courtyard and narrow flights of stairs going up and down. She had formed the impression from her visit to Lunar Antique Tiles that interesting *azulejos* were hidden in dusty crypts, and this was to be no exception. Petite as she was, Lacey almost had to duck to get down into the cellar. She arrived in a tomb-like room lit by a single, naked bulb and smelling of lavender and chalk. Several hundred *azulejos* were arranged on neat shelves. After a few minutes of browsing, she recognized that this collection was more selective than Lunar's. From the simple geometric brilliance of sixteenth-century Muejar pieces, through the tin-glaze Majolica style of the seventeenth century, into the porcelain color explosion of the eighteenth century, and finally to the regularized hand-made production of the nineteenth century, this collection had been carefully curated to showcase only unblemished specimens. Unlike Lunar, which varnished its collection with the authenticity of chips and fades, this collection had been restored to original perfection. Lacey felt as if she were visiting a crypt of Portuguese history in which each epoch had been frozen forever in time.

"May I help you?" The clerk had come silently down the stairs. Lacey had not heard her and jerked around.

"Oh, yeah, thanks. I..." She had meant to say something different at first, to come sideways to the question, but now it seemed that she should get straight to it. "I have this." She reached into her pocket and pulled out the two pieces of the broken rat tile. "This is broken. Can you fix it?"

The clerk looked at Lacey inquisitively and took the pieces. "Yes, of course it can be done. You could glue it yourself."

"But I've been told that to mend a broken tile—that is very difficult. It takes a master."

The clerk looked at her again. She took a moment to answer. "Yes, maybe, but we do not do repairs for customers here. We only sell tiles. I can give you the name—"

"Cisterno Vazio," Lacey broke in. "In Lisbon, I was told that he could fix a tile like this, to make it look beautiful again, like all of these." She gestured around the crypt. When the clerk did not answer, Lacey added in a whisper: "This piece is very special to me." Lacey made a "come closer" gesture with her index finger. Obedient but apprehensive, the clerk leaned in. "They call me 'The Mouse.'"

"Let me see," said the clerk, whirling around with a little shudder and disappearing up the stairs, still clutching the *azulejo* pieces in her hand.

Minutes passed in the darkness of the crypt. From the voices on the first floor, it seemed that the Germans and the Americans had both left the shop and two or three new bevies of customers entered. Lacey nervously checked her phone—no new message from her mother, and a curt "Are you OK?" from Inês. She pocketed the phone and crept to the edge of the stairs. There was no sound from the upper floor. Lacey went back over to the tiles and tried to inspect them, but she found that she couldn't focus on *azulejos*. She had just decided that no one was coming and that she should go back upstairs and retrieve her broken tile when a quiet voice came from the landing. "Good morning, Señorita."

For the second time in ten minutes, Lacey nearly jumped out of her skin. She was used to taking others by surprise, not being taken, but something about the cellar had made her twice be caught unawares. Or maybe it wasn't so much the cellar but the people in this shop, people who were used to moving stealthily.

Her interlocutor was a man of maybe sixty. Long gray hair and a scraggly beard, uncharacteristic of a Portuguese man of his generation, spilled onto his shoulders and chest. His deep black eyes lay sunken behind dark glasses and his shoulders were hunched as if he spent most of his days looking down. In two bony hands he held the pieces of Lacey's broken tile.

"Good morning," she answered, a bit too late. "Thanks for coming down. That tile—can you fix it?"

He answered without looking down at the tile. "Yes, of course." His English was flawless, slightly posh. "Can you come back in three days?"

"Sure, but there's something else." Lacey fished deliberately into a pocket, then slowly her hand emerged and handed the man a small object. "This one is also broken, but I don't have the rest of it."

He looked at what she handed him, then betraying the slightest hint of surprise, brought it closer to his eyes and stared intently. Then he handed back the object—a three-by-three-inch tile fragment picturing the tips of human toes—and asked very quietly: "How did you come to have this?"

"Well," answered Lacey, livening up. "It wasn't as hard as you might think. I pretty much have the run of the place now when Inês is out. Tia Leonor just lets me in like I'm part of the family, and I know exactly where Inês hides her things—behind those *azulejos* on the wall. And this"—she gestured to the tile fragment—"well, I first came upon it when I was burgling Inês's office on a different assignment, and then we kinda became friends and she told me all about it."

The man handed all three tile pieces back to Lacey and sat wearily on the steps, never taking his eyes off her.

"And how did you find me?" he asked sadly.

"That would be trade secrets, of course, so I can't tell you all of it, but maybe just the fun parts? So after Inês took me to Boca do Inferno and told me about Aleister Crowley faking his death, the idea just jumped out that you had faked your death too, Mr. Fonseca. Of course, that raised lots of questions, but it also answered many, like why you took the money from the safe before going to meet Alfonso Guimarães. Inês said that it was to buy out his share of the Crooked Queen, but it always seemed more likely to me that you needed the money to bribe the coroner and then to live off wherever you planned to disappear to."

He nodded, and his shoulders seemed to droop even further. "You see that I do not live in luxury," he added without sounding defensive. "But you have told me why you looked for me, but not how you found me."

"Really not so hard. You obviously have been hiding these past five years, but not too well, because no one was looking for you. Your trail started with *azulejos*. They were your passion, but you knew that they were not your wife's, and that she would sell your collection after your passing. You knew that she would take them to Miguel Pereira, who you have worked with for many years. You did not trust him well enough to share your secret, but you did know how he deals in tiles well enough to set yourself up here in Coimbra and deal with him at a distance. In that way, you were able to buy back many of your own *azulejos* and set yourself up in the *azulejo* trade. Miguel may not know that you are alive, but he did give me the one piece I needed. Well, really it's the three pieces I needed—the broken rat tile, now in two pieces, and the name of the dealer in Coimbra who had bought many of the Fonseca tiles—Cisterno Vazio.

"That had to be you, of course. Inês told me that you love to play with words. What is a Cisterno Vazio? In Greek, *kistē* meant a chest or box, but by the time it became *cisterna* in Latin, it was a well. Vazio comes from the Latin *vacīvus*, so vacuum, or empty. Empty well. But of course an empty well is a dry well. That makes it a *fons sicca*, a spring that has dried up during the summer. Fonseca is Cisterno Vazio, and Cisterno Vazio is you."

Ricardo gave her a wan smile. "You are friends with my daughter, then? You are like her."

Lacey blushed. "Yeah, we've hit it off pretty well."

"And she sent you to find me?"

"Not exactly. At first, she believed that you were dead. She wanted me to discover the truth about your... your murder. And to find the Crooked Queen. Where is it, by the way?"

He rose emphatically and his face came suddenly alive with a flash of anger. "No, that I do not have! You should ask Guimarães about that."

"Then why did you disappear? Why did you do this to your family?"

He slumped back down onto the stairs, his shoulders drooping more forlornly than before. "You cannot ask me that," he said in a low voice. Then, a bit louder: "There is a great shame in my past. A secret shame that would hurt my family more than my death. You must not ask me about it. Please, do not ask me about it."

His head fell into his hands, and he seemed ready to weep.

Lacey wrung her hands. She was much better as a snoop than as a priest. She thought of Inês. Inês was her friend, and she had promised to help her. Friends had been in short supply on the lonely road Lacey had chosen to walk since dropping out of law school. She looked back at Ricardo, a once proud man crouched in a dim crypt that housed the one passion left in his life. She thought again of Inês and remembered that her friend was still keeping secrets of her own. Secrets that she had not shared with Lacey.

"OK, Mr. Fonseca," she answered at last. "I won't say anything for now. I can't promise you that I will never say anything to Inês, but there are more things I'd like to understand before knowing what I should do." Then, suddenly feeling very awkward, she added: "Look, I'm not actually sure how any of this is my business. I came to Portugal to do a totally different job and I... well, I just sort of stumbled into your family's..." She was suddenly at a loss for words.

"Fools, lies, and skeletons?" he asked gently.

"Yes, that's exactly what Inês said!"

"As I said, you and she are very much alike. Now, good day, Ms...?"

But before she could answer he disappeared up the stairs, still holding the broken pieces of the rat tile.

Lacey did not linger any longer at the Passeio Lusitano. She flitted through the shop, avoiding the sales clerk's eye, and passed back out into the sultry Rua da Matemática. She was halfway back to the Pensao do Cabra when she stopped suddenly in her tracks. "Wait a sec," she said, half aloud. When Inês had mentioned fools, lies, in skeletons, it had been in reference to the Guimarães family, not her own.

Chapter 11

THE ESTATE OF TEARS

Lacey still had not made it back to the hotel when her phone rang. It was Inês. Lacey stared at the screen for a moment, reluctant to answer. Then, remembering that Inês had texted a few minutes before and realizing that she would be unable to avoid her friend for long, she answered.

"Mousie, are you OK?" Inês sounded worried. Lacey remembered that the last time they had been together—two days before outside the Igreja de São Roque—Lacey had just escaped being crushed by a car.

"Yeah, I'm fine. What's up?" She tried to sound casual and unconcerned.

"Where are you?"

Lacey hesitated. She had just promised Ricardo not to say anything for now, and questions about her whereabouts would inevitably lead to him. On the other hand, Inês already knew that she was leaving Lisbon, and probably guessed that she would come to Coimbra.

"Coimbra. I came up on the train yesterday."

"I thought so. Have you seen it yet?"

"Seen what?"

"The Quinta das Lágrimas. I assume that's why you came."

Of course that's what Inês would have assumed, and Lacey felt foolish for not leading with that as her cover story. "Not yet. I wanted to look around the city first, see the university."

"Good. Then we will stay there together tonight. It's a magical place, Mousie. I will show it to you. I know the proprietor and will make the reservation. My treat. What time is it now? Ten o'clock? I will catch the next train and meet you there at 1:30."

"Oh, you don't have to go out of your way—" began Lacey, but Inês cut her off.

"Nonsense, of course I will come. *Ciao, menina.*"

And so the matter was settled by fiat. Although Lacey still felt ambivalent about what to say to Inês now that Ricardo had walked out of his tomb like Lazarus, it was also a relief to have her schedule for the next day or two decided for her. She had left Lisbon in a hurry with the sole goal of confirming that Cisterno Vazio was Ricardo Fonseca and had not given much thought to what she would do if she were successful in that endeavor.

Also, the Quinta das Lágrimas had been growing in her mind ever since Inês first mentioned her namesake's love story and the theft of the Crooked Queen. Inês, Leonor, and Pedrinho had all called it a magical place. Whatever could that mean? Lacey's work had taken her to many exotic places—corporate boardrooms, smugglers' dens, love nests, counterfeiting studios, and the like—but never to a *magical* place. Some vestige of Iowa farm girl within stirred to walk through the tall stalks of a cornfield and emerge in an enchanted realm.

Lacey shook her head and slapped herself on the cheek. Romantic balderdash! This was no trip to Disneyland, but rather an opportunity to visit the scene of the crime; get to the bottom of the Crooked Queen's theft; delve into Inês's *fools, lies, and skeletons*; dig for the truth. She was on the case, and the case had better beware.

Still, there were two hours to kill and a university to visit. In shadowboxing with Inês, she could not afford to slip up on small things. Lacey had said that she had wanted to see the university, and it would not pay for Inês to ask her how she liked it and have to admit that she hadn't gone. It was a short walk up the hill to the university. Soon, she found herself in a wide courtyard flanked by academic buildings. She was surprised, and a bit disappointed, to find that many of the university's buildings were of twentieth-century vintage and seemed austere, almost Stalinist. Lacey consulted her phone and learned that the place to visit—the only one that Inês was certain to ask about—was the Biblioteca Joanina, the eighteenth-century library. A student pointed her to a magnificent Baroque building on the outskirts of the courtyard. She made her way to the doors, where a docent relieved her of ten euros for admission.

The late morning had grown sweltering and Lacey was grateful to step into the library's cool darkness. She was greeted by walls of carved teakwood, gilded arches, floors of rose, white and gray marbled tiles, and ornately frescoed ceilings. If it hadn't been for the shelves upon shelves of ancient books, she would have thought it a church. Curiosity piqued, Lacey browsed along the shelves, looking for familiar titles and linguistic challenges. Jumbles of Latin, Greek, Italian, French, and Portuguese riddled at her from the shallow recesses of the teakwood. Here was Dionysius of Halicarnassus's *Roman Antiquities*, here something styled a "book of hours" that looked to be at least five hundred years old and too fragile to touch—whatever could a book of hours be?—and now something more familiar, Homer's *Opera Omnia*. Before long, Lacey was engrossed in deciphering titles and had entirely forgotten about meeting Inês. Also, the temptation was rising in her soul to take a book off the shelf for perusal. A sign at the entrance had made it very clear that the books were *not* to be touched by mere mortal tourists, but the docent seemed asleep at the front door and, really, what would be the harm of a quick peek inside?

Original sin arrived not in the form of a serpent, but of a leather-bound *Collected Works of Lucian of Samosata* in Latin translation. Resistance was futile. This was the very work that had caused Lacey's brush with heresy in Bible college. It had been generally known to the college's prefects that the second-century satirist had skewered the gods and superstitions of the pagans, but generally unknown to those same good people that Lucian's *Death of Peregrine* took vicious aim at the Christian religion also: *These misguided creatures start with the general conviction that they are immortal for all time, which explains the contempt of death and voluntary self-devotion which are so common among them.* Lacey had discovered all this quite by accident while reading *Peregrine* in Greek, and then, quite innocently, in her opinion, drafting an English translation and posting it, with critical annotation, on a college bulletin board colloquially known as the Areopagus. Alas, this Areopagus turned out to be less open for inquiry than its Athenian namesake, and the matter escalated from the janitor to the chaplain to the rector of Greek to the chairman of theology, and finally to the dean of students, in whose spacious office Lacey spent a miserable afternoon reminiscent of an auto-da-fé. She had been saved at length by a sympathetic librarian who promised to banish Lucian to the Restricted Books crypt, rumored to double as an incinerator. That had been the last she had seen of Lucian. Until now.

With one more glance in the direction of the absent docent, Lacey slipped Lucian from the shelf. She never had the chance to consummate her sin. At that very moment, something wiggly, furry, and decidedly creepy fluttered pell-mell onto her head, tangling briefly with her hair before swooping away with an indignant bout of chirping. Lacey let out a muffled shriek, fumbled the book back onto the shelf, and beelined for the exit, hands over head and crouching like a coal miner. Brushing by the now fully alert docent, she scampered out the door and away from the library.

It wasn't until she was back at the *Pensao do Cabra* and ensconced in the safety of her room that she allowed herself to think about what had just happened. A quick Google search confirmed her suspicion that the visitor to her head had been a bat. Apparently, bats had resided in the Joanina Library since the nineteenth century and were tolerated because they ate flies and gnats that otherwise might molest old books. Lacey had never been particularly squeamish about creepy-crawly things and chastised herself for overreacting. But the bat incident underlined the intermittent apprehension that had come and gone in waves since São Roque. Was Lacey Papparin becoming... mousy? That play on her nickname had never occurred to Lacey because it was so far out of her character, but now it picked at her mind. Was she the fearless field mouse that broke the corporate law firm mold, or a shivering little rodent trapped in the corner? And now the broken mouse tile assumed a darker new meaning. It had been broken when she was attacked, and it had not been repaired. *To mend a broken tile is very difficult; it takes a master.* Was the mouse tile irreparably broken? Was she?

To her credit, Lacey did not suppress these inner daggers at once. Her mother had taught her many things, but perhaps none more valuable than that the time to move on from anything unpleasant—sorrows, betrayals, annoyances, disappointments, anxieties, hurts, and fears—was after letting them linger inside for just long enough. "Everything has to run its course," Daisy would say. "Take it for a jog now, or it will take you for a marathon later." Lacey sat in her room with a deep cup of dark coffee and allowed play to the feelings of vulnerability that had been flickering in and out throughout her stay in Portugal. After a quarter of an hour, she rose, collected her few things, and checked out of the hotel.

It was a twenty-minute walk from the old city, across the river, to the Santa Clara district—much faster than by car since the closest way across the water was a footbridge. Lacey stopped at a sundries store and purchased some clothing and toiletries, then wandered along the Mondego's east bank, watching the lazy summer waters ease by the city. When she came to the Pedro e Inês bridge, she saw with slight apprehension why it was nicknamed "the bridge to nowhere." From each bank, a cantilevered walkway enclosed in a balustrade of blue, pink, yellow, and green glass ran out into the river with the appearance that the sides would miss each other in the middle. It was only by seeing pedestrians successfully navigating the bridge that Lacey realized that the displacement of the two halves was an optical illusion, a metaphor for the displaced love of the bridge's namesakes. Lacey crossed the bridge slowly, enjoying the play on her cheeks of the water-chilled breezes. There was no rush to reach her destination—Inês shouldn't be there for at least another hour.

Ten minutes later, Lacey reached a closed wrought iron gate marking the entrance to a fence of limestone, plaster, and iron rails that enclosed an impenetrable wall of foliage—the grounds of the Quinta das Lágrimas. She rang the call button, and an obsequious male voice answered in English. She announced herself as a guest, and the gate immediately swung open inward. Lacey found herself walking down a shiny cobblestone drive underneath a canopy of trees. To her right, she caught glimpses of guests in plaid waddling about a lush golf course. She hoped that Inês didn't golf. If Lacey had needed another reason to drop out of law school, the expectation that she would have to play golf to entertain clients would have sufficed.

After several hundred shaded meters, the driveway brought her to the steps of a single-story Baroque building graced with tall windows and painted dandelion yellow. She ascended the broad limestone steps and was met by a uniformed doorman. He gave her a doubtful look, as though guests usually didn't arrive on foot with no luggage, but nonetheless opened the door and welcomed her to the Quinta. Lacey's first impression of the building's interior was that it was trying to seem older than it actually was, like a girl wearing her mother's heels. Thick draperies stifled almost every glint of sunlit, and little lamps shed timid, parsimonious light as if admitting their failure to compensate for the sun's exclusion. The furniture was stuffy and archaic, the walls white and austere. If passionate love was the Quinta's ethos, the reception area was perhaps a jilted lover.

A young man behind the reception desk greeted Lacey pleasantly and asked if her party—apparently meaning her parents—would be checking in. Blushing slightly, Lacey explained that she was meeting a friend—Inês Fonseca—who probably hadn't arrived yet.

"Oh yes, Ms. Fonseca, of course. Then welcome! Is this your first time at the Quinta, Ms...?"

"Papparin. Lacey Papparin. And, yes, this is my first time."

"Welcome, welcome. The Quinta is a place you won't forget."

"I've heard that it's magical," said Lacey amicably.

"Oh yes." And then, lowering his voice, added: "And maybe haunted too."

Lacey took this in stride. "I've heard that the ghost of Inês de Castro sometimes wanders the halls at night, weeping on her way to be crowned queen. Have you seen her?"

He looked around uncomfortably. There was no one else in the reception area. Still, he hesitated. "Well, the bosses really don't like us to talk about that much, except maybe with British tourists because they come here *because* of that."

"So you *have* seen her."

"I didn't say that," he retorted indignantly.

"Yes, you did. If you hadn't seen her, you would have said that right away, since you obviously don't want to talk about it."

"OK, OK," he said, looking around again and then leaning over the counter and lowering his voice even further. "I can't be sure. My mother says that the church teaches that there are no such things as ghosts, but I guess they also teach that we shouldn't tell lies, and I did see something once. I was here alone at the reception, late at night. There was a little knock at the door, which was strange, because it wasn't locked. I went to open it, but there was no one there. When I turned back to the desk I saw..." He stopped and shivered.

"You saw what?" asked Lacey eagerly, once again forgetting herself.

"I saw a pale shadow moving across the room. It seemed like a woman dressed in long white robes. And her neck was... it was bent."

"The Crooked Queen," whispered Lacey.

He nodded, shivered, nodded again, and then straightened up. "Now, let's get you a room, Ms. Papparin. May I see your passport?"

While she handed it over, the clerk scanned a computer screen. "Ah, Ms. Fonseca called in a reservation for two rooms just an hour or two ago, but she didn't say in which wing of the building. Do you prefer the palace or the four elements building?"

"Four elements building?"

"Yes, you wouldn't have seen that when you arrived. It's tucked away to the side. Most of the palace building was built after a fire to the original chateau in 1879, so it's a little old-fashioned. But the four elements building was designed much more recently, following principles of oriental Zen philosophy by the modernist architect—"

"Did you say modernist?" He looked puzzled, so she added quickly: "The old wing, please."

"Of course. Room number ten, then. My favorite. Do you, er, have any luggage?"

"Nope, traveling light. Just this bag." She took the electronic key card, which seemed to clash with the lobby's efforts at antiquity, and thanked the clerk for his help. Following his directions, she wandered out of the lobby into a maze of narrow hallways connecting the reception building to the palace wing and the pool deck and gardens behind. Pedro and Inês memorabilia adorned the walls. There were oil paintings of various scenes of the lovers' lives—their rendezvouses by a shady fountain, Inês's child clinging to his mother as she pled for her life, dead Inês receiving the homage of her unwilling subjects under Pedro's wrathful eye. There were other objects of remembrance too: maps of the gardens in ancient days, embroidered tapestries transcribing verses of Camões, *azulejo*s depicting the royal coat of arms, medieval weapons, and a burnished suit of armor. Lacey studied these carefully, wondering if any of them might be valuable, like The Crooked Queen.

The door to Room 10 opened with a click, and she slipped into a very different atmosphere than the fusty hallway. The curtains were pulled back from the ample windows, allowing a cascade of light to spill over the gardens and cast a golden-green aura onto the milky whiteness of the sheets, coverlet, and walls. The only saturated color appeared in a headboard of rich azure velvet and the dark, wooden floor planks. A recess wide enough for a single chair was notched into the far wall, inviting the guest to shelter privately with a book or deep thoughts. The only artwork was a pair of cubist paintings of Pedro and Inês. Lacey was drawn to them at once. Pedro had no face and few discernable features other than overly large hands clutching a bloody sword. Inês's bald head tilted slightly to the side, neither quite alive nor dead. The queen held some sort of impish creature—Lacey could not discern exactly what—limply in her arms, but the eye was instantly drawn to an oval of slashing crimson lines at the queen's abdomen and twin spurts of red on her arms. Involuntarily, Lacey ran her finger across the queen's belly. She jerked back suddenly. Did it really feel damp and sticky?

A rap at the door startled Lacey. She scurried across the room and opened the door, expecting a hotel attendant. But it was Inês.

"Oh, hi; you're earlier than I expected," said Lacey.

"*Ciao,* Mousie," Inês answered, stepping into the room and closing the door behind her. "Portuguese trains are efficient. I made good time." She looked over Lacey carefully, as if expecting to find something troubling, then gave the American a little peck on each cheek. "So, what do you think of it?"

"Well," said Lacey carefully. "The walk-in is fabulous, and this room is so interesting. I was just looking over those paintings. So…" She trailed off and gestured toward the far wall, as though to make the pictures speak for themselves.

"Oh yes, they are everywhere here." Inês lowered her voice. "You know that Inês's ghost still haunts this place, right?"

"I read that somewhere," Lacey answered, not wishing to reveal her conversation with the clerk but wondering if Inês already knew about it. "Do you believe in ghosts?"

"Of course," her friend answered, sounding incredulous at the question. "But let's not speak of that now. There's so much to show you. Give me ten minutes to unpack; then we can walk through the gardens."

"How about the rest of the buildings?" asked Lacey.

"They are not so interesting. It's the gardens that have centuries of history to tell."

"But the Crooked Queen was stolen from inside the building, no?"

"Yes, of course." Inês gave Lacey a quick glance. "We should speak with Santiago. He can show us the room where it was taken. Maybe before dinner. He's not in yet. But the gardens first. Meet me outside in ten minutes."

Ten minutes later, Lacey exited the rear of the palace onto a cobblestone terrace. Although it was still early afternoon, the air seemed cool, damp, and fragrant with the aroma of flowers and trees. Two bougainvillea vines grew up the walls of the old palace, their vivid red flowers springing out from the stucco's pallor. A stone path covered by a canopy of foliage led away from the building past a grove of bamboo, while a network of intimate fountains and pools, apparently linked by an underground watercourse, gurgled busily.

Lacey stood with her back against the warmth of the building and took in the beginning of the gardens. Inês did not arrive in five minutes, and then barely made it another ten. By the time she showed up, Lacey had grown so drowsy leaning against the wall and absorbing the garden's enchantment that she started when her friend touched her shoulder.

"Ay, oh, hi. I was just looking at that oak tree over there. Don't think I've ever seen one quite like it."

Inês laughed. "You will see many things here for the first time. These botanical gardens were planted over two hundred years ago and have grown ever richer in Portugal's warm sun and soil. And maybe a bit from the magic of this place too. That is an Australian silver oak. You will not see many of those in Europe or America."

Lacey gave her a respectful glance. "You seem to know your trees."

"I know them like you know your *azulejos*," Inês said with another little laugh. "See that tree there? It's a spiny-leaf podocarp, also from Australia, and also very rare. There are only two of them in all of Portugal. And here," she began to amble forward, "you can see a European hackberry. Majestic, isn't it? Now this stand of timber bamboo comes from Japan. Look at how tall and straight they grow. And that date palm there—you will only find it in the Canary Islands, and here of course. We are now in what they call the Romantic Garden. Come, let me show you more wonders."

They wandered along the stone path past the bamboo grove and came to a pavilion with glass walls. Tables and chairs were set up inside but did not seem to be in immediate use. Inês stopped, seemed on the verge of entering, then reconsidered. "I used to think that this was where I would have my wedding reception," she said with a sigh, and then moved on. Inês had never mentioned any romantic relationships. Lacey briefly considered asking but decided to hold her tongue for the present. In a place like this, there would surely be more opportunities to speak of love.

On the far side of the pavilion, the canopied courtyard came to an end. To the right, the property opened up to the golf course and a swanky clubhouse. Thankfully, Inês showed no interest in divot digging. Straight ahead and sloping to the left, dense woods closed off the view. "This way," said Inês. She led the way to a stone staircase almost hidden in the curtilage of the trees. They ascended steeply and found themselves on a narrow gravel trail. The two women walked in silence for a few moments until an old limestone wall, perhaps ten feet tall, appeared on the right.

"What's this wall?" asked Lacey. "It seems out of place."

Inês scrutinized it carefully. "I don't know. There are many different aspects to these grounds. They were not all put together at once as part of a single design but grew from the land over time according to the desires and purposes of many different masters. But now look at this plaque." She stepped beyond the wall and came to a slate of white marble inscribed with a few lines in Portuguese. "Do your magic, Mousie."

The plaque read:

(Contra-romance de Ines e Pedro)

nom Ines. E foste minha.
Como Ines sobre a pedra estavas nua
E o meu punhal eu o enterroi
No coracao da lua
Como Ines so depois foste rainha

Manuel Alegre

Lacey studied the writing carefully and bit her lip uncertainly. "Who is Manuel Alegre?" she asked slowly.

Inês laughed. "You're stalling! That is obviously the name of the poet. But now you must do the translation."

"OK, OK. Well, the title is easy. It says *Contra romance de Ines e Pedro*, which means 'against the romance of Ines and Pedro.' By the way, why doesn't it have the little accent mark over the *e* in Ines?"

"You're stalling again! The answer is easy: the stone carver was lazy about the accent mark. And you have been lazy about the title."

"Really?" She sounded genuinely dejected.

"Look carefully. *Contra* and *romance* are hyphenated; it's *contra-romance*, not *contra romance*. Also, do you really think a poet in this place would be against the romance of Pedro and Inês? He might as well be against gravity!"

Lacey wrinkled her nose with waning confidence. "You have a point. It's not against their romance, but a counter-romance. Or... wait. *Roman* in French means a novel or a story. So maybe the poet is telling a counter-story, a different story, about Pedro and Inês."

"That's better. Now go on."

"OK. *Teu nom Ines. E foste minha.* Your name is Ines, and you were mine."

"Good."

"*Como Ines sobre a pedra estavas nua.* Like Ines on the stone, you were nude, or naked. But I'm confused. Who's he talking to now?"

"Keep going. Maybe you'll get it."

"All right. *E o meu punhal eu o enterroi.* OK, OK. He interred or buried something. But what? A *punhal*. His *pugnus*, his fist? He buried his fist? That sounds OK for a bar fight, but not the stuff for an epic romance."

"You're being too literal. What do you bury that you hold in your fist?"

"Hmmm. Lots of things. A garden trowel? A fork? But I'm guessing a sword or a knife."

"*Bem*. Punhal, dagger. He buried his dagger. But where and why?"

"Where: *No coracao da lua*. I already gave you *quem vê cara não vê coração* when we first met. He buried his dagger in the heart of the moon. And why: *Como Ines so depois foste rainha*. Like Ines only later were you queen."

"So what does it all mean?"

"Hmmm. I've got each of the words, but I'm not sure how they all fit together."

"Exactly!"

"Exactly what?"

Inês, who had begun to walk forward, stopped suddenly and looked Lacey in the eyes, almost belligerently. "Exactly what you need to be thinking." And then she walked on.

Wary of the sudden change in her friend's mood, Lacey decided not to press it for now and walked along the trail for a few minutes in silence. Soon, the gravel path narrowed at the entrance to another woods where the trail became dirt. Although the temperature had been near ninety degrees when Lacey walked over from the city, inside the belly of the verdant woods it felt chilly. Goose pimples ran over her arms.

Just inside the woods, Inês stopped abruptly and gestured toward a palm tree that soared over a hundred feet, shattering the tree line with its exuberant fronds. "Here is something from your continent, Mousie." Her tone seemed cordial again. "A desert fan palm from Baja, in Mexico. And now we have left the Romantic Garden and are entering the area of the Medieval Garden, the heart of the story of Pedro and Inês. Watch out for the roots. It's dark in here and easy to trip."

The somber path wound down through the tree canopy and descended toward a stone archway overgrown with vines. Red ribbons had been tied in many of the trees, some bright and shiny, others old and tattered. "What are the ribbons for?" asked Lacey.

"Tourists leave them as symbols of undying love. Although, I know of people who return to cut them down when things don't work out." She laughed again, a bit hoarsely. "Look, there is my favorite tree of all.

The banyan, from India. This one is three hundred years old. The banyan is known as a strangler because it starts life growing onto another tree and then sends more and more roots down until it strangles its host and takes over."

Lacey studied the tree intently. It was a magnificent specimen, with hundreds of sinuous terrestrial branches spreading away from the body like long fingers searching for something just beyond the tree's reach. Something about the tree's aggressive expansionism and its darkening of the adjacent woods made her uneasy. "It seems strange," she said slowly, "for a strangler to grow in a place that's supposed to be romantic."

For the first time that afternoon, Inês seemed surprised by something Lacey had said. "Really?" she asked. "I don't think that at all. I think it's really quite natural. But speaking of romance, here is the Fonte des Amores—the fountain of the loves."

The two women walked to a place where a cruciform channel opened at a rocky outcrop in the base of an old stone wall. Clear, gentle water percolated from the base of the rock, filled the cross, and then meandered down the length of the channel for about fifty feet before trickling off the edge of a retaining wall. Inês dipped a finger into the water. "This is the holy of holies—the place where Pedro and Inês met secretly when she was banished to the convent that used to be next to these grounds." Her voice seemed to choke up suddenly, but Lacey dared not look to see if there were tears on her cheeks. In any event, Inês recovered quickly and brusquely moved the tour along. "Now we are almost at the Fonte das Lágrimas, where Inês was murdered, but I must show you two interesting things along the way."

They wandered away from the lovers' fountain and its protective banyan tree and came to two soaring sequoia trees. "These grounds are historically important, and not only because of Pedro and Inês. Remember Napoleon?"

"Short dude; took over lots of Europe."

"Including Portugal. Or he tried. Portugal has always been allied with England—it just works that way. So Napoleon tried to take Portugal. The

Duke of Wellington brought an English army to Portugal and eventually pushed the French army out. At the time, this property was owned by a soldier named António Maria Osório Cabral de Castro, who fought several battles alongside Wellington. Castro brought Wellington to visit the Quinta, and the Duke fell in love. You see, everyone falls in love here! Wellington planted these sequoias to commemorate his visit."

"I think I like them better than the banyan," offered Lacey.

"But then tell me what you think of the next trees," said Inês, moving along the path. They came to two small deciduous trees that Lacey would never have noticed amid their more impressive peers. "What do you make of these?"

"Well, they're quite ordinary, I have to admit."

"That's because you see them in summer. In spring, you would not be able to miss them because of their deep pink flowers. *For everything there is a season, and a time for every purpose under Heaven.* Their botanical name is *cercis siliquastrum,* but their popular name is Judas tree. Can you guess why?"

"Ugh. Judas hanged himself from a tree—at least that's the Bible story in Matthew's gospel. It's a bit different in the Book of Acts. There he fell headlong in a potter's field and his guts spilled out."

"But maybe both accounts are right! He hanged himself from a tree until the rope burst, and then he fell headlong and his guts spilled out. Anyway, that's the story with the Judas tree. It originated in Palestine and used to have white flowers, but after Judas hanged himself on it and spilled his blood, the flowers became red."

"The banyan tree is growing on me," said Lacey with a shiver, not realizing the irony until the words left her lips. Feeling that even her metaphors were betraying her, she quickly added: "What a cheerful place this is!"

"Steel yourself, Mousie. It's about to get even better. Here we are at the Fonte das Lágrimas, the Fountain of Tears."

They had come about fifty yards from the Fonte dos Amores to a place where the water trickled from within the side of the hill, through a narrow channel at the base of a rock façade. Just inside the channel, the rock at the bottom had a dark reddish hue.

"You don't need to say," said Lacey mournfully. "Leonor already told me about the rock being stained with Inês's blood."

"Yes, that's the legend. Of course, no educated person believes that today, right? It's just a red fungus. But tell me, Mousie, how is it that, for hundreds of years, this fungus has grown only in this one place in the Quinta grounds?"

"I dunno. The conditions are just right here?"

"Or..."

"Or... ?"

"It's haunted."

Lacey looked around uneasily. Although she had seen a few other guests around the hotel, they had been quite alone on their walk and she was not feeling entirely comfortable with her friend's moody behavior. It was one thing to trade ghost stories in the stodgy enclosure of the hotel, and quite another to stare at the uncanny patch of red at the scene of the ancient murder. Her mind wandered to the weird and impenetrable poem, the scarlet ribbons decaying in the branches, the strangulating banyan sending forth its spiny fingers, the whispering Judas trees, and the red stain on the rock. She began to think that she did not like the place as much as she had expected.

A minute had passed, and Lacey had made no answer to the "haunted" comment. Apparently believing that hers was the last word on the topic, Inês moved on from the Fountain of Tears. The channel that fed the dark pool flowed on into a reservoir also fed by another channel farther down the trail. That pool spilled over into a larger reservoir adjacent to an open amphitheater and little patches of formal gardens. Here, the trees opened to a vista across the reservoirs and amphitheater and toward Coimbra over the river.

"We have seen the historical parts, the heart of the Quinta and the story of Pedro and Inês," said Inês. "There is much more of course, but it is more to be felt than seen or told about. Maybe our paths should separate for a while, Mousie. I wish to visit the herb gardens near the pools. But you should go the long way back to the hotel. If you go that way. "She gestured to a stone path running laterally next to the upper reservoir. "You will find yourself again on the paths through the woods. They are older even than the paths that we have already walked. Older, less traveled, and even more full of memories. Walk that way and feel Old Portugal. You will find that the paths loop back around and come back to the hotel. Let's meet back in the lobby in an hour, shall we? Then we will find Santiago and ask about this business of the Crooked Queen."

Although she didn't say so, Lacey felt relieved at having time away from Inês and quickly accepted her suggestion. Something unexplained had changed in her friend's attitude. From early on, Lacey had understood that Inês was not showing all of her cards—and nor was Lacey. But there had been an understanding between them, a unity of purpose, that seemed to be fraying with every step deeper into the Quinta's fabled grounds. Lacey watched over her shoulder as Inês disappeared into the herb gardens, and then continued along the ledge of the upper reservoir back toward the woods.

Beyond the Fonte dos Amores and reservoir, Lacey came to a stone staircase. At its head, the thick woods closed around a narrow gravel path leading upward. As she walked along, it seemed that the trees bent closer and closer into the trail, to the point that she was forced to walk with a bowed head. Periodically, she came across the remnants of a crumbled stone wall or a decrepit wooden handrail, but the hotel apparently had decided to leave this trail to the vagaries of time. Fallen trees lay across the path and thorn bushes reached out to grab unwary victims. At one point, the foliage became so dense that Lacey had to crawl on hands and knees to secure passage. She began to wonder if Inês had been aware of the condition of the trail and, if so, why she had sent her friend this way. *Old Portugal indeed!*

Lacey had just decided that she would abandon the trail and head back down when there was a cacophonous barking of dogs, coming from the direction of the fountains and Medieval Garden. She was not afraid of dogs, but coming in the midst of the forsaken woods, the sound rattled her already uneven nerves. Lacey doubled her speed along the trail. Thorns and branches snagged her clothes and tore at her hair, but the pricks and pokes only spurred her to move even more quickly. Before long, she was half crouching, half running through the dense woods. All of the pleasant arboreal chill had now dissipated. Perspiration dripped from her face.

At last, the woods receded and sunlight dappled the trail. Lacey saw with relief that she was near the golf course and clubhouse. Feeling foolish for having been spooked, she resolved to finish her walk back to the hotel with dignity. As she strolled causally down the hill into the Romantic Gardens, the sun began to beat onto her face and she reached for her sunglasses, which she had pushed onto her head when she had entered the woods. They were gone, doubtless fallen prey to the tendrils of the woods. "They're cheap; I can buy another pair," she said to herself, not wanting to admit that she would not have gone back for a pair of Armanis either.

Chapter 12

THE CROOKED QUEEN

Back in Room 10—perhaps because of the sun dipping below the tree line—the portraits of Pedro and Inês had acquired a darker tenor. Inês, especially, cut a grotesque figure. Her head seemed more lopsided than before and the bloody ring on her belly had spread with the coming of the shadows. Thinking with embarrassment of her panic in the woods, Lacey had to resist the temptation to remove the portrait from the wall. Nonetheless, she did not linger in the room. Well before the appointed meeting time, she slipped back into the hallway and closed the door on the leering portraits.

No one but the receptionist was around, so she set off to explore the rest of the old wing. To the right of the reception area was an inviting reading room, the kind of place where one might lose oneself in a paperback novel. It opened into a library crammed floor to floor with dusty books. Lacey took a quick glance and moved on. One library encounter would suffice for the day. At the far end, a shabby wooden door led out of the reading room. It was closed and there was nothing indicating whether guests were welcome to pass through, or what lay beyond. Moved by curiosity, Lacey walked over and grasped the handle. It was not locked; the door opened with a creaking sound.

Stepping through, Lacey was surprised to find herself on a narrow balcony overlooking an aged chapel thirty feet below. The wooden balustrade looked so decrepit that she dared not lean on it as she surveyed the room from the acrophobic eyrie. The chapel seemed to be in a state of desuetude. There was a small sitting area with a few disorganized chairs and a recessed chancel housing a bare altar. A bouquet of withered red roses lay forlorn in the middle of the room. The queer room was strangely out of place from the rest of the hotel and grounds.

A voice came suddenly from the reading room: "So you found it." Inês stepped through the door, accompanied by a middle-aged man dressed primly in a gray suit.

"Oh, hi," said Lacey, a bit flustered. "Found what?"

"The scene of the crime. I assume that is what you were looking for, Mousie?"

"Not really," admitted Lacey truthfully. "I was just exploring the hotel to kill time." She glanced at her watch, noticing that it was still a few minutes before she and Inês were supposed to meet in the reception area. "But this is where the Crooked Queen was stolen?"

"Yes," answered Inês. "Let me introduce Santiago. He was here at the time."

Santiago nodded curtly. "Yes, that's true."

He paused, as if waiting for Lacey to begin asking questions. Lacey said nothing. Santiago stood in stony silence. Lacey began chewing her nails. It was irritating that they were behaving as if she were a tourist asking questions about the menu. She was still in Portugal as a favor to Inês; they had come to the Quinta as a favor to Inês.

"Well, tell her about what happened," Inês said after seeing that neither of the other two was going to budge. Santiago gave her a glance, and then said: "There is not much to know. This is the palace chapel. It is not used much now. The door is always double-bolted at street level to protect against unauthorized access to the hotel. The windows do not open. Guests can only see the chapel from here. After we learned of the historic importance of *A Rainha Torta*, we moved the tableau from the lobby here to keep it safe."

"It would have been hard to view from up here," commented Lacey.

"It wasn't on display for the benefit of guests," said Santiago sharply. "We wanted to keep it safe during the lawsuit."

"That worked out well," said Lacey, despite herself.

"You cannot blame the hotel," retorted Santiago. "This was the plan agreed upon by both families. We even added a sensor and an alarm to the tripod where the *azulejos* were sitting. When I checked it at night, all was well. In the morning, it was gone. The door had not opened. The windows had not been broken. No one unusual was in the building. Its disappearance is a mystery. Like a locked door mystery in a detective book, but this one is real."

"Someone must have gone over the railing, climbed down into the chapel, disconnected the alarm, hoisted *The Crooked Queen* back up, and then slipped through the hotel when no one was looking," offered Lacey. Her more cooperative tone covered the study she made of both of their faces. Inês and Santiago nodded. "*Sim*," said Inês, "that's what the police said."

"Well then," said Lacey, "I'm sure it's no good asking about fingerprints or security cameras. Anyone sophisticated enough to pull this off would have covered their tracks."

"Of course," said Santiago, a bit more warmly. "Is there anything else?"

"No, no. But thank you for your time."

Santiago disappeared quickly into the reading room, leaving the two women gazing gloomily over the rickety railing into the chapel. Inês waited until Santiago was out of earshot, and then asked: "I'm sorry that Santiago wasn't so helpful—it's just that he feels responsible, and it's hard being caught between our two families. Did you learn anything useful, Mousie?"

"Actually, he was very helpful," answered Lacey. "That gives me plenty to go on."

"OK," said Inês doubtfully. "But now we should be thinking about dinner. The hotel has a five-star restaurant. Do you have anything else you can, uh, wear?"

Lacey looked abashedly at the grimy shorts and T-shirt she had been wearing for the last several days. "Uh, not really. I kinda left Lisbon in a hurry."

"Not a problem. I brought a few extra things. They may be a bit big for you, but we'll make do."

Lacey opened her mouth to protest but couldn't find a graceful way out. So, half an hour later, she found herself in a black silk dress three inches too short and three inches too wide as she entered the restaurant with her benefactor, self-conscious and anxious about the evening. The room fronted the Romantic Garden, and the two women were seated at a table for two, covered with a white tablecloth and tucked comfortably against a rounded window overlooking the trees and fountains where their promenade had begun that afternoon. Evening was falling over the grounds. The gardens already looked more ethereal than they had in the dazzling afternoon light.

In the intervening thirty minutes, Lacey had been pondering what to say over dinner. She was beginning to feel that it might be time for a candid talk. Was Inês still interested in locating the Crooked Queen? She wasn't giving many signs of it. Lacey had tentatively decided that the time for the tête-à-tête might be after they had each imbibed a half glass of port. Inês had apparently been entertaining similar thoughts and moved preemptively: "OK, Mousie. Tonight, let's just enjoy the Quinta. This is one of the best restaurants in Portugal. My treat. We can do business tomorrow morning."

Before Lacey could answer, the waiter arrived with menus. Inês dismissed them with a wave of her hand. "*Os sete pratos*," she declared imperiously.

"Wow, seven courses," said Lacey apprehensively. "I'm not sure I'll be able to do justice to that."

"Believe me, *menina*—you will."

The law firm had not exactly liked to trot her out in front of clients, so Lacey had little experience with fancy meals. She quickly understood that the seven courses were manageably sized and lost her fear of not getting through them. The meal was as scrumptious as Inês had promised. No sooner had the sommelier poured the wine (looking a tad disapproving that they had begun with port) than the waiter appeared with two small plates of spicy *chouriço* sausage in a filo dough pastry shell. The pastry was so crisp and buttery that Lacey was still chasing the flakes to the corner of her plate when the next course arrived.

"Chocolate?" asked Lacey, surprised to see a sweet so early.

"Chocolate bomb with liquor," explained Inês. "It's good to mix savory and sweet in the palette. Now watch the liquor. Once you explode the bomb, the liquor runs for its life."

Lacey tapped cautiously at the chocolate shell with her spoon.

Inês laughed. "You would make a terrible terrorist! That's no way to explode a bomb! Watch me." She gave the shell an authoritative flick with her spoon. As the liquor came burbling out, she scooped up chocolate flakes and liquor with fluid dispatch.

"Oh yeah," said Lacey with enthusiasm and followed suit.

The liquor and port combined to ease the tensions of the day, and she soon found herself laughing with Inês in enjoyment of the feast. The restaurant was slowly filling with patrons and the mood was light. Next to arrive was a reduced pineapple cube with wasabi infusion. "I didn't know that wasabi was Portuguese," said Lacey with a giggle.

"It's from one of our former colonies, I'm sure," answered Inês with a smirk. "Remember, we used to rule the world."

They had barely started the pineapple when a course arrived that Lacey momentarily thought she might not be able to stomach. "Raw egg swimming in a cream sauce with herbs," said Inês proudly.

"Really?" asked Lacey, steeling herself.

"Relax; you'll love it." Inês leaned forward with a spoon, apparently to demonstrate some technique. Her elbow caught a water glass and sent it spilling into Lacey's lap.

"Ay, *menina*, I'm so sorry," she cried, tossing her napkin as a sop.

"No worries; it's your dress."

"But you shouldn't have to finish supper all drenched. Look, I have another dress hanging in the closet in my room. It's blue and white, and it might fit you better anyway."

Lacey protested that she was fine, but Inês insisted. Taking Inês's key card, she hurried to change, anxious not to interrupt their high spirits. On the way down the hotel's corridors, Lacey found herself a little shaky on her feet. The port and liquor were more than compensating for the day's earlier awkwardness.

A few minutes later, wearing a dry dress that didn't fit her any better than the wet one, she arrived back at the table to find that she had been lapped. A plate of sushi and watercress had joined her untouched egg and cream, and her wine glass had been topped off. Inês insisted that she not hurry to catch up. "Enjoy it," she said, drawing on the port, and encouraging Lacey to do the same. The two were soon back to their merriment. For the fun of it, Lacey launched into an analysis of the other patrons in the restaurant.

"That couple over there..."

"You mean the guy in the purple shirt with the lady half his age?"

"Yeah, but she's older than you think, and he's younger. She's Eastern European, probably Romanian, and works in the hospitality business."

"Now how can you possibly know that?"

"Trade secrets, my dear, but if you want a few clues. Well, I caught a snippet of her voice coming back to the table. There's the accent and there's the attitude. A quieter and deeper tone than someone from, say, Holland or Norway. As to the hospitality business, look at the way the maître d' is treating her—less polite and formal than a guest, more important than a friend or family."

"You're making that up!"

"No, no, really, and the guy..." As she launched her dissection of the man who wasn't as old as he looked, Lacey began to feel awkward. She wasn't quite sure why, but an unfamiliar sensation was growing subtly in her. As Lacey looked at the subject of her dissection, she found it difficult to identify the sorts of concrete things to which she usually applied her trade secrets. His hairline, shoes, rings, posture, clothes, and tone of voice were not speaking to her as they usually would have. On the other hand, she began to see things about the man that she could not explain but seemed indubitably true. "He's loved three times in his life," she said slowly, "and twice his heart was broken. He is not yet in love with the woman he's with now but will be by Christmas."

Inês put down her glass and looked at Lacey with deep interest. "Go on," she said.

"He... he will break her heart. But it won't be his fault. He will break her heart by dying. In three years. In an accident. At the beach." Her voice faltered.

Inês reached across the table and took her hand. "Are you OK?" she asked with concern.

Lacey surprised herself by not feeling embarrassed. "Yes, I'm OK. You said this place is magical. I'm beginning to smell the fairy dust." As she spoke, it occurred to her that she didn't recognize her own voice. It seemed to be floating outside of her and directed by a greater intelligence than her own.

Inês laughed, as if uncertain whether Lacey was joking. Clarification was briefly averted as the waiter arrived with the next course—Angus beef with asparagus and baby carrots. The conversation paused while they ate. But now that she had started, Lacey felt she could not stop. Bisecting an asparagus spear, she asked: "How about you, Inês? Have we come all the way to the Quinta das Lágrimas for you to keep your heart closed to me? Who is your love?"

Inês was unoffended by the question. "Well, Mousie, you are bold to ask! But I think that you are younger than I am and so you should go first."

"My lover," said Lacey with a flourish of her napkin, "is Ares, god of war, who rides his red chariot across the sky drawn by the fire-breathing steeds Phlogios, Phobos, Aithôn, and Konabos." She had no idea why she said this, but it sounded remarkable when she did, and she indulged in a drink of wine to celebrate. "Now your turn."

Inês feigned to understand "your turn" as referring to the wine rather than answering the question. She drank deeply from her glass, then sat back in her chair and watched Lacey closely. But Lacey had gone too far to back down. She drank again quickly, then said: "You must tell me who you love, Inês. Surely in this epicenter of romance you would tell me that!"

Inês sat quietly, as if toying with competing impulses. Her brow furrowed and her lips moved silently. Now it was Lacey's turn to watch and read her friend's face, but she found it difficult to see Inês Fonseca across the table. Instead, she fancied that she saw the figure of Inês de Castro, not a decapitated corpse or ethereal ghost, but a young woman of flesh and blood. Whichever Inês it was lifted a flagon of wine to her red lips, her face sad and worn beyond her years.

"Are you sure you're feeling all right?" The question clearly came from Inês Fonseca. She was peering intently back at Lacey.

"Yes, yes, I'm fine," answered Lacey. In fact, she wasn't sure if the strange way that she was feeling should be counted as less than fine or more than fine. "It's just that it's as if I'm seeing you for the first time. It's the magic, you know."

Inês was on the verge of saying something, but at that moment the waiter arrived and placed a small plate and bowl before each of them. Inês seized on the intervention. "And here are the answers to your question, Mousie. Who are my loves? You should know that already. Why sweets, of course! Here are the sixth and seventh courses. Chocolate cake and ice cream!"

Lacey reached for the dishes mechanically. She was no longer hungry—whether because she had eaten her fill or something else she wasn't sure—but it would have been rude not to finish the gourmet meal. Inês attacked the desserts with no sign of abated appetite. Their conversation lagged, but both women cast veiled glances at each other, occasionally meeting each other's eyes. When they did, Lacey found that she tried to hold the gaze, but Inês quickly backed away. They finished their food and drained the last dregs of their wine. Inês summoned the waiter, settled the account, and rose from her chair.

"Come, Mousie," she said. "You need some fresh air. Let's go for a walk. Night is falling and you'll see how different things look under the stars."

Something in the suggestion of a walk sapped Lacey's exuberance. Memories of her flight from the old upper trail that afternoon sent goosebumps down her arms. Outside the round windows, the shades of night had fallen on the Romantic Garden. Lacey rose uncertainly. She found that she no longer felt shaky but rather light and airy, as if she were standing on a velvet cushion. "Thanks so much for this wonderful meal," she said with genuine gratitude, "but I'm getting a little sleepy. I think I'll turn in for the night."

"Nonsense," retorted Inês jovially. "You've just been galloping across the sky with Ares. A walk in the gardens will settle you down for a good night's rest."

Lacey was not sure that a walk in the darkened woods past the scene of a royal murder would have this effect, but she felt indebted to Inês and embarrassed to admit unease about walking the trail again at night. Inês took her by the hand and led the way through a glass door exiting onto the patio at the border of the Romantic Garden. At once, Lacey felt silly for her apprehension. The gardens were lit with hundreds of lights strung in the trees. Their sparkles danced through the garden's leaves and flowers and spilled onto the burbling streams and fountains.

"How beautiful," said Lacey spontaneously.

Inês nodded. "Yes, it's beautiful. This is never said in the legends, but I believe that Pedro and Inês met here mostly at night. It would have been too risky for them during the day."

They walked past the bamboo stand, now an army of stern sentinels casting spiny shadows over the trail. They came to the glass pavilion, now rendered desolate by the curtain of night. At the end of the Romantic Gardens, they ascended the trail and passed the sleeping golf course on the right. Here the canopy ended, and with it the overhead lights. To the east, across the river, the lights of Coimbra burned dimly. Overhead, a crescent moon sat low on the horizon. It became very dark. Lacey's spirits sank. The shades of apprehension that had sent her running along the trail that afternoon crept back into her mind. She tried to walk closer to Inês. But Inês had turned cold and grim, like the moody version of herself that had surfaced that afternoon.

"Where are we going?" asked Lacey, worried that her voice sounded tremulous.

"Back to the fountains," answered Inês tersely. "You should see them at night."

"Are you sure it's..." her voice trailed off.

"It's what?"

"It's safe?"

By way of answer, Inês picked up her pace. They passed the ruined wall and the marble slate with the inscrutable poem. *He buried his dagger in the heart of the moon.* The words came back to Lacey, now pregnant with sinister meaning. She felt her spirits sink into her stomach, and then suddenly wrench themselves free from her body and alight above her. She was looking down on herself, she and Inês descending the ancient stairs toward the strangling banyan and the Fonte dos Amores. From another plane she heard her own voice, muffled and distant, whimpering: "Let's turn back. I don't want to go down there."

But still the two women kept walking—past the sinister banyan, past the lovers' fountain. There were dim floodlights on the old stone walls, but their illumination disappeared into the black recesses of the exotic trees. Now, looking down from above, Lacey could hardly see her own body along the inky path to the Fountain of Tears. She could not see Inês at all.

And then came a horrifying realization. A solitary, wan shaft of light fell across the path, and Lacey realized that Inês was no longer with her. She looked around desperately in every direction, but her friend had vanished into the night. She was alone. Alone before the Fountain of

Tears. All was very quiet, save for the burbling of the little brook spilling out from the rock and flowing through its channel into the crimson pool.

Lacey could not move. Slowly, inexorably, like a spirit dragged to Hades, she sunk back into herself and became a body rooted in place as steadfastly as the banyan. Beyond all will, her eyes locked onto the bloody fountain, and she stood as dead, awaiting the pronouncement of her doom. How long she waited that way—whether a minute or an hour—she could never say. The only sensation that she could remember later was that of growing very cold and wishing that she had a sweater. And also the feeling that she had transcended both hope and fear and had come to a juncture of true sight where, for a moment, she would see not through a glass darkly but face to face.

When the queen rose from the pool, she did not seem to be in a hurry, and she did not seem wet. First, slowly, the jeweled tips of her crown emerged from the lapping water. Then rose her tilted head, swathed in an embroidered circlet of white that met the red-stained kerchief about her neck. The bloody stain spilled over her bosom and onto the waist of her white robes. Her arms lay lifeless at her sides, hidden in lacey sleeves. Only the tips of her fingers emerged to smooth the edges of her robe. But Lacey barely saw these things because her eyes were locked with the queen's. And what eyes! Colorless, lifeless, without white, iris, or pupil. Eyes as dead as stone, yet full of malice older than stone itself.

The queen stepped from the pool, not disturbing the waters with her passing. Her bare feet moved noiselessly over the flagstones, leaving no wet footprints behind. Ten yards from Lacey, she stopped. Her arms left her sides and spread open wide. There was no doubt as to the meaning. It was a command. Lacey was to come.

What would have happened next if it had not been for the barking of a dog became a matter that Lacey would relive in nightmares for the rest of her life. But a dog did bark. Perhaps it was one of the same dogs whose barking had sent Lacey scurrying along in apprehension that afternoon. Now, its sudden forlorn yammering broke the spell and unleashed Lacey's body and mind. She could feel again—fear, horror, madness.

They jolted through every artery and nerve in her body. With a scream, she lurched back from the specter. Stumbling, falling, she tore back along the treacherous path. The black banyan loomed up ahead and seemed to launch every one of its terrible tentacles to grab the fleeing woman. Twice she fell on its roots, certain that she would never rise again. But somehow her feet found the path again. Now she was ascending the stairs, back into the closure of the wooded trail where the dark was near total. She ran with no thought but only will.

Suddenly, a figure loomed ahead in the darkness. The scream died on Lacey's lips as she stumbled into the arms of Inês. Sobbing uncontrollably, she clung to her friend and buried her head in the silk of her dress. Inês was speaking urgently—whether asking questions or giving instructions Lacey could not tell. All she understood was that her friend was holding her close and leading her quickly back toward the Quinta and away from the horror at the fountains.

What happened next remained forever shrouded in Lacey's memory. Somehow, they reached the sanctuary of the hotel. Lacey was vaguely aware of Inês pulling back the covers of the bed and easing her head onto the pillow. She remembered begging something through inchoate words and clinging to her friend's hand, and that Inês was sitting on the edge of the bed when total darkness overtook her.

Chapter 13

ADEUS, TO GOD

Lacey awoke slowly, heavily. She blinked her eyes, looked around the room, and for a moment could not place where she was. Then the previous day's events crept slowly back into her consciousness in nearly perfect chronological order: finding Ricardo Fonseca alive, the bat in the library, the walk to the Quinta, the conversation with the receptionist, Inês's moody behavior walking the grounds, panicked flight along the old upper trail, the strained conversation in the chapel, the seven-course dinner, venturing out again in the dark, and the dreadful encounter with the ghost of Inês de Castro at the Fountain of Tears. Had some or all of it been a dream? Gingerly, she pulled back the covers and saw that she was still dressed in Inês's blue and red dress. It had been real—all too real.

The curtains were drawn, but dazzling sunlight managed to spill in through the seams and lent the room a cheerful air of morning. Inês had been sitting on the edge of the bed when Lacey fell asleep, but she must have left at some point during the night. The room looked the same except for something that Lacey knew was different but could not place at first. And then she remembered what it was. The ghoulish paintings of Pedro and Inês had been removed. They were nowhere to be seen.

On the bathroom vanity, Lacey found a note from Inês written on Quinta das Lágrimas stationery. It read: "Dear Mousie. I'm so sorry about yesterday. What happened to you was awful, and it was my fault. When you wake up, give me a call. Inês." Lacey checked her phone. It was a little bit after 8:00 a.m., and there was a text from Inês to the same effect. She texted back simply *I'm up*, then hopped into the shower. When she emerged and had dressed there was a text back from Inês: *Meet me for breakfast on the patio outside the restaurant at 8:30.*

The palace wing of the hotel seemed friendlier in the morning than it had in the afternoon and evening. Maids were already bustling about the halls looking for unoccupied rooms to clean and opening windows to let in the crisp morning air. Several other guests passed Lacey on their way to breakfast and wished her cheery good mornings. Even the Pedro and Inês memorabilia on the walls seemed less burdened with the weight of history and more kitschy.

As she walked, Lacey mulled the previous day's events. Should she have told Inês about finding her father? Would that have changed the course of subsequent events? And the ghost. Did she really see it, or had the day's uncanny occurrences primed her to imagine it? Really, was she losing her mind? And now what should she say to Inês? What about the fruitless search for the Crooked Queen? Was it time to pack up and go home? *I'm not a quitter*, she thought. And then she remembered dropping out of law school and realized that sometimes she was.

Inês was already seated at a round glass table on the terrace outside the hotel adjoining the Romantic Gardens. Her eyes seemed red and swollen as if she had been crying. As soon as Lacey arrived, she jumped up, ran over, and gave the American a hug. "I'm so sorry about everything," she said, sounding near tears again.

"Sorry about what?" asked Lacey cautiously as they took their seats.

"Everything, everything! It's my fault for asking you to do this. You have been almost killed by a madman, and last night..."

"About last night," said Lacey, searching Inês's face. "What exactly did happen?"

Inês lowered her voice. "First some coffee and food. We shouldn't discuss such things on empty stomachs."

Whether because of the previous evening's seven-course meal or subsequent events, at first Lacey didn't feel much like eating. Nonetheless, seeing that she would get nothing further out of Inês until she had broken her fast, she accepted a token breakfast of a galão, two scrambled eggs with dill and parsley, and a slice of thick, crusty bread with marmalade and butter. A few bites into it, she realized that she *was* hungry and accepted Inês's proffer of sliced pineapple and sausages. And when the waiter offered a tray of *pasteis de natas,* she found it impolite to decline.

While they ate, Lacey tried to watch Inês surreptitiously while seeming to take in the morning. If the hotel seemed friendlier by morning light, the Romantic Garden seemed less romantic. Dappled sunlight had replaced the canopy of stars and the dull murmur of guests eating breakfast drowned out the gurgling of the fountains. The bamboo stand, now draped in shade, looked neither impressive nor foreboding, but something that one might see as background in a picture book of the Far East. The gardens had become a cheerful place but gone were both the magic and dread of night.

As for Inês, the morning had done her no favors. She had been crying—that was clear—but there was more. Her hair had as much of an air of dishevelment as is possible in a short bob. Her fingernails, usually manicured to perfection, seemed to have been chewed, as though Lacey's bad habits were starting to rub off on her friend. Overall, she wore an air of melancholy, belied only by her ability to keep pace with Lacey on breakfast. Whatever sorrows, doubts, or secrets the two women kept to their own counsel, they remained sisters in the apparent conviction that there is no sin so great as a wasted Portuguese breakfast.

When they had finished eating, the two women sat back with refreshed cups of coffee and looked at each other with the frank understanding that business could no longer be averted. "Well," said Lacey, "about last night."

"Yes, last night. But first, I have to apologize to you for my behavior yesterday, *menina*. I know that I was not polite to you at times. There are just so many things..."

"Like what?"

"Fools, lies, and skeletons."

"Maybe you should tell me everything."

"And maybe you should too."

"Maybe. But let's start with last night. When we went back out after supper. Why did you disappear?"

"Disappear? So you don't remember? That's my fault too. You were acting strangely from the end of supper, and I should never have stopped to take the call."

"The call?"

"From my mother. She called as we were entering the Medieval Garden. I thought it might be urgent and stopped to speak with her. We spoke for a few minutes, and I thought you were waiting with me in the dark. But when I looked up, you had disappeared. I thought you had returned to the hotel, and so I went back to look for you. But you were not in your room or anywhere else around the building. I hurried back along the trail. As I was about to reach the fountains, you came running and crashed into me. You were shaking violently and crying, 'Inês, Inês, Inês.' I'm so sorry to have frightened you like that."

"You didn't frighten me, and I wasn't crying your name," said Lacey deliberately, searching her friend's face. "It was the other Inês. I saw her. At the Fountain of Tears."

Inês sat stock still across the table, her eyes wide. "You saw… you saw Inês de Castro?"

Lacey nodded. "You seem surprised," she added coolly. "Weren't you telling me yesterday afternoon that the fountain is haunted?"

"Yes, but that's just a story people tell." She paused. "Are you sure of this?"

"Why wouldn't you believe me?"

"I believe you, menina, I do. But what you saw … was it real? You were acting so strangely at dinner. At first I thought it was just the wine, but as we walked outside you seemed like such a different person. I'm so worried for you. This is all my fault."

"You keep saying that, but what's your fault?"

"Dragging you into my family's dirty business. Exposing you to danger. Don't you see what's happening? You're cracking; you're losing it, Mousie."

"Me, losing it?" Lacey tried to say it sharply, but the words came out more squeaky than sharp. In fact, what Inês had just said was exactly what she had been worrying about before she had even arrived at the Quinta das Lágrimas.

"Please don't be offended, Lacey." It was the first time in many days that Inês had used Lacey's proper name. "This is not your fault, but mine. You are so young, so extraordinary, but for everything else you are also so innocent. I have pulled you into something too deep, too sinister."

"You're forgetting that this is what I do," said Lacey dryly.

Inês shook her head. "Not this time. It's time to let go. I can't ask you to keep doing this. You should go home."

Lacey had expected that this might be coming and had herself wondered whether it was time to move on, but now that Inês said it, she felt a contrarian resolve. "But we haven't found it yet," she said. "We haven't found the Crooked Queen."

"No, no, we haven't, but nor have we gotten any closer. Please, Mousie. Please go home. I will always be in your debt for doing this for me. I will always remember. But the *azulejos*—they are just old tiles. They are not worth the loss of you. Or of me."

"And your father?"

Their eyes met. For a moment, Lacey thought that Inês might waiver, but then she blinked twice and said: "My father is dead. Or, if he is still alive somewhere, he is beyond our reach. Finding the *azulejos* will not bring him back."

Lacey sat back in her chair. The breakfast hour was waning in the Romantic Gardens. Most of the other guests had left and the waiters had cleared their tables. The dull roar of conversation had lapsed, replaced by the gurgling of the brooks and the singing of the birds. Their urgent conversation seemed alien, boorish.

"And what will you do?" Lacey inquired at length.

"Me? Portugal is so small, but the world is a wide, wide place. Once we ruled it. Or perhaps my life will go on as it is. Is that such a bad thing?"

"No, of course not. Then will you come back with me to Lisbon?"

"Not yet. I will stay here a day or two to say goodbye to this place that I once loved and now will never see again. No, no, don't ask me why. It just is that way. But you should go on back to Lisbon. Don't stay there long. Get your things and go straight to the airport. Stay at an airport hotel until you can get a flight. It could still be dangerous. Please, Mousie, for my sake, watch yourself, and go home. It's time to say *Adeus*, to God."

They both rose spontaneously from their chairs and embraced. Inês seemed more composed. There was no trace of a sniffle or tear. Her embrace was resolute but warm. For her part, Lacey felt a surging strength as well. Although uncertain of her next steps or safety, the doubt about herself that had been growing in her mind dissipated into the trifling air of the Romantic Garden bathed in the morning glow. She considered renewing the earlier suggestion that both women come clean on everything they were holding back, but she quickly decided to let things be. They had reached a moment of mutual understanding that, however tentative, felt like a decision. The path lay forward, not back.

After a ritual two-cheek peck, Lacey returned to her room, leaving Inês seated at the table, staring wistfully into the trees, *her* trees. Lacey had little to pack. Still, she did not reemerge from the room for some time. For the better part of an hour she sat quietly in the snug recess, pulling together her thoughts. At around ten o'clock, she checked out at the front desk, leaving Inês's borrowed dress to be cleaned and returned to her friend's room. Then, quiet as a church mouse, she took a final tour of the Quinta before making her departure.

Her first stop was the old chapel balcony—the scene of the newer of the two crimes now tarnishing the Quinta's legacy. She sat for a few minutes behind the rickety balustrade and studied every detail. It was just as she had left it yesterday, probably as it had been left for many decades. There was no need to take pictures or notes; every observation of importance she absorbed, labeled, and filed in the recesses of her mind.

After consulting the train schedule, she rose and left the hotel through a rear exit in the Four Elements wing. It brought her out near a swimming pool where a few tourists were sunning themselves on deck chairs. Lacey skirted the building in the direction of the Romantic Gardens. After verifying that Inês had left the breakfast area, she walked quickly and quietly through the gardens, past the golf course, and onto the trail toward the Medieval Gardens. When she reached the area just above the fountains, she stopped, took out her phone, made a call, then moved on without any conversation.

Her stop at the Fountain of Tears was not a long one. She stood at the edge of the pool for maybe a minute or two, peering intently into the water. Then she stooped down, dipped her hand under the surface, and felt around for something. Appearing satisfied with whatever she had found or not found, she moved on to her final destination. It was the herb garden that Inês had visited by herself the previous afternoon. Here Lacey lingered for a quarter of an hour, meticulously inspecting the flowers and plants and occasionally consulting with her phone. A close observer might have seen her collect a few specimens and tuck them under her shirt. Inspection completed, she walked briskly past the amphitheater and across the open meadows back toward the Quinta's exit and the city of Coimbra. A dog barked in the distance. Another answered. She did not look back.

Chapter 14

GIDEON'S FLEECE

This time, Lacey slept the entire trip as the Alfa Pendular swept across the heartland of old Portugal. It was not until the train slowed for its arrival at the Oriente station that she opened her eyes again and gave thought to being back in Lisbon. In the past two days, two people had made urgent requests of her—Ricardo to keep his secret; Inês for her to go home immediately. She had made a promise to Ricardo, and though her moral commitments may not have remained as stark as those propounded in Bible college, she felt an obligation to honor her word. On the other hand, whatever else Inês may have hoped or understood, Lacey had not promised anything with respect to staying or leaving. That she would have returned home days ago apart from Inês's request for help and that Inês had now revoked her request seemed relevant but not dispositive. Contrary to Inês's suggestion that they were no closer to locating the Crooked Queen, Lacey had collected several clues. The Mouse was at the locus of a dangerous mystery, and it was not in her nature to scurry away from it.

The immediate question was what to do about retrieving her things from the Airbnb. As Inês had warned, Lacey could not stay there safely anymore. If Black Jacket or anyone else was still looking for her, they might have traced her to the apartment and might even now be watching for her. The words *mouse trap* suggested themselves uncomfortably.

But Lacey was not prepared to abandon her personal effects so easily, particularly in mind of her skittish behavior in Coimbra. Pride in profession was slowly reasserting itself. On balance, she decided that it was reasonable to drop in quickly to the Airbnb, retrieve her things, and then find a secure hotel for the night.

She took the metro to Rossio Square and emerged beneath the towering obelisk upholding a statute of Dom Pedro IV, the first emperor of Brazil. It was midafternoon and the square was only lightly populated. Lacey made her way past a baroque fountain of cherubs pouring water onto mermaids. It was unclear why the mermaids needed to be bathed, since they already resided in the sea, but such questions would have to wait for a more leisurely moment. At present, her mind was preoccupied with sneaking in and out of the Airbnb.

As she left the square and wandered up the streets of the Alfama, the words *Gideon's fleece* came to mind. It was a story that probably she hadn't thought about since Sunday school, but suddenly the words impressed themselves as significant: *So Gideon said to God, "If you will save Israel by my hand as You have said—look, I shall put a fleece of wool on the threshing floor; if there is dew on the fleece only, and it is dry on the ground, then I shall know that You will save Israel by my hand as you have said."* A test, a sign. Good idea. But what to use for a fleece?

Such problems were peppercorns to the Mouse. She approached the apartment through a maze of jigging and jagging alleys and stopped in a little plaza at the intersection of two of the larger streets two blocks from the apartment. There was a café, drug store, shaded fountain, and steady trickle of pedestrians passing through. Lacey found a discrete corner between two crumbling walls and set up a vigil. She watched the plaza for half an hour, cataloging and considering about twenty different candidates. The housewife on her way home from shopping might have been interested in the job, but she had quarreled with her husband that morning over money and seemed flighty. The civil engineer with the thick glasses would have been perfect, apart from the fact that he wasn't a woman. The accountant in the red dress had a gambling problem and might just take the money and run. But now the middle-aged bookstore clerk finishing her espresso at the café—she was reasonably smart, not overly educated, bored with life, and looking for love—in other words, perfect.

Lacey walked over to the table casually and pulled up a chair. "Speak English?" she asked the bookstore clerk.

"Yes, a little," said the woman uncertainly, as though wondering if she was about to be taken in by a Jehovah's Witness or political recruiter.

"Good. I wonder if you would like to make twenty euros for fifteen minutes of work? It's a very easy job."

The woman looked distrustful. "Yes? What is the job?"

Lacey giggled nervously. "Well, I need something from my apartment, but I'm afraid that I can't go and get it myself. My upstairs neighbor asked me to go to the cinema today on a date, and I said that I couldn't because I'm out of town. But if I go back to the apartment and am seen..."

The clerk still looked uncertain. "Yes? But is this neighbor... a bad one?"

"Oh, no, no," declaimed Lacey. "The sweetest old thing. Just not my type, you know."

The clerk mulled this information. Perhaps the neighbor would be *her* type. "OK," she said. "Twenty euro?"

"Twenty euro." Lacey presented her with the money, the key to her apartment, and the description of the item she wanted to be retrieved. She had considered the possibility of asking for all of her effects, but there seemed no plausible way to spin that request. So she settled on a folder of papers on the night table.

The clerk took off in the direction of the apartment. Once she had disappeared around the corner, Lacey sped off on a different route to the same place. If someone was watching, they could be concealed in any number of places, so she would need to be cautious in her choice of a lookout spot. Just down the street from the Airbnb was an apartment with a recessed entryway. Lacey approached it quickly from the eaves of an adjacent building and slipped into a dark corner. She had an open view of the Airbnb's brick patio with the potted geraniums, marble table, and folding wooden chairs.

A few moments later, the store clerk approached from another street. She passed through the patio, unlocked the door, and entered the ground-floor apartment. Lacey watched like a hawk. A mother and two children walked by on their way home from school. A moped, then a taxi, passed by in opposite directions. Lacey began to relax. Maybe this had been overkill.

Or not. She felt it before she saw it. It is difficult to explain such things, but in her line of work those who only apprehend danger once they see it do not remain long in the profession. Suddenly, Lacey knew that someone was coming. Goosebumps flared on her arms. And then she saw him. A slight man, hooded and stealthy, crept up toward the apartment. He passed through the patio gate, came to the apartment's window, and peered in through the glass. A moment later, he slipped away and hurried back down the street. Lacey could not see where he stopped, but she was certain that he had. Before he disappeared from view, she caught a glimpse of his shrouded face. It was Pedrinho Guimarães.

At the same moment Pedrinho disappeared from view, the store clerk burst out of the apartment without the folder. Her face was drawn and frightened. She hurried quickly down the street, casting glances back over her head in the direction of the apartment.

Lacey hesitated no longer. She could only guess what the clerk had seen inside the apartment. It was only mildly reassuring that she had escaped unharmed. No doubt the folder and apartment key were gone now, and probably with them all of her clothing, effects, and suitcase. That was inconvenient, but less so than ending up in a coffin thousands of miles from home. She had to get away, and quickly.

As Lacey hurried down the street away from the apartment, keeping out of sight as much as possible by skirting buildings and ducking behind shrubs and street signs, she realized that she had failed to form a clear plan as to where to go next in the event that Gideon's fleece came back wet. Then another disturbing thought came to her—the recollection that Gideon had thought that one test was insufficient, and had put out a second test, reversing the order of wet fleece and dry ground, before going to battle. And then her sixth sense kicked in again, and she knew she was being followed.

Lacey had kept her wits enough not to turn around and look. That would have been as good as an invitation to her pursuer to seize the moment before she tried to flee. Instead, Lacey kept walking furtively but at a steady pace. She now knew where she must go. To a public place, a place with many people where she might either shake her pursuer or at least dissuade him from trying to harm her. A few twists and turns away, on the main road from the Baixa to the Alfama, stood the Sé, Lisbon's historic cathedral. She had meant to visit it before leaving Lisbon but had never gotten around to it. Now it would be her sanctuary.

Maybe. It was probably a good thing that Lacey had not had the time to study the Sé's history and learn, for instance, that just a few decades after King Pedro I mourned the murder of his Castilian lover, an angry mob suspected Bishop Dom Martinho Annes of conspiring with the Castilians, chased him into the cathedral's north tower, and tossed him out the window. Defenestration is merely one act in the Sé's bloody annals. The cathedral stands on the edge of a bluff overlooking the river estuary, where from the earliest civilization, it has witnessed the brutally contending wills of peoples, cultures, and religions. Archaeological excavations in the cathedral cloister, some still ongoing, have uncovered the layers of medieval Christendom crushing the red walls of a Moorish mosque, and under that, vestiges of the Visigoths effacing an old Roman road laid over fragments of Phoenician pottery. In more ways than one, it is a place to be buried.

These were not thoughts that Lacey was having as she turned onto the Largo da Sé, a thoroughfare bustling with trolleys, taxis, and tourist carts. A hundred yards up the winding road she could see the cathedral's fortress-like façade, jagged crenellations, vaulted entryway, and twin bell towers. She quickened her pace and allowed herself a half glance to the rear. With a twinge of fear, she saw her pursuer. It was Black Jacket. The jacket was gone and his eyes concealed in dark sunglasses, but there was no doubt about the malice on his mind. He was thirty yards behind and had quickened his own pace when she had quickened hers. It was now a race to the cathedral.

Lacey broke into a run, looking around wildly in the hopes of seeing a policeman. The streets were thick with tourists, but there was no sign of the law. What was the saying? *When seconds count, the police are only minutes away?* There would be safety in numbers at the cathedral, wouldn't there? She dodged through tourists in an inverse of the chase that had begun her adventures on the Feast of Saint Anthony. It had been an even race then and was again today.

In the fleeting moments before Lacey reached the cathedral's steps, she gave one more look behind her. For the moment, Black Jacket had disappeared into the crowd. But down the Largo da Sé another familiar figure was hurrying toward the cathedral. It was Pedrinho Guimarães. And he seemed not to be alone. Although in the blur of the crowd she could not make out the figure, it seemed that Pedrinho was himself being followed by someone—a short, stout woman. "How many people do they think it takes to catch a mouse?" she muttered to herself as she passed underneath the Sé's somber archway.

To her dismay, the only personnel at the door were two elderly nuns handing out rosary beads. They did not look capable of repelling a stray dog. Lacey accepted a string of beads as an insurance policy and passed inside the iron-bound wooden doors. It was gothically dark inside. The present cathedral structure was built during the Reconquista period with more military than spiritual functions in mind. Along the western aisle a rose window played stingy with the sunlight, leaving most of the illumination to fall dimly from aisle windows barely more than slits and, at the far end, the transept's lantern tower. A few candles flickered from alcoves channeling the prayers of the saints. Beyond the transept opened the Chapel of the Blessed Sacrament, crowned by a wrought iron chandelier. Further in yet, Lacey could barely make out the beginnings of a dim baptistery swathed by a wall of seventeenth-century glazed *azulejos*. There would be no time to study them today.

Lacey veered toward the aisle to her right on the eastern and darker side of the cathedral. Several hundred tourists were milling about. Her pounding heart slowed its rhythm. It was unlikely that her pursuers would try anything overt as long as she stayed around crowds. She looked back toward the door. A dozen or more people had entered behind her, but there was no sign of Black Jacket, Pedrinho, or the third pursuer. Uncertain of her next move, she found a concealed place behind a stone column where she could keep an eye on the door. For several anxious minutes, she watched and waited. Still, there was no sign of pursuit. Then it dawned on her that they were waiting outside for her to exit. True to the cathedral's military design, the front door was the only apparent entry and exit. Like Adonijah fleeing Solomon, she had managed to grab the horns of the altar, but the moment she relinquished them and stepped back outside, they would be waiting.

But there must be another exit. Stealthily, Lacey moved farther along the dark eastern aisle until she located a box of cathedral brochures. The map confirmed that there was no other way out through the cathedral but also invited tourists to visit the adjacent cloister, including a site of archaeological excavations. No exit was advertised here either, but an open-air cloister seemed a more promising place to search for unauthorized exits than the confines of a martial cathedral.

A multinational tour group following a guide trudged past her, whispering and snapping pictures. Lacey saw her opportunity and melted into the rear of the group. She gave the door one more glance as they arrived at the entrance to the cloister where a docent was collecting seven euros per person. Still, no one. Lacey stepped through the turnstile and into the passage to the cloister. If someone came after her, they would have to find her in the crowd.

The group entered a corridor with a ribbed arch ceiling. To the right, the passage opened intermittently onto an enclosed courtyard where the late afternoon sun spilled onto the grass. After the tomblike cathedral, the glimpse of sun and grass brought back a touch of life. But here were other tombs as well. To the left, recesses opened into sepulchers where the ancient kings, bishops, and noblemen of Lisbon lay ensconced in marble sarcophagi. They passed the tomb of King Afonso IV, father of Pedro I and murderer of Inês de Castro. After her recent experience in Coimbra, Lacey felt more sympathetic toward the king than she would have expected. Moving on, here was João Anes, Lisbon's first archbishop, and here a nobleman named Lopo Fernandes Pacheco, whose dog the artist had carved devotedly sitting at his dead master's feet. They passed yet another recess, but this one had no tomb. Instead, it was occupied by a suit of plated armor. The empty knight stood erect and vigilant, warding off foes with a deadly looking halberd.

As the tour group continued down the cloister corridors, stopping intermittently for explanations by the guide, Lacey looked for an opportunity to peel off and search for an exit from the cathedral. They came to a place where an excavated pit with boardwalks and scaffolding opened off the cloister's medieval corridors—the archaeological site advertised in the cathedral brochure. Twenty or thirty feet down in the pit lay the dusty ruins of old stone walls—the uncovered remains of the Moors, Romans, and their predecessors. Excavations were evidently ongoing, but the ruins were deserted. The tour guide gestured at the ruins, indicated that the group might return later, and continued down the corridor. Lacey slipped away from the group, out of the cloister, and onto a narrow and thinly railed boardwalk.

Instantly, she fell into temptation. In contrast to the cathedral's tomblike aura, the excavation site seemed full of life. Walking on the perimeter on the boardwalk, Lacey could make out the path of an old Roman road. Her mind's eye could see the adjacent shops filled with toga-clad merchants hawking their wares to passersby hurrying along toward the Zeus temple. She could smell the aroma of roasting fowl and herbs from the Roman kitchen and recoiled from the reek of the open sewer, whose remnants remained plainly visible in the maze of broken walls, floors, and streets. At the broken red walls of the old Moorish mosque, she could hear the prayers of the faithful, perhaps gathered for one last stand before the onslaught of the re-conquistadors. From every stone, nook, and crevice, the sounds, smells, and visions of ancient cultures—not dead or buried but alive and imperious—flooded over Lacey. Momentarily, she forgot about her peril and searching for an exit and allowed herself to be lost in the lives of men and women whose bodies had long since departed but whose spirits never would.

Another ancient story—the story of Gideon—returned to her, unbidden. What about it? Gideon had divided his men into those that cupped the water in their hands to drink and those that lapped the river like dogs. Those that cupped the water remained upright and alert. They remained in his army. Those that lapped like dogs could be caught easily unawares. He sent them home. Vigilance. Vigilance!

Too late. The heavy blow landed on her legs suddenly from behind. She fell hard on the boardwalk, dangerously close to the edge and already underneath the protective railing. She looked down and saw a thirty-foot drop into a Visigothic cistern. She looked up and saw the figure of Black Jacket standing triumphantly over her. His eyes remained shrouded in dark sunglasses, but his mouth was twisted into a malevolent leer.

"*Adeus, puta*," he rasped, cocking a black-booted foot to administer the *coup de grâce*.

The blow never fell. With a *swoosh*ing sound the shaft of a halberd fell from behind Black Jacket, cracking him on the side of the head. He staggered back, bellowing, spitting blood, and raising his fists toward the unexpected assailant. The medieval weapon flashed again, this time showing not just the wooden shaft but the grim pike head, bristling with blades and spikes to cleave bone and marrow. It was accompanied by a primeval battle roar that seemed to rise from the deepest recesses of the archeological pit, older than the Moors, Visigoths, Romans, Phoenicians, and Celts. Black Jacket took one look at his adversary, wiped the blood from his mouth, and fled for his life.

Lacey propped herself on her elbows and looked up in a daze. Had she encountered a second medieval phantom in as many days? The wielder of the halberd approached, lowered the weapon, and reached out a hand. Lacey met her rescuer's eyes, then flopped back weakly to the ground. The word that left her lips was the last one she would have dreamed of speaking at that moment.

"Mom?"

Chapter 15

AN UNEXPECTED GUEST

"**W**ell, honey, I was bored."

Daisy Papparin removed a kettle from the stove, poured two cups of herbal tea, and joined her daughter in the sitting area near the window. They were lodged in a spacious but sterile efficiency suite with green and mauve wallpaper and a fully stocked minibar in the Lisbon Marriott. It was the kind of lifeless corporate room that Lacey would never have taken on her own. But considering the circumstances, her mother's taste in hotels was the least of her issues.

"Wait a minute!" Lacey was wearing pajamas and reclining lazily in an oversized sitting chair, her slippered feet propped on an ottoman. "You're running away from Glennis and the grandkids, aren't you?"

Daisy smoothed her blouse and took a long sip of tea. She was a short woman, just this side of plump, with shoulder-length salt-and-pepper hair and a round, cherubic face a decade too young for her aging hair and spinster glasses. Wrinkled khaki culottes sagged above her bare feet, only slightly less pressed than her green polyester blouse that could not have cost more than $9.99 on the sale rack at Bloomingdale's. She took another sip of tea, then mimicked her daughter by propping her feet on the ottoman.

"Running away from your brother?" she asked innocently. "Why would I do that?"

"Glennis, Mom. The way that woman takes advantage of you, I can't say I blame you."

"Oh, honey, don't be so hard on your sister-in-law. She's had a rough life."

Lacey snorted. "Yeah, right. I suppose it's a real burden having to drive an extra three miles to the spa. Admit it, Mom, she's a wench and you're running away from her."

"Well, there's more to it than that. I was worried about *you*."

"But *why*? *How*?"

"Your work is so dangerous. Of course I worry!"

"But how do you know about my work? How did you know that I'm not studying for the bar? How did you find me here?"

"Of course you weren't studying for the bar. You would have had to go to law school for that."

"You mean that all this time... ? Why didn't you say anything? Why did you pretend to think that I was in law school?"

"Oh, honey, you know. I didn't want to be nosy. It's your life." She paused, sipped her tea, and then shot Lacey a furtive, guilty look. "And maybe I was a bit worried that if you knew that I knew you would make it harder for me to keep tabs on what you were up to."

Lacey nearly spilled her tea. "What do you mean 'keep tabs on what you were up to?' Have you been spying on me?"

"Well... yes."

"But how, how, *how*?"

Daisy giggled. Anyone who overheard it would have been forgiven for thinking it was one of Lacey's own giggles. "You can't expect me to give up my trade secrets, honey."

This time, Lacey did spill her tea. Not a trickle, but a full gushing wave of hot tea. The tea tsunami leaped from her cup and landed on her pajama pants. Lacey jumped up and danced about ridiculously while her mother made matters worse by fussing at her lap with a napkin.

"Stop it, stop it, Mom! I'm OK." Lacey dashed back into the bedroom and reemerged a moment later in fresh pajamas, grateful that they had dropped by the Airbnb to grab her effects on the way to the hotel. "What did you say? Did you say your *trade secrets?*" Her voice was shrill.

"Oh, that's just a little expression I have, honey. I didn't mean..."

"*Your* little expression, Mom? That's *my* little expression!"

Daisy removed her feet from the ottoman and say up primly. Her face wore a sympathetic but firm look. "Of course it's your expression, honey. You got it from me. I'm sure that you don't remember this, but it was something I used to say when you and Tristan were little. Like when he burned his report card in the back yard and I turned up another copy of it. Or when your French teacher gave you an F because she thought you had cheated to write a perfect test but then your grade showed up as an A on your report card. Trade secrets!"

Lacey slumped in her chair, looking utterly crestfallen.

"What's wrong, sweetheart?" asked Daisy with concern. "You don't think that I'm upset when you say 'trade secrets,' do you? It's really quite a compliment to the way I brought you up. Although"—and here Daisy's face took on a somewhat scolding expression—"I can't approve of you lying about things. That just isn't right. From now on, you'll tell me the truth, won't you?"

Lacey nodded forlornly. "It looks like I can't keep anything from you anyway." She paused, set down her tea cup, then reached over and took her mother's hands. "I just don't want you worrying about me, Mom. You've had enough to worry about over the years—like raising us as a single mom. I just wanted things to be happy at home, like they always were, even after Dad wasn't there anymore."

Daisy caressed her daughter's hands. "You know that I can't stop worrying about you whatever you do. I don't know that I would have worried about you any less in law school, swimming with all of those sharks. At least what you do is honestly dangerous. Do you know what I mean?"

"Yes!" answered Lacey, straightening from her slouch. "That's exactly it. My work is honestly dangerous—even when it's dishonest—which is what I like about it. But, c'mon, Mom, you've gotta tell me how you tracked me here. If for no other reason because I've gotta worry about who else might be able to track me."

"Oh, you don't have to worry about that, sweetie. Tracking you is easy, but only for me. You must have forgotten that I cosigned for your credit card when you went off to college. I get activity reports in real-time." Seeing the look on her daughter's face she quickly added, "Don't worry, I respect your privacy. Unless it involves figuring out where you are."

"Thanks, Mom. That's very decent of you." Lacey took the tea mugs to the kitchenette and refilled them. She returned, proffered her mother's mug, and settled in comfortably. "OK, now that you're here, do something useful and tell me how you tracked me to the cathedral."

"I already did something useful, didn't I? Whacking that nasty man with the thingamajigger."

"Yeah, and thank you, Mom. This is kinda embarrassing to say, but you probably saved my life. That's the second time that guy..." She trailed off nervously, still not sure she was ready to tell her mother everything.

"Oh?" asked Daisy.

"Let's get to that in a minute. First, tell me how you found me."

"Well, I knew where you were staying in Lisbon, of course, so when I decided to come—oh, and maybe I did need a break from the grandkids—I just took a taxi to the little apartment that you were renting in that cute little neighborhood with the narrow streets. I arrived there yesterday and found that you weren't there. I thought about texting or calling you, but then decided it would be more fun to give you a little surprise. Well, I waited until late but you didn't show up, so I came here and got a room."

"I was out of town."

"Yes, I know, in... how do you pronounce it?"

"Co-eem-bra."

"You don't have to say the last bit quite so loudly, do you?"

"Whatever, Mom. So you figured out that I was out of town, then what?"

"I saw that you bought a train ticket back to Lisbon and decided to have dinner waiting for you when you got home, just like old times."

"Uh, that means that you got into my apartment?"

"Well, that wasn't hard. Mr. Reis, your landlord, is so understanding. I just told him the truth, of course—that I was your mother visiting from Iowa. Such a nice family man." She lowered her voice confidentially. "I think he might be a Catholic."

"So he let you in."

"Yes, right away. Such a cozy little apartment. I packed your bags first—I thought we should move out after dinner—then started making chicken-à-la-king. That was always your favorite in high school. Couldn't find any eggs at the supermarket, though."

"Did you try asking someone?" Lacey knew this question was diversionary, but after being initially flabbergasted, she had begun to feel quite warm and comfortable and was rather curious to learn more about this heretofore unknown side of her mother.

"Well, yes, but they just laughed and pointed back at me." Daisy sounded mildly hurt.

"In what language did you try asking them?" asked Lacey, archly.

"Portuguese, of course." Daisy now sounded puzzled. "That's what they speak here, isn't it?"

"They do, but you don't. What exactly did you say?"

"Here. I wrote it down from the dictionary." Daisy retrieved a slip of paper from her pocket. "Ohn-day est-a-oh as ah-voes."

"Let me see that," said Lacey, taking the paper from her mother. She scrutinized the writing on the paper for a moment, and then started giggling. "I see the problem. The phrase you wanted to say was *onde estão os ovos*, which would have been, 'Where are the eggs?' I think what you actually said came out more like *onde estão as avós*, which means, 'Where are the grandmothers.' So they did answer your question!"

Daisy flushed and snatched back the slip of paper. "It's my first time in foreign parts," she sniffed with injured dignity. "But I suppose you would have done better than that. You always were so gifted with languages."

She said this without the slightest hint of resentment or irony, only simple pride in her daughter. Lacey instantly felt ashamed of herself. In the space of a few minutes, she had gone from seeing her mother as an innocent, parochial widow concerned only with the sweetness and light of home to see in her the prototype of the Mouse herself.

"Thanks, Mom," she said softly. "You've done very well. But go back to my apartment. So you're there happily making chicken-à-la-king. Then what?"

"Well, I heard the door opening and figured it was you and was wondering what you'd say when you saw me there cooking. But it was someone else. A woman, who must have been Portuguese. Well, she took one look at me and got this fearful look on her face, then turned around and ran away."

Lacey burst out laughing. "She thought you were the upstairs neighbor!"

"What upstairs neighbor?"

"Oh, just someone I invented. I suppose I wasn't clear about their gender. Never mind. Go on."

"Where was I? Oh yes. The lady ran out the door, and I ran after her, just to see if she was OK. When I got outside, I caught a glimpse of you, of all people, way, way down the street. Just a little glimpse because I think you didn't want to be seen, but I'd know your little trot anywhere. So I started following after you as fast as I could. I'm not a spring chicken, you know, so I was afraid I was going to lose you. But I'd be darned if I didn't get some help on that score. Just as I was about to lose you from my sight, I saw this big, mean-looking man—the same one who roughed you up in the church—start taking after you. And then, just a bit later, I see this other, much smaller guy, taking off after him. So it was sort of like Hansel and Gretel following cookie crumbs to find you."

"The smaller guy. What did he look like?"

"I mostly saw him from the side and the back, and I was running, you know. But he was a small guy with a thin face, light-colored hair, and glasses like John Lennon."

"Pedrinho. I saw him too."

"Who's that?"

"I'll fill you in later. Let's finish your story. So you're running after me behind the two guys who were chasing me. What happened when they got to the church? Did they split up?"

"No, I don't think they were together to begin with."

"What do you mean?"

"I mean that they weren't working together, or on the same side, or however you'd put it. The little guy was clearly trying to stay out of the big guy's sight. When the big guy got to the church, he didn't go in right away, but stood around on the front steps, as though deciding what to do. The little guy ducked behind a car until the big guy finally went in."

"That's... interesting." Lacey sat back and sipped her tea thoughtfully. "So what did you do?"

"Well, I wanted to see what they were going to do, so I waited until the big guy went in. As soon as he did, the little guy followed him, and I followed the little guy. When I got inside the church, it was dark and I couldn't see the little guy. He seemed to have disappeared. But I did see the big guy, and he didn't seem to have good intentions. So I kept on his trail into the cloister. When I saw you split off from the group and him start charging toward you... well, I grabbed that thingamajigger, and the rest is a bit of a blur. I think I might have gotten mad and shouted something." She blushed.

"You roared like a bull and whacked him, Mom, and it worked beautifully." Lacey giggled.

"But why was he after you?" Despite having shown a grittier side of herself than her daughter could have believed possible, Daisy sounded genuinely perplexed by why anyone could want to hurt her daughter.

Now it was Lacey's turn to be uncertain. "I don't know, exactly, but it's all connected to something called the Crooked Queen."

"Really?" asked her mother, in a voice that clearly meant, "Tell me everything."

Lacey looked her mother over long and hard. How much should she be told? Lacey wasn't used to telling her *anything* about her work, her adventures, her real life. Over the years, she had fallen into the habit of pressing her mother hard about all of the details of Daisy's life back home while offering half-truths and outright lies about her own. She had justified this as protecting her mother from disappointment and worry, but now she saw that her motives had been different. The one she was really protecting—by maintaining a fantasy land in Iowa to palliate all of her own disappointments and worries—was herself.

Still, it wasn't easy to let go of her long-acquired habits. Lacey had taught herself to read everyone and trust no one. Even with Inês, her ersatz client and instant friend, she had not allowed herself total openness. She had held back bits and pieces, even as she knew—or perhaps *because* she knew—that Inês was holding back too. Did it have to be like this with her own mother? Had her own mother ever held back on Lacey? Of course she had. Even as Lacey was trying to deceive Daisy, Daisy had deceived Lacey into thinking that Daisy herself was deceived. They had both been deceivers; it was just that Daisy was the more effective one. And now that the truth of Lacey's life was out in the open, would anything change by Lacey telling her mother everything?

Lacey sighed deeply. "OK, Mom. Since you're here, you might as well know the story. Maybe you can help me. Help me again, that is."

She started at the beginning of her trip to Portugal, now almost two weeks ago, and meticulously recounted her adventures. The job for the pharmaceutical company. Chasing Black Jacket through the streets of Lisbon during Saint Anthony's feast. Undercover at the Casa Fonseca. Dead end on the pharmaceutical case. Discovery by Inês. The backstory of the Crooked Queen and Ricardo Fonseca's disappearance. The face-off between the Guimarães and Fonseca clans at the Castelo São Jorge.

Fleeing in the thunderstorm, and Leonor's surreptitious grab at Beatriz's handbag. The visit to the Boca do Inferno and Lacey's suspicion that Ricardo was still alive. Rui and Dinis unloading oriental rugs at the dock. Visitation with the supposed bones of Ricardo Fonseca. Fado with Leonor, and Rui's rude appearance. Lunar Antique Tiles and Black Jacket's first attack. Trapping Beatriz at the embassy, and the uncomfortable confrontation with Pedrinho outside. Flight to Coimbra and discovering Ricardo Fonseca. And, of course, everything at the Quinta das Lágrimas, including the ghost of Inês de Castro. It all came out. Or, at least most of it.

Daisy sat listening with alternating expressions of fascination and dismay. Periodically, she took a little journalist's pad from her pocket and scribbled a note. Her brow knitted with chagrin at the accounts of Black Jacket, and her eyes moistened at the romance of Pedro and Inês. The discovery of Ricardo Fonseca alive seemed to fill her with wonder and joy, as though her daughter had brought back Lazarus from the dead. But it was the ghost of Inês de Castro at the Fountain of Tears that seemed to capture her imagination, and her pad overflowed with notes. When Lacey finished her tale, Daisy read over her notes, sat back with closed eyes for several minutes as in deep thought, then sat up abruptly and said: "Well, the ghost didn't do it, so whodunnit?"

"Oh, Mom," answered Lacey wearily, "they *all* dunnit. Isn't that clear by now? Fools, lies, and skeletons. It's all of them!"

"What do you mean? All of them couldn't have taken the Wicked Queen."

"Crooked Queen, Mom. You're thinking of Jezebel or Snow White. And, no, of course all of them didn't take it. But I'm beginning to wonder how central the *azulejos* are to any of this. There are many secrets here—secrets and great shames and spying eyes. Like what happened those many years ago at the tomb of St. James in Galicia? Whatever it was, it connects Beatriz and Leonor, and not in a friendly way. And who hired Black Jacket to steal the briefcase from the Café Luís de Camões, and why is that person intent on me not getting closer to the truth about the disappearance of the Crooked Queen? And what sent Ricardo Fonseca into hiding? And why are Rui and Dinis in business together, and what are they hiding? And, most of all, who is blackmailing Inês?"

"Blackmail?" said Daisy with a shiver.

"Yes, blackmail. Why did she bring me to the Quinta das Lágrimas? To see the sites? No, her goal was to scare me off the trail of the Crooked Queen, to send me home."

"But why would she do that? She was the one who asked you to look for the Wicked Queen in the first place."

"Crooked Queen, Mom. That's what she asked, but is that what she really meant? And even if that's what she really meant, she clearly had changed her mind. She was scared, Mom, scared of something that she wouldn't tell me. Someone has scared her, and I think it's blackmail."

"But who's blackmailing her?"

"Two leading candidates. Beatriz..."

"Yes, she sounds like not a very nice person. And you said she told you she had secrets on the Fonseca family that should never get out."

"And Leonor."

"Wait, I thought that she is your friend's aunt. Why would she be blackmailing her own niece?"

"Leonor's relationship with her sister's family is complicated. She clearly hates Rui and resents her sister. She's treated like the poor stepchild of the family. She had something to do with Ricardo's disappearance—I'm sure of it." Lacey paused for a moment, thinking. "The pieces are coming together. I can see all of the puzzle now. But there's one character who's sort of a corner piece, and I can't quite figure out which corner he belongs in."

"Who's that?"

"Black Jacket. Here's what I don't get. He stole the briefcase from Dinis Guimarães and Farid Hasanova. And then he started coming after me. He's obviously not the sort of dude to be doing any of this on his own. Classic hired thug. So who's he working for? I would have thought that he was Dinis's hired thug, but obviously he can't be working for Dinis if he's nicking briefcases from him." She paused for another moment, and then added: "Or can he?"

"You ask such interesting questions, sweetie. How are we going to answer them?"

"*We?*"

"Well, I'm here now and, as you said, I might come in useful again."

Lacey laughed. "Yeah, Mom, I have no doubt that you'll be very useful indeed."

"I will be!" Daisy sat up straight in her chair and did a poor imitation of a military salute. "But what is it that you want to do? If your friend wants you to back off, are you helping her by staying involved? Couldn't you be putting her in greater danger?"

Lacey sat back and thought for a moment. "Maybe," she said slowly, at last. "But thus far the physical danger has been all mine. I think I can still help Inês by defanging a few serpents."

"You mean Beatriz and Leonor?"

"Maybe, eventually. But first an easier target."

"Dear me, you have an easy target?"

"You'll see."

Chapter 16

PRINCE HUSAIN'S FLYING CARPET

Rui Fonseca bounded up the Avenida da Liberdade like a jackrabbit on caffeine. From head to toe, he was groomed to perfection. Every hair on his head had been greased into submission. Donna Maria had picked over his face like a mother baboon searching for any stray whisker or zit. A starched white collar bit into his bulging neck to accommodate a red power tie flapping over an austere blue suit. Wingtip shoes shone dazzlingly in the afternoon Lisbon sun, the product of two brands of shoe polish, three brushes, and a morning's worth of cursing. If attire was the measure, Rui Fonseca was ready for prime time.

But the movement of his body and the twitching of his head bespoke a man less than certain of impending success. He was practically running, not because he was late for his appointment, but because he could not contain the nervous energy welling up from the pit of his stomach. Every now and then he slowed to a walk, wiped his forehead with a white handkerchief, and muttered to himself in Portuguese. Twice, he stumbled over the cobblestones, once nearly going to the ground. And every half block he removed the letter from his coat pocket, scrutinized its content with perplexity, and then stuffed it back into his pocket with imprecations.

The letter. It was the letter's arrival the previous day that had begun Rui's tormented path to this moment. Donna Maria had brought it to him at lunch in his father's office, where he had been pretending to go over account statements, after a courier left the letter with Leonor at the front desk. His mother stood over him imperiously as he examined the envelope, realized its meaning, broke into a sweat, and, with shaking hands, eased open the top with one of his father's letter openers. There could be no doubt of its authenticity. Emblazoned at the top of the heavy, musty-smelling stationery was the crest of crests—the white letters LSE over a crimson background.

Rui read the letter quickly. His face drooped. His cheeks sagged. He glanced up anxiously at Donna Maria's hardened face, then read it again, this time parsing every syllable of every word. Then he threw the letter down onto the desk and demanded in Portuguese in a tone of exasperation: "What does it mean?"

Donna Maria took the letter and read it out loud in her posh English: "Dear Mr. Fonseca. The Admissions Committee of the London School of Economics is in receipt of your application for admission to the Executive Global Masters in Management programme, together with your university transcript from the University of Lisbon and letters of reference. We are not impressed. You seem very dull."

"*Mãe de Deus!*" shrieked Donna Maria.

"Wait, *mamae*, there's more," demanded Rui plaintively. "Read the rest."

Donna Maria adjusted her glasses, drew a deep breath, and continued. "You seem very dull," she repeated.

"Don't read that part again!" screeched Rui. "Get to the rest of it."

Donna Maria rapped him on the head with her knuckles and read on. "Nonetheless, in light of your sister's superior performance at LSE..."

At that moment, Inês walked into the office. "What's the commotion?" she asked.

Rui jumped up from his chair, pushed his sister out the door, slammed it closed, and returned to his father's swivel chair, where he sat in a quivering heap while his mother continued to read the letter.

"Nonetheless, in light of your sister's superior performance at LSE, we have decided to give you one last chance. If you will be so kind as to come to our Lisbon office (at the address given above) at three o'clock tomorrow promptly (that means not a minute before or a minute later), our Lisbon admissions officer will conduct an interview of your person to determine your intellectual aptitude, proficiency with the English language, moral character, and personal hygiene."

Donna Maria, who by now was white and quaking, paused and then added, "There's one more line in the letter. It says... I can't believe what it says."

"Read it!" screamed Rui.

"It says... It says... It says: 'Don't screw this up, Rui.'"

"What *is* this?" Rui demanded, grabbing the letter out of his mother's hands and shaking like a leaf in a windstorm.

Donna Maria sank tremulously into the visitor chair. "What this is, Rui, is your last chance."

She might have added: "Your last chance that none of us expected." For, of course, *no one* had expected that Rui would be accepted to the Executive Global Masters in Management programme at LSE. Every other MBA program to which he had applied, around the continent and United Kingdom, had said no, and without hesitation. There were the small matters of his abysmal university grades, his suspension in two separate semesters for cheating, his marginal performance on the English aptitude tests, and that two of his academic references—unbeknownst to Rui, although he might have guessed—called him, respectively, an "idiot" and a "lying, stealing, cheating bastard whose head is in the clouds only when it's not up his butt."

Rui was surely not going to get into LSE, but he desperately needed to, and the family desperately wanted him to, which is why everyone kept thinking that maybe, just maybe, he had a desperate chance. After all, Inês had distinguished herself brilliantly there—first-class honors, three special merit awards, and two offers of post-graduate scholarships—and her LSE days of glory comprised the first, second, and third paragraphs of Rui's tri-paragraph admittance essay. When LSE did not reject his application within three days of submission, like all of the other schools, a hushed rumor began circulating in the family (mostly the extended family; the immediate family knew Rui) that maybe they were taking his application seriously. Rui was seen at odd hours with his head in an unusual place—not in the clouds or up his butt—but stuffed into a book, and an English dictionary at that.

Another rumor circulated in the family. Rui was becoming *serious*. He would go to LSE and become a cultivated man of affairs. He would return to step into his late father's shoes and lead the Casa Fonseca into a future of prosperity. (It did not occur to almost anyone that Inês, having already succeeded brilliantly at LSE and at the firm, was a far more likely candidate to save the import/export house.)

So it was that the coming of the letter fell like a thunderbolt from the hammer of Zeus. Despite Rui's insistence that only portions of his interview invitation be communicated to the family, the entire contents of the letter were somehow leaked, such that by the time of his interview every aunt, uncle, godfather, godmother, cousin, nephew, niece, grandparent, mistress, boyfriend, family priest, and family shrink had heard that LSE thought Rui was dull. For Rui, there was only one path out of Hades. He must show them otherwise. He must conquer the interview and gain the coveted acceptance to LSE.

Rui mopped at his brow and glanced again at his watch. 2:51 p.m. He had arrived at the appointed destination—a disappointingly common-looking office building just off the Avenida da Liberdade. LSE's office was on the ninth floor. From the time he entered the building, it should take about three minutes to summon the elevator and arrive at the office. So to make it at exactly 3:00 p.m., as the letter said, he should enter the building at 2:57. Six minutes to kill. Rui reread the letter. Then he read the dictionary, aloud: *Aardvark: a nocturnal burrowing mammal with long ears, a tubular snout, and a long extensible tongue, feeding on ants and termites. Aardvarks are native to Africa and have no close relatives. Abacus: an oblong frame with rows of wires or grooves along which beads are slid, used for calculating.*

It was 2:57 p.m. Showtime. Rui stuffed the dictionary into his pocket, mopped his brow one last time, and entered the foyer. A single elevator waited, doors open. As Rui approached, the doors suddenly closed, and the lights indicated that it was ascending. He looked nervously at his watch. Still time to make it. The lights indicated that the elevator had reached the eleventh floor and stopped. Good, now it was starting back down. It reached the tenth floor, and then stopped again. After a long pause, it went down to the eighth floor and stopped. Rui looked at his watch again. 2:58. He cursed and mashed the call button. The elevator left the eighth floor but on its way back up. Rui broke out into a new sweat and released a torrent of curses. On cue, the elevator plunged downward, leaving a trail of descending lights. Then, on the second floor, it stopped. Rui checked his watch. 2:59. He mashed the call button with existential violence and released a fresh string of curses. Stubbornly, vengefully, the elevator sat a floor above him. Now in full panic, Rui cast about for a stairwell. There was one off to the side of the foyer. Rui dashed for it, grabbed the handrailing, and started up the stairs. At that moment, a loud *ding* announced the elevator's arrival in the lobby. Now spewing curses volcanically, Rui dashed back down toward the elevator. He arrived just in time to see the doors closing. The steel jaws closed with a snap, the strip of interior light vanished, and the elevator seemed to rocket up toward the top of the building. Spent of curses, Rui took a gigantic gasp of breath and sprinted for the stairs.

At 3:02 p.m., Rui pushed through the door of a nondescript office on the ninth floor, announced by an exterior plaque to be the Lisbon office of the London School of Economics. If he had not been drenched with sweat and panting convulsively, and further, if he had been even minimally observant, he might have espied certain factors casting doubt on the office's authenticity. Like the fact that the interior consisted of a single small room, appointed with cheap rented furniture, including two chairs, one desk, and a battered floor lamp. Like the fact that the single poster hung on the wall advertised river cruises on the Nile. Or the fact that the single person in the room, a middle-aged woman behind the desk, looked much more like a homemaker from Iowa than a graduate admissions officer.

"You're late," said the admissions officer with a pleasant smile. "Two minutes late. Didn't you read our letter? Or maybe you didn't understand it?"

"Yes, please," gasped Rui.

"*Yes, please*, what? That you didn't read it or that you didn't understand it?"

"Yes, please, sorry," begged Rui, flopping himself into the chair across from the desk without invitation.

"I'm not sure why you're sitting down," said the woman, still very pleasant. "You weren't here when you were supposed to be, so I'm not sure we can have the interview."

"Oh no, yes, yes," said Rui, grasping for the proper idiom. "Please to have interview. The..." for a moment, he seemed to be reaching for his dictionary, "the... elevator no work."

The admissions officer looked at him critically over the rim of her glasses. If Rui had bothered to notice fine distinctions, it surely would have occurred to him by now that her accent seemed rather un-British, or, as his mother would have put it, more Helen Hunt than Helen Mirren. In fact, that thought came close to occurring to him once, but the fog of self-induced and circumstantially induced anxiety kept the thought from ever landing squarely in his frontal lobe.

"Well," said the admissions officer after a long pause, "I will report your story about the malfunctioning elevator to London. They make the final decisions, of course. My recommendation is just a recommendation." She reached deliberately for a red pen on the desk and jotted a large note in a small notepad.

"Oh, thank you, thank you," murmured Rui, feverishly adjusting his tie and wondering if it would be better to mop his face with the handkerchief or let the sweat keep dribbling off his chin.

"Then let's begin. Today's interview will consist of a reading, comprehension, and analysis test. You will read a passage aloud. I will stop you occasionally to ask you questions about the passage. Any questions?"

"That is all?" asked Rui suspiciously. He had assumed that they would be asking him questions about himself. The task at hand seemed to have nothing to do with his past performance or, indeed, with anything about himself at all. That was a relief. Questions about himself would not have been favorable terrain.

"That is all," agreed the officer gravely. She reached into a desk drawer, took out a stapled set of papers, and handed them to him. "Our passage today is from *The Arabian Nights; One Thousand and One Nights*. Have you heard of it?"

"Yes, yes, of course," nodded Rui, lying.

"Good. You will be reading the story of *Prince Husain's Flying Carpets*. Please begin."

Rui looked at the story packet. There appeared to be about six or seven pages, and the print was fine. At a glance, he could tell that there were many big words. It would not be easy, but he must succeed. His future was on the line. Rui straightened his posture and began.

"*Prince Husain's Flying Carpets*. The Great Sultan"—he pronounced it *slut-an*—"of Persia had three sons."

"Let me stop you right there," interrupted the admissions officer. "What is a sultan?"

"Eh, I do not know, exactly."

She frowned and, after choosing the red pen, wrote a note in her pad. "And Persia, I hope you've heard of that."

"Yes," agreed Rui. "Persia. I have heard."

"Do you know where Persia is?" she persisted.

"Eh, maybe somewhere in *Médio Oriente*."

"That's not English. Anyway, Iran. Iran is Persia."

"Yes, Iran. I know that."

"But you didn't a minute ago. That's why we changed the story to Persia—to see if you knew where that was. In the actual story, the sultan lives in India. But if I had asked you where India is, you would just have said India."

Rui wasn't sure if he was supposed to agree, so he said nothing.

"Keep going," said the officer.

"The slut-an's three sons were named Husain, Ali, and Ahmed. The slut-an also took care of his niece, named..." Rui paused and mouthed out syllables to himself. "She was named Nou-ron-ni-har, and her father had died so the slut-an took care of her." He looked up to see if the officer wished to ask him a question, but she just watched him impassively from behind the desk.

"The slut-an planned to marry Nouronihar to a rich foreign noble, but all three of his sons desired to marry her instead."

Wham! The officer slammed her fist on the table with a cacophonous blow. Rui jumped out of his chair.

"That's disgusting!" inveighed the officer, glaring at Rui. "They wanted to marry their own cousin? What kind of filth is this you're telling me?"

"I-I don't know," he stammered. "It's just what paper says."

"Likely story," glowered the officer, jotting two or three notes with the red pen. "Well, keep going, if you must."

Shaking, Rui obliged. "Since all of the sons wished to gain their cousin's hand..." The officer snorted loudly. "The slut-an decided to stage a competition. Each of the three princes would travel to a faraway land to collect the greatest treasure he could find. Whichever one found the rarest and most valuable treasure would be granted Nouronihar's hand in marriage."

"And what do you think of that?" demanded the officer.

"Eh, OK, I guess. Whichever one brings best treasure gets the girl."

"And you think that would comply with the European Declaration of Human Rights? Whichever man happens to find the shiniest jewel or teapot gets to buy this poor, helpless girl, whatever she thinks about it?"

"Oh no, no, it's terrible."

"Then why did you say it's OK?"

"I no really understand."

"I'm beginning to get that impression." The scarlet ink flowed like blood.

Rui could feel the interview slipping away. He must turn things around now, in the next paragraph. "Husain, the oldest of the three sons, traveled far away to the Kingdom of Bisnagar. He went to the market and found a merchant selling a very plain-looking carpet for a huge sum of money."

"Now that's interesting," interrupted the officer again. "Why do you think a merchant would offer a simple rug for a large sum of money?"

Rui felt his pulse quickening. This was his chance. The medieval wheel of fortune had spun in his favor for once. "Carpets, rugs, they can be very valuable if they are the right ones," he said knowingly.

"Oh yes?" asked the officer with interest. "And what makes a rug the right one?"

"It must be made of the best materials by someone who knows how to do it. And especially, it must come from right place. Right place. Customer care a lot about where rug come from. Not Bangladesh or Morocco. Right place."

"You seem to know a lot about rugs, Mr. Fonseca." It was the first time she had used his name, and it gave him a thrill of encouragement.

"Yes, yes, know much about rugs. Ask more."

"OK then. Where would someone go to buy a rug here in Lisbon? Not just any old rug—the right rug, as you said."

"Maybe from me," said Rui with a smile that he thought straddled the line between nous and mystery.

"Really? So you deal in rugs? Could you find me a rug—the right rug—if I wanted one?"

Rui couldn't believe how far fortune had definitely spun in his favor. "But of course. The right rug. A perfect rug. And from special place. Maybe I go get one now?"

"No, keep reading."

It was disappointing that she had not gone for a bribe immediately. Maybe this was just her way of haggling. That was one thing that Rui did understand. He read on. "Husain asked the merchant why he was charging such a high price for the rug. The merchant answered that it was a magical rug that would transport its owner wherever he wanted to go. So Husain bought the rug. It was the worst decision of his life."

Something about the last sentence revived Rui's worries. As he had been reading, it had gradually dawned on him that he *had* actually heard this story before. Did someone fall off the magic carpet and die? That didn't ring a bell. As he now remembered the story, it hadn't been a sinister one at all but ended in a happy marriage. How could buying the carpet be the worst decision of Husain's life? Feeling again like a sheep being led to the slaughter but seeing no other course, he read on.

"Husain rode the rug back to the hotel. When he arrived, a mob of policemen was waiting for him. They arrested him and threw him into a prison full of rats and murderers."

Rui glanced up fearfully at the officer. She was surveying him with cool eyes. "Why do you think they arrested him, Rui?"

"Don't know, don't know," he answered, a bit too sharply.

"Then read on."

Three drops of sweat slipped from the end of his nose and plopped messily onto the paper. He wiped at his nose furiously with the sleeve of his jacket. "A lawyer came to visit Husain in jail. He explained that Husain had been arrested for buying an illegal rug. The kingdom of Bisnagar had declared an embargo on rugs made in the kingdom of Samarkand, like the one that Husain had bought."

"Oh dear, dear," clucked the officer. "That sounds very bad for poor Husain, doesn't it?"

"Why, no, I no understand," said Rui sulkily.

"You don't understand? I thought you were a big expert on rugs. Surely you know that from time to time countries embargo rugs from certain other countries over political disagreements. You knew that, didn't you?"

"I no understand," insisted Rui petulantly. He shot a glance behind him toward the door.

"Then read on a bit more. That may help."

Rui looked at the sheet and began to mumble inaudibly. "I'm sorry, Mr. Fonseca," said the officer. "I can't understand what you're reading. Please read comprehensibly."

Rui took a deep breath and read: "Of course, Husain knew that he had done wrong. The rug had been expensive because it was illegal. And now he faced a life of imprisonment in the terrible jails of Bisnagar."

Rui put the papers down on the desk. "I need go to toilet," he muttered, rising from his chair.

"A few more questions before you go, if you don't mind."

Rui paused.

The officer leaned forward and took off her glasses. "Mr. Fonseca, when you said that you could get me the right rug from the right place, exactly what did you mean?"

The interview was lost; now he had to protect other interests. Rui bolted, whirling away from the chair and running toward the door. He did not have to open it. The door opened suddenly, and a third person entered the room. Rui fell back toward the chair, gasping in terror.

"Mademoiselle Gertrude LeClerc!" he exclaimed, stumbling into the chair.

There could be no doubt about it. The grim Swiss inspector was back, with austere brown hair, exaggerated nose and bosom, thick glasses, unsmiling suit, low heels, ponderous briefcase, and all. She entered the interview suite and slammed the door irrevocably behind her. The way was barred. There would be no flight for Rui.

"Mr. Fonseca!" she roared, advancing toward him with the briefcase deployed as a mace. "It's ever so good to see you again. Now perhaps we can get the answers that you hid during the dawn raid."

He shrank from her toward the desk.

"Keep your distance, sir!" commanded the officer, rapping his head with a stapler from behind. This sort of physical chastisement was entirely familiar to Rui, having been practiced by his mother, aunt, and sister for most of his life. Whimpering, he sat stiffly in the chair.

"So, tell us about your little side business with Dinis Guimarães, will you?" asked the inspector. She had come around to the side of the desk to face him with the officer. In theory, this left open the path to the door. But there was no chance that Rui would make a run for it again. He was a beaten man, and everyone knew it.

"What business?" he asked weakly.

"No more games, Mr. Fonseca," retorted Mademoiselle LeClerc sternly. "You are already in a great deal of trouble. The Casa Fonseca's membership in the Association of Importers and Exporters International—well, that is already done. But now we are talking about crimes, *crimes*, Mr. Fonseca. And not just any crimes. International crimes, monstrous crimes. The sort of crimes in which the CIA and KGB take a great interest. Oh yes, Mr. Fonseca, the kinds of crimes that lead to waterboarding."

It is uncertain whether the insinuation was rendered more or less terrible by the fact that Rui had never heard of waterboarding. In any event, the threat had its desired effect. Rui hunched over into a fetal position and began crying.

"Yes, yes," he blubbered. "Dinis make me do it. He promise me much *dinheiro*, much money, but he never pay me what he promise. Talk to him, talk to him!"

"You can be sure that we will," said Mademoiselle LeClerc, tapping her briefcase on the desk. "But now you must tell us everything. These rugs that you and Dinis keep at the docks, where do they come from?"

"Persia."

"So you do know where Persia is!" exclaimed the admissions officer.

"And you also know that Persia is Iran and that the European Union has an embargo against Iranian rugs for political reasons. Don't you know that, Rui?" said Mademoiselle LeClerc. "And that makes Persian rugs very scarce and valuable, doesn't it, Rui? And very illegal."

"Yes, yes." He moaned.

"Good. Your cooperation is noted. Now tell me about a man named Farid Hasanova."

"Who?" He sounded genuinely confused.

"Farid Hasanova. About two weeks ago, Dinis met him at a café near the Praca de Camões. A man in a black leather jacket stole a briefcase that Farid and Dinis were arguing over. What was in that briefcase?"

"Oh yes, briefcase. Papers for shipment of rugs. The man—what you call him?"

"Farid."

"Yes, Farid. He sell us rugs. Very nice rugs. Very much *dinheiro*. Buyers of rugs want papers to say how old and valuable are the rugs. But those papers, they cannot come with the rugs in case *polícia* come to where we unpack rugs from boat. Papers with the rugs say rugs from India. So Dinis meet man to pay for the rugs and get real papers. Sometimes they argue over money. But this day, Dinis tell me Duarte Vasconcelos show up and steal papers. Dinis very angry."

"Duarte Vasconcelos. Who is he?"

"Duarte? Oh, everyone know Duarte. Whenever you need bad job for cheap, Duarte."

"So did Dinis ever get the briefcase back?"

"No, no. Duarte, he say he give briefcase to American girl."

For a moment, Mademoiselle LeClerc seemed to lose her train of thought. But she recovered quickly and pressed forward. "The American girl? You mean that friend of your sister's from LSE?"

"Yes, yes. She's a spy."

"Is that what Dinis said?"

"Yes, a spy. Dinis no know who she working for, but maybe Inês. But Dinis want her gone. Dinis very angry."

"Yes, you said that. So Dinis spoke with Duarte who said the American girl had the briefcase. Then what?"

"Then Dinis pay Duarte to make American girl go away."

The admissions officer sprang to her feet, grabbed Rui by the hair, and twisted viciously. He yelped and tried to squirm away. "*Go away?* You mean he sent that thug to kill her! She's somebody's daughter, don't you know?!"

"Aye, aye, aye!" squealed Rui. She let go of him. "No, not to kill. Just scare her a bit. But Duarte, how you say, he get carried away sometimes."

Neither Mademoiselle LeClerc nor the admissions officer seemed receptive to this exculpatory account. The Swiss inspector folded her arms. "This is serious, very serious, Mr. Fonseca. You have admitted to two crimes now—smuggling and being an accessory to attempted murder."

"No, please, no," pleaded Rui. "Duarte and the girl, I have nothing to do. I just help Dinis with rugs. He make me do it, and he no pay me like he say."

The inspector and officer exchanged a glance that Rui did not see because his face was buried in his hands. "Very well, Mr. Fonseca," said Mademoiselle LeClerc. "Although you are a stinking little weasel, the Association of Importers and Exporters International will take into account your cooperation in deciding whether to escalate this matter to further authorities. Here is what you must do. Go back to Dinis and tell him that if there is any further trouble with the American girl, the municipal police, the CIA, and the KGB will be informed of his smuggling ring. Do you understand me very clearly?"

"Oh yes, Mademoiselle, very clearly."

"And besides telling this to Dinis, you will not say a word about what happened here to anyone. You will tell everyone that your interview with LSE was fine and that you will hear their decision in due course."

"Yes, yes." Rui rose from his chair and began staggering for the door.

"One more question before you go." He stopped at the threshold, trembling and waiting for the axe to fall.

"Where is the Crooked Queen, Rui?"

"What?" he asked with confusion.

"*A Rainha Torta*. Who has it?"

"No, this, this I do not know."

"I believe that those may be the first completely true words you've spoken all afternoon," said Mademoiselle LeClerc drily. But Rui did not wait to hear her. He was out the door and dashing madly down the stairs with no thought but to escape.

The two women waited behind in silence until Rui was far away. When it was clear that he had gone and would not be back, Mademoiselle LeClerc began a rapid metamorphosis. In short order, a suit coat, brown wig, glasses, prosthetic nose, and artificial bosoms were shed, revealing the willowy figure of Lacey Papparin.

"Well?" asked her mother.

"Well, well, well," answered Lacey. "That confirmed things I suspected and solved the mystery of Black Jacket. He's a freelance thug who appears to be just smart enough to play everyone against the middle. Stealing from Dinis and then being hired by him—that's good business, if you can get it."

"But who actually hired him to steal the briefcase? Surely not Inês?"

"No, not Inês. But maybe someone close to her. Rui has been very useful after all."

"You know, I started feeling a bit sorry for him when he realized that we weren't actually interviewing him for that university. But then..." A wave of anger came over Daisy's face.

"Yeah, yeah, Mom, always looking out for me, aren't you? But I don't think that Rui had anything to do with Black Jacket's attacks on me. He's just a little twerp, really. That was all Dinis. But thank you, anyway."

"Any time, dear. And now I could use some supper. This detective stuff is hard work. What's that fish you've been telling me about again?"

"*Bacalhau*, Mom. They have a hundred ways of making it here. I recommend the simplest preparation: Just a broiled side of cod on the bone with boiled new potatoes sprinkled with olive oil and black olives on the side. And a bottle of port, if you'll join me. I know a place. And maybe we can catch some fado over dinner. It's like a window into the soul of Portugal. You should really hear it before we leave Lisbon."

"And when will that be?"

"Soon, and maybe sooner than we want. But we have a little bit more work to do before we can leave in good conscience."

"All righty then. What's next?"

"Portugal's a place for food; let's move up the food chain."

Chapter 17

RECIPROCAL REVERSE BLACKMAIL

The pool deck at the Lisbon Marriott is usually sublime at eleven o'clock in the morning in early July, and today was no exception. The pool nestled reclusively within a green sward dotted with palms, conifers, and oaks. Tall buildings enclosed its muted green waters on three sides, shading them from the harshest rays of the summer sun. Overhead, a perfect azure sky, dotted with fleecy clouds, announced an amnesty from worry. At the pool's edge, white deck chairs invited patrons from the adjacent hotel restaurant to lay back and soak in the Mediterranean climate.

Not many had answered its call yet today. Night had come late, and the day was still young. At present, the only hotel denizens enjoying the pool were two Lufthansa flight attendants loitering on deck chairs and drinking margaritas that they would need later in the day to stomach the passengers on the flight back to Munich. A little girl and her father wandered out of the hotel. The girl dipped her toes into the water, squealed twice, and then beelined back to the hotel. July or no July, the surrounding buildings' shade kept the water at temperatures favored by Northern Europeans and penguins.

To this happy valley came now two unhappy interlopers, not together nor initially even conscious of one another. They walked a few seconds apart down the long, glass-enclosed hotel corridor connecting the elevator lobby to the poolside restaurant. Their high heels clicked briskly on the white marble flooring; their posture was erect and suspicious; their dark, unfriendly clothing announced zero tolerance for pleasantries. Apart from this, the two women were as different as could be. One was short and plump with a mane of salt-and-pepper hair. A crucifix hung about her neck and, as she walked, she clutched at its silver transcendence and murmured the rosary in Latin. The other seemed at least a decade younger (although we should never judge a book by its cover). She sported a coiffure of copper curls that seemed to strike at her collar like cobras. As she walked, she clutched at her purse and muttered a string of epithets under her breath in Portuguese, French, English, and Polish—the latter recalled from the last words of an ex-boyfriend from Krakow as he took his leave from her apartment possessed of only boxer shorts and a cigar.

Leonor was first to arrive at the reception kiosk, which, given the interstitial hour, was not manned by restaurant personnel. She rested her elbows on the kiosk and cast about for someone to help her. Someone arrived sure enough, but the last person that Leonor was expecting. Beatriz came up behind her from down the long marble hall, proud and erect but not expecting to see Leonor either. The two women caught sight of each other at the same moment and froze into granite statues. A full moment passed before either was able to get a word out, and when they did, it was the same word, expressed with all the vituperation that forty years of nurtured hatred can produce: "You!"

Beatriz was the first to get out a follow-up to the accusatory pronoun. "How dare you summon me here, you loathsome creature! I'll take you to the law. You'll be locked away for the rest of your pitiful little life."

"What a fine thing for you to say, you horrible Medusa!" yelled Leonor, brandishing her crucifix as if to ward off an evil spirit. "The crime you describe is your own. How dare you threaten me! How dare you summon me here like some poor underling of your sickening company!"

"What is this nonsense you're talking?" retorted Beatriz, advancing within spitting range of her foe. "I came here because of the vile note you sent me. Don't pretend it's the opposite!"

"Don't you pretend, you disgusting monster!"

Just when escalation to physical violence seemed likely, the faceoff came to an abrupt denouement as the same realization seemed to fall on both women at the same moment. Both robotically reached into a pocket and pulled out a cream-colored envelope addressed with their own name in neat cursive calligraphy. Both summoned a single sheet of folded, cream-colored stationery from the envelope and surveyed its contents for at least the tenth time. Then slowly, gradually, the two women looked up into each other's eyes. Unbidden, their hands reached out and performed that choreographed exchange whose mastery some ten millennia ago paved the way for civilization—the perfectly simultaneous barter that leaves neither party a debtor nor creditor for even a microsecond.

And then both read, in each other's letter, exactly the same message in Portuguese that they had read the previous day in their own: *Your secrets are known by your enemies. If you wish them to stay secret, come tomorrow at 11 to the Marriott Hotel restaurant.*

A logician might have informed the women that it was still possible that the other was the author of the note and had simply faked a note to herself as well. But Beatriz and Leonor were not ruled at this moment by logic, but rather by instinct and emotion, and they knew at once that both of them were victims of some third power. Their eyes left each other's and looked about with dread for the puppet master.

Their dread turned into befuddlement when the puppet master walked out of the restaurant and turned out to be a plump, ordinary woman of about their own age. Any doubts about her nationality that might have lingered after consideration of her attire, physical attitude, and apparent lack of self-awareness about being a guest in a foreign country evaporated after she opened her mouth and said, in perfect American: "Hello, ladies. Thanks for coming. Care for some tea and pastries? This is a great country for pastries, you know."

Leonor and Beatriz stared back at her, dumbfounded.

"Sorry," the woman added quickly. "I should have introduced myself. My name's Daisy Papparin. I believe that both of you have met my daughter, Lacey. I just learned that people call her the Mouse, which doesn't seem quite appropriate for my little girl, but '*c'est la vie*,' as they say in Germany."

Neither of the Portuguese women flinched an eyelash.

"Well," said Daisy, apparently uncertain if she should just continue, "I suppose you're wondering why Lacey asked you here, although she's pretty sure that you're smart enough to have figured it out by now. Did you, by the way?"

No answer.

"OK then, Lacey will explain it all to you. I'm just her assistant today. My job is to greet you and show you to your seats."

"Our seats?" inquired Leonor, daring at last to speak. Her tone was neither incredulous nor hostile, but something closer to genuine perplexity.

Daisy laughed. "Your choice, if you want to stand. I don't suppose this business has to take all that long, although based on what Lacey told me about the two of you, we all might want to grab some tea before we get started. And some of those delicious pastries. If I'd know about your pastries over here, I would have come on over years ago." She laughed agreeably to show that she meant it as a genuine compliment but got no traction with her audience.

"OK then," she continued, "let me show you to your seats. Lacey wants you on opposite sides of the restaurant. As you can see, it's totally empty right now, so this will be easy. Leonor, you take that little table near the window over there." She gestured vaguely in the direction of a far corner overlooking the pool. "And Beatriz—wow, those are some gorgeous curls you have; I'll have to ask you where you get your hair done later—you can take this table here near the entrance. Oh, and one more thing. You'll need to leave your phones with me."

"What?" both women demanded in unison.

"I know, I know," said Daisy with contrition. "You won't be able to follow the soaps for a few minutes. I thought it might be a little rude to ask and tried to talk Lacey out of it, but I'm sorry to say that she insists. You see, you're not supposed to be talking to each other while we do this little... this little exercise."

"As if!" Beatriz snorted derisively.

"I have nothing to say to *her*," insisted Leonor with injured pride.

"Well that makes things easy," said Daisy with a wide smile. "No need for the phones, so they can go right into this bag." She held out a crinkled El Corte Inglés shopping bag.

Leonor and Beatriz stared at her incredulously. They did not reach for their phones.

"Now don't worry," Daisy said reassuringly. "I won't eat them. Not with all of those pastries over near the salad bar."

Slowly, Leonor reached into her purse, pulled out a phone, and dropped it into the bag. Beatriz resisted longer, muttering passive-aggressively under her breath while tapping her heels loudly against the marble floor and looking around as if expecting someone to show up and put an end to this nonsense. No paladin came. Sighing loudly, she retrieved her own phone, made a great show of turning it off as though Daisy were likely to begin using it for long-distance calls, and then dropped it into the bag in a manner calculated to cause a noisy collision with Leonor's phone.

"Thank you," said Daisy. "Now that we have all the preliminaries settled, please go to your tables. Lacey will be out shortly. If you need anything, I'll be right over there." She gestured toward a table halfway between their appointed stations.

Leonor and Beatriz walked reluctantly to their tables and sat down. A waiter came by to take their orders. Neither ordered anything. They sat waiting—Leonor nervously and Beatriz sullenly.

Five minutes later, Lacey made her appearance. All traces of Mademoiselle Gertrude LeClerc from Geneva were gone. Once again there was a waifish young woman with a shoulder-length bob of brown hair, mildly freckled cheeks, and a face free of makeup or guile. She was dressed casually in knee-length hiking shorts, a red polo shirt, and brown leather sandals and carried nothing but a closed dossier. She entered the restaurant, passed Beatriz without acknowledgment, and made her way over to Leonor.

"Hi, Tia," she said, sitting down. "I'm sorry to do this to you, but I think you'll see that it's for your own good, and for your family's too."

"What have I done to you?" demanded Leonor, seizing her by the hand.

"Nothing, Tia. You've only been kind to me. That evening of fado—wow, still feeling the love from that one. Unfortunately, the things that you have done have spillover effects that nearly led to me being killed—twice, actually."

Leonor gasped and took Lacey's other hand.

"But we've taken care of that now, and this isn't about me at all. It's about your family—really, both of your families. Stuff has been going on too long, and it's time for it to stop."

"Yes, yes," burbled Leonor, nearly in tears. "But it's *them*. It's *her*. They are the bad ones, Lacey. Don't you see that?"

"Oh yeah, I see that. And I know that you are a good and decent person, Tia, and that I won't be saying the same when I talk to Medusa in a minute—although even she has hurts that run deep too. But I'm not here to judge you, or Beatriz, or anyone. Somehow, I got pulled into your family business, and since I'm already in the middle of it, I'm going to straighten a couple of things out before pulling myself out of the briar patch."

"But what do you want from me?"

"I'll tell you that in a bit, but first let's talk about your blackmailing Beatriz?"

"Me blackmailing Beatriz?" Leonor protested with innocence. "No, no, Lacey, you have it all backward. She's the one who's been trying to blackmail me."

"Of course she has. I'll talk to her about that next. But you've been doing your own little bit of extortion too."

"But how did you figure that out?" It was a confession, but also a genuine question.

"Honestly, it took me a while to see it, which isn't something I like to admit. It started with one clue—one that I mentioned to you at the end of our dinner together, but that I misinterpreted. That night at the castle, when the downpour started and everyone was fleeing, and Beatriz slipped and fell, I saw you put your hand into her handbag. At the time, I assumed that you were taking something. When I asked you about it, you flatly denied stealing anything. At first, I assumed that you were lying, like most people would in that circumstance. But then I asked myself whether you were the kind of person to tell a lie, and that didn't seem consistent with the person I got to know over dinner. So if you hadn't taken anything from Beatriz's purse, what was the explanation for what I saw? That you were *putting* something into her purse. But what sort of thing would someone want to slip secretly into someone else's purse? Something anonymous. An anonymous note."

"Inês was right about you," said Leonor mournfully. "You are an extraordinary young woman."

"Did she really say that about me?" asked Lacey happily. Then, remembering herself, she continued. "OK, that's how I got to the part about the note, but now I had to figure out what an anonymous note might say. Blackmail was the best guess, among other things, because I came to realize that Beatriz was blackmailing *you*—but we'll get to that in a minute."

"Please do," said Leonor, perking up a bit.

"So what was the secret that you had on Leonor?" Lacey continued. "That one took me a while to crack. I guessed that it had something to do with the stolen briefcase that got me into this mess in the first place, but I couldn't quite place what it was. There was the weird fact that Dinis and Rui were in some sort of shady business together—weird, because your two families hate each other so much. Could you be blackmailing her about that when it involved your own nephew? But then, after seeing how Rui treated you at the restaurant and how upset it made you, it occurred to me that you wouldn't necessarily mind getting your nephew in some hot water too. After my mom and I cornered Rui and got the truth out of him, it finally became clear. Dinis's business wasn't just shady; it was big-time illegal. He roped Rui into helping him, but if anyone was going down hard, it was going to be Dinis. And, by extension the CATIE import/export house, through which Dinis was laundering most of his transactions in illegal Persian rugs. Alfonso, he might have sold his son down the river to save his business if things got ugly, but Beatriz—she's a different story. As nasty as she can be, she was once devout, and she's a mother. She was always going to save her son. You knew this. And somehow you found out about Rui's illicit side business. That gave you a great opening—dirt on Dinis that could give you leverage over Beatriz."

"Yes, yes," agreed Leonor energetically, "I knew that my worthless nephew was in some sort of bad business with that Guimarães brute. But I could never prove exactly what they were up to."

Lacey smiled. "Oh, I think you're more resourceful than that, Tia. You sit at that pretty front desk and see everything and everyone that comes in and out of the Casa Fonseca. Including Duarte Vasconcelos. He must have come by at some point to do some dirty work for Rui, and you got to talking with him, because you're the gatekeeper, and that's what gatekeepers do. So you asked what he was doing for Rui and Dinis, and he told you, because a guy like that likes nothing better than to dip his finger in two tills at once. And then you found out that Dinis was having a meeting with Farid Hasanova to get the genuine papers for the shipment of carpets, and you saw your chance to get the hard proof on Dinis that you had been looking for. Black Jacket—Duarte—of course said yes to the money and nipped the suitcase from the café. Unfortunately, I happened to be trying to steal the same suitcase, but that's another story."

"I'm so sorry," said Leonor, with genuine penitence in her voice. "Sorry for what?"

"I put you in danger, and I just understood that now. Yes, yes, it's all true what you say. I wanted—*I needed*—something to hold against Beatriz. After Duarte brought me the bag, he asked me what I should say when Dinis found him—because Dinis was certainly going to find him. I paid him a lot of money not to say it was me, because I needed to keep Beatriz guessing. I told him to make up some story—any story—about working for someone else. I see now that Dinis thought that it was you. I'm so sorry I put you in danger." She sniffed and caressed her crucifix.

"No worries. Danger is in my job description. But, just to round out the story, exactly what did you say in the note you stuffed into Beatriz's purse at the castle?"

"It was anonymous, as you guessed. It just said that someone was in possession of proof about Dinis's illegal dealings that could be very damaging to him and CATIE. There was no demand for now. Just a warning to Beatriz to behave herself because someone was watching." Leonor sighed. "I was so worried about how to give her the note. All evening, I was looking for my chance. And then when that crazy storm came..."

"Lots of interesting things happened during that storm," said Lacey thoughtfully. "Anyway, I think that's as much of the story as we need to go over right now."

"But I don't understand," said Leonor plaintively. "What do you mean to do with it?"

Lacey patted the older woman affectionately on the hands. "Nothing to hurt you, Tia. Only something that will free you. But I'll come to that in a few minutes. First, I have to have a chat with Medusa. Do you happen to have a mirror? If I look at her directly, I might turn into stone."

Leonor let out a hearty laugh, the first such merriment that Lacey had ever heard from the dour spinster. Across the room, Beatriz apparently heard the laughter and gave such an awful scowl that it seemed actually capable of turning someone to stone.

"I'll be back soon," said Lacey. "While I'm talking to Beatriz, why don't you have some tea and *pasteis de natas* with my mom?"

"I would like that!" said Leonor with enthusiasm.

At a signal from Lacey, Daisy came over to take her daughter's place. She slid easily into a chair across from Leonor, and the two women quickly fell into amiable conversation.

Beatriz's reception of Lacey was less cordial. She snarled as Lacey approached, her face crimson and screwed up into a terrible expression somewhere between rage and apoplexy. "How dare you do this to me?! I'll see you locked up in prison, you wretched little inbred cousin-marrier!"

"That's OK," answered Lacey with a winsome smile. "I've heard that your prisons have gotten way better since the revolution. There's even cable and room service. But as between me and Dinis, my money's on him to land behind bars."

Beatriz tried to make a dangerous face but mostly succeeded in looking uncertain. "Why, of what crime do you accuse my Dinis?"

"Well, where to begin? There's smuggling, of course, but also extortion, money laundering, racketeering, first-degree assault, attempted murder, and tax evasion."

"*Tax evasion?*" demanded Beatriz incredulously.

"Aha! So you don't feign innocence as to the others. And if you think that your precious Dinis will wiggle his way out on the list of things he actually did, just remember that the feds got Al Capone on tax evasion. Everyone does tax evasion, and as soon as the cops start looking for the bad stuff, they always find at least bad books. But who needs tax evasion as to Dinis? There are documents showing the smuggling, and a witness"—here Lacey waved her hand toward her mother—"on the attempted murder."

Beatriz lowered her eyes and smoothed her bronzed curls. She seemed to be weighing her options. At length, she asked simply: "What do you want from me?"

"We'll get to that in a few minutes. First, let's start with Galicia. What happened at the Cathedral of St. James in Santiago de Compostela?"

A flicker of triumph and derision returned to Beatriz's eyes. "Ask her." She gestured in the direction of Leonor, who seemed to be in rapt conversation with Daisy and didn't seem to notice her enemy's gesture.

"But I asked you."

"And why should I tell you?"

Lacey answered with silence. Beatriz looked around the restaurant again, as if certain someone would come to her rescue. A waiter, pretending to arrange the menus, surveyed his patrons' curious behavior. Apart from that, the dining room remained empty. She was trapped.

"Oh all right then," she snapped. "What do you want to know?"

"To get to Galicia, why don't we start in Coimbra? When you were a university student, living in the *república* on the Rua São Salvador."

"How do you—" Beatriz started to ask, but Lacey cut her off quickly.

"We'll be here all day if you start asking silly questions. When you were at the university, you dated Ricardo Fonseca for a while, didn't you?"

"Worst mistake of my life," she hissed.

"Maybe, but you didn't see it that way when he dumped you, did you?"

She rose from her chair like a viper ready to strike. "Why would you assume that *he* dumped *me*?" she demanded, dripping with venom.

"Because why else would you be out for revenge?"

"*Me*, take revenge on those little worms?"

"You're no good at denial, Beatriz. You should have said *that little worm*, not *those little worms*. But, of course, you did take your revenge on *them*. You took it then, and you've been taking it ever since."

"They had it coming."

"No, you just acted out of spite. At first you were hurt and just lashed out at the closest victim. You were a decent person then—religious, devout. But over time you acquired a taste for revenge. The more you got, the more you wanted."

"It's like a good wine," said Beatriz, her lips curled with malice. She had seated herself again and almost seemed calmed by the recounting of her sins.

Lacey continued. "Your first victim was Leonor. The poor innocent thing had a mortal crush on Ricardo too, but the closest she could get to him was to date his roommate—who is now your husband. When Ricardo dumped you to date Leonor's sister, that broke both your heart and hers. But that didn't stop you from meting out more punishment on her. She was Maria's sister, and punishing Leonor meant punishing Maria. So you stole Alfonso Guimarães from Leonor, even though you didn't love him then, and don't love him now."

"Love is so overrated," scoffed Beatriz. "At least he's good in business, which is more than I can say for your pathetic friends."

"It was cruel of you, Beatriz. Cruel to Leonor. And cruel to yourself. She became an old maid. But you became... you."

"Don't lecture me with your morals, as if you had any!"

"You're right, Beatriz. My own morals—and heaven knows my mother has some work to do in that department—have nothing to do with this. But you once had morals too. And Galicia was where you finally lost them, wasn't it?"

Beatriz laughed wickedly. "*I* lost *my* morals in Galicia? Oh no, you have it backward. You should be at the other table for that accusation."

"Oh Beatriz," said Lacey sadly. "I almost do feel sorry for you. When you left for Galicia, you were still full of piety—piety and hope. And so was Leonor. She made a mistake, and the cost was her innocence. But you made a choice, and the cost was your soul."

"Oh, come on! What are you? Some kind of hillbilly priestess?"

"OK then, let's stick to the facts. In 1975, Ricardo and Maria were married. The revolution had come, and Ricardo and Alfonso were estranged. But the following year both you and Leonor happened to go on the same pilgrimage to the tomb of St. James in Galicia. Both of you were still on the road searching for something, and St. James is the patron saint of pilgrims. You walked the last hundred kilometers to the cathedral along the Camino de Santiago, the way of St. James. When you arrived..."

"Yes, yes," said Beatriz excitedly. "When we arrived, *he* was there. He had come to Spain on business, or that's what he said. But maybe he had come for another reason—to take advantage of a stupid little hussy who couldn't stop thinking about her sister's husband, even on the holiest of pilgrimages."

"So are you now a hillbilly priestess?"

"I saw what I saw. Oh yes, I saw it and took pictures to prove it. He thought he could treat me like some low-life wench. Oh no! I saw what I saw and took what I took."

"There you go again," said Lacey, again sounding sad. "That was the end of Leonor's innocence, but yours too. It's been eating you all of these years, hasn't it? The weight of hatred and malice. They say that revenge is a dish best served cold. But you've been serving it for years and years, and it's turning you to stone, just like Medusa when Hercules turned the mirror on her."

Unexpectedly, Beatriz said nothing in reply. Despite her premonitions about the powers of Medusa, Lacey met her eyes and held them until the older woman turned away.

"It would have been easy to ruin Ricardo and Maria at once, wouldn't it? But you strung it out. For year after long year, you sat on your prize, hinting to Ricardo at what you knew, what you could prove. He probably begged you to let it go, offered you money. But you didn't want his money. After a string of other boyfriends, you came back to Alfonso. His business was booming; he was rich. And by marrying him, you could injure Leonor again and keep watch on the Casa Fonseca. Watch, wait, and ruin."

"You make it sound like this was my whole life," said Beatriz sullenly. "You have no idea about my life. I did many things. I married. I traveled. I worked with the business. I had children."

"You did. But you never forgot your thirst for vengeance on the Fonsecas. As your husband fought them in business, you goaded him to make it even more personal. And whenever Ricardo Fonseca seemed to win an advantage, you brought him back down with a little word or note."

"Don't blame his failures on me. My husband was always a better businessman."

Lacey recognized the diversionary effort and ignored it. "And then came the opportunity that you had been waiting for to get your revenge in the present and in the past. The Crooked Queen. I can't believe that you cared that much about the *azulejos* themselves, or even the money. The Queen was the symbol of everything that you held against the Fonsecas. Coimbra, the university, the early years, the revolution. When the lawsuit first happened, it would have been so easy for you to play your ace and make Ricardo give up the Queen. If you had told your husband about Galicia, that's what he would have done at once. But you played your husband too. And the theft of the Queen would give you exactly the leverage you craved."

Beatriz grew hot again. "Now you're really talking nonsense. We didn't steal the damn *azulejos*. It was them!"

"I believe that you didn't take the Queen. But once it was gone, you saw your chance to break Ricardo Fonseca. You told him that he not only had to return it but that he had to confess to having stolen it. Or else. It would have ruined him, in business and as a man."

"And why shouldn't I have made a thief confess? A thief! A thief!" She was on the edge of her seat again, making as if to rise and strike.

"But that's where you miscalculated. Ricardo didn't have it either. When he told you that, you gave him an ultimatum. Produce the Crooked Queen and confess, or you would reveal what happened in Galicia. You drove him off the cliff."

Beatriz slumped in her chair, dejected again. "I thought he had it," she murmured. "If he didn't, who did?"

"That's for me to know and you to find out—probably never," answered Lacey with a smile. "But now we have the story out. Is there anything you want to add?"

Beatriz just shook her head.

"Good," said Lacey. "Now I need to go and talk to Leonor again. I don't think it will take very long. While I'm gone, you might want to say the rosary or something."

Beatriz again said nothing. Lacey rose and walked over to where her mother and Leonor were eating pastries and drinking tea, seeming for all the world like two old friends. She sat with them for only a few minutes. Beatriz could not hear what they said, because they spoke in low voices, but she could see that the conversation was serious. As Lacey spoke, Leonor nodded her head frequently. When Lacey finished speaking, she nodded her head vigorously. Lacey left the table and returned to Beatriz.

"Very good," she said. "Half of the game is played, and with success."

"What game?" asked Beatriz suspiciously.

"Reciprocal reverse blackmail."

"*What?*"

"Don't worry, the name sounds fancy, but the rules are really very simple. There are two contestants—you and Leonor. Each of you has been blackmailing the other, and the other's family. You may have guessed by now that Leonor is the one who left the note in your purse at the Castelo de São Jorge. She has irrefutable proof that your son is involved in illegal smuggling. The release of that information would ruin your son, certainly, and probably your family's business too. Whatever your son's sins, I do not think it right for her to hold that over you, do you?"

Beatriz, who could see where this was headed and didn't like it, could not avoid shaking her head.

"Good. Further, as we established a few minutes ago, you have been blackmailing the Fonseca family and Leonor for decades. She does not think that is right either. Nor do I. Where I come into the picture is that I have these dirty secrets about both of you and am therefore able to blackmail both of you at the same time. But I have no interest in ruining either of your lives—Leonor, because I am actually quite fond of her, and you, because—well, this is hard to say, but I really do think that you deserve a chance at redemption from the person you've become, just like that poor girl Matilde Maria Teixeira who was a teenage mom and is now going to be studying on a Fulbright Scholarship at Duke—I moved her into the *yes* pile after you left."

"You did *what?*" roared Beatriz.

"Now, now, don't go showing your nasty old self just when I'm about to give you a chance at redemption. We haven't finished the rules of the game yet. Right now, I'm blackmailing both of you on a short fuse. I'm asking each of you to promise to walk away from blackmailing the other. If both of you refuse, then I'll just walk out of here, shake the dust off my sandals, and leave you to your own fate. If both of you agree, we'll be rid of this nonsense forever. But if one of you agrees and the other disagrees, well then, I'll have to act on the information I have against the recalcitrant party. Now do you understand the rules of the game?"

"Yes," said Beatriz through gritted teeth.

"I should also tell you that Leonor has already agreed to give up on blackmailing you. I suppose you see where that leaves things, according to the rules of the game."

Beatriz nodded grimly.

"One final rule I have to tell you. In order for me to trust your word, you will need to take an oath. My mom always said that I shouldn't take oaths—something about letting your yes be yes and your no be no—but I'm afraid that I have no choice in this matter but to ask for one. It seemed only fair to make both of you take the same oath, and there was only one that I could think of that would do the trick. You must swear by the Cathedral of St. James in Santiago de Compostela."

Five minutes later, Leonor and Beatriz left the restaurant. Not together, of course. They had not become friends, nor even relinquished being enemies. But they both seemed to walk with a somewhat lighter step than when they had entered. Leonor was caressing her crucifix but not so much in supplication or alarm as in thanksgiving. For her part, Beatriz might still have been mistaken for a character out of Greek mythology, but one might charitably think of Ariadne rather than Medusa. She seemed to be talking to herself as though trying to figure out what had just happened and whether there might not be some silver lining in it.

Daisy and Lacey stayed for an early lunch because they were Americans and didn't think it odd to eat before noon. Plus, they had plans to make and places to see. Their days in Lisbon were fast closing, and there remained things to do in that wonderful, fallen capital of an empire.

Chapter 18

BON VOYAGE

"I think it's time that we drop in on them, don't you, sweetie?" Daisy sat on the deck holding a glass of lemonade. A hundred feet below, the gray-green waters of the North Atlantic sparkled in the morning sun, barely troubled by the passage of ninety thousand tons of steel. The affairs of humanity remained a largely uninteresting story to these waters. They had been there long before the humans arrived on their little wooden boats and would be there long after the last big ships motored through.

"I dunno," answered Lacey lazily from the other chair on the deck. Her bare feet were propped up on the rails. She took a slow sip from a half-finished margarita and eyed her mother. "After the craziness of these last few weeks, it's nice just to sit here, don't ya think?"

"Well, it certainly is very relaxing being in here, but I can't say that I've enjoyed the part about sneaking around so they don't see us. I thought that he came close in the castle in that Spanish city. What do they call it again?"

"Cádiz. But I thought you were starting to enjoy this cloak-and-dagger stuff, Mom."

"Oh, it's a bit of a thrill—doing what you do. But you have to remember that I'm a homebody. This is only my third time outside of Iowa, ya know. You're going to have to give me some time to get used to it."

Lacey sat up with a sigh. "I suppose you're right, Mom. We've come this far. Let's get it over with."

They rose and stepped back into a stateroom appointed with a double bed, sitting table, and loveseat. The room was serenaded pleasantly with mismatched colors. The carpet was French blue with a tan brocade and shocks of red flowers, the walls speckled beige, the coverlet purple and chartreuse, the loveseat dandelion yellow, and a tropical modernist print on the wall some combination of green, aqua, and goldenrod. Daisy, dressed for the beach in a Hawaiian shirt and culottes, fit right in.

Lacey, who had been wearing exercise shorts and a tank top, stepped into the tight closet, the sort of thing that she could still do and her mother—beyond Lacey by two babies and twenty-five years, couldn't— and emerged moments later in well-pressed slacks, a white blouse, and penny loafers. "Go as you want, Mom," she said. "For me, this is still business."

"Where do you think they'll be?" asked Daisy as they exited the room into an interior passageway of garish colors.

Lacey glanced at her watch. "Catching a late coffee in the Sugarcane Bar. That's where they've been this time the last two days."

They met a few other passengers as they traversed the belly of the beast. The weather was fine and most of their fellow travelers were above deck enjoying the cruise ship's decadent inventory of amenities—swimming pools, water slides, basketball courts, lounge chairs, restaurants, and spas. Inside the passageway, there was no pitch or roll, nothing to hint that they were seafarers. The ship's technology had stripped away the sea's undulations and perils. There would be no seasickness, danger from storms or pirates, or lack of food or drink on this crossing. Modern ingenuity had erased the hardships of life at sea. Maybe it had erased its romance too. But Lacey wasn't worried about such things as she walked the steady, sterile passageway and climbed the stairs toward the upper decks. Her mind was on unfinished business, business that she had not meant to start but now knew that she must end.

Nestled in the ship's interior next to a sprawling atrium, the Sugarcane Bar traded sea views for intimacy. Along one wall, curtained windows backed by blue lights from the atrium made a feeble pretense of oceanic authenticity. But patrons came for the views of each other, not the scenery. Overhead lights were kept dim even in the morning hours. At the bar, the black stools were spaced far apart for those wishing solitude or, by drawing two together, to create space from others. On the black marble floors, red leather chairs were arranged in twos or threes around little wooden tables that could barely accommodate two plates and glasses.

Lacey and Daisy paused at the entrance. Few patrons had come this early to the nocturnal joint. A father and young daughter sent away from their cabin by a mother in need of time alone sipped fruit slushies and played checkers. A retired couple fought to control a tablet with pictures of their grandchildren. And, in a remote corner on the far side of the bar, a young couple canoodled over their morning coffee. On them the mother and daughter's gaze fell. Oblivious to their audience, the couple sipped, whispered, laughed, and cuddled. They were young, at sea, carefree, and in love. But such conjunctions never last.

Daisy gave her daughter a little push in the back. Lacey sighed deeply. Her mother gave her another encouraging push. Slowly, she started across the room. The couple in the corner did not notice the two women's approach until they were right in front of the table. Then, in startled unison, two pairs of eyes, round as saucers, turned upon the visitors.

"Mind if we join you?" asked Lacey in a meek voice.

There was no answer from Inês Fonseca or Pedrinho Guimarães.

Lacey waited a moment and repeated the question in a slightly louder voice.

Inês buried her face in her hands. Pedrinho, composing himself with pallor, gestured that they should sit down. Since Lacey seemed presently incapable of logistics, Daisy pulled up two chairs and pushed her daughter into one of them. A long and heavy silence followed.

At last, Inês raised her face. There were no tears on her cheeks, but her eyes were red. She groped for Lacey's hands, but they were not offered.

"I'm so sorry, *menina*," she said in a hoarse whisper.

This time, Lacey did not say, "For what?" or "That's OK." She just sat with her eyes on the table. After another spell of silence, she said simply: "This is my mom."

"I'm so sorry, Mrs. Papparin," said Inês.

"Don't apologize to me, honey," said Daisy, cheerfully taking the younger woman's hand. "I got a trip to Europe and a cruise out of this. We have cruises on the Mississippi in Iowa—you probably didn't know that—but they're nothing like this."

Another lull. No one seemed to be up for comparing riverboats and the *Norwegian Star*. At length, Pedrinho asked in a voice of mixed shame and wonder: "How did you find us?"

"Don't bother," Inês snapped, sitting up straight. "Those are her trade secrets."

Lacey snorted. "Don't flatter yourselves. You left more crumbs than Hansel and Gretel."

"Really?" asked Pedrinho.

"Really," agreed Lacey. For a moment, she seemed to be debating whether to say more; then her old zest won out. "Yeah, OK, Inês doesn't like to fly, right. She told me she wouldn't be caught dead on an airplane. So, when you two flew the coop, you weren't flying but going by sea or land. Land would only take you somewhere else in Europe. The Fonsecas' thoughts are always on the old empire. Inês pretty much gave it away over breakfast at the Quinta das Lágrimas. And then it all clicked. What better way for you to start your new life than by eloping on a cruise to Rio de Janeiro? On arrival, you could blend right in and disappear."

"But how did you know which ship we would take?" asked Pedrinho.

"I'm afraid *that* would be a trade secret," answered Lacey primly.

"She got that expression from me," stage-whispered Daisy. No one seemed to notice her editorial.

"How long have you known?" asked Inês sorrowfully.

"About what?" answered Lacey.

"About us."

"Well, most knowledge is a matter of probabilities, so I didn't really *know* until I saw you two lovebirds over here in the corner. But I had suspicions early on, and the probability got higher with time."

Inês exchanged Daisy's hand for Pedrinho's. She looked earnestly into Lacey's eyes. "Please don't be angry with me, Mousie. Please tell me everything. I've been dreading this moment for a long time."

"You knew that I knew?"

"Yes, and I knew that you knew that I knew that you knew. You're an extraordinary young woman."

"So why didn't you tell me everything?"

"Because the words would never come. Because I was afraid that you would think me selfish or evil. Because I had promised Pedrinho that it would be our own secret forever."

Lacey said nothing in reply.

"Please, please," said Inês again on the verge of tears. "At least let's come clean to each other now. Tell me everything, Mousie. And let's do this the old way. Let's order some food first."

"Not this time," replied Lacey morosely. She paused, then launched in. "OK, before that night at the castle you screwed up, Inês. You told me all about the evil Guimarães clan, but you never told me that Pedrinho overlapped with you in London. Then you asked him if he remembered me from LSE. That question would have made perfect sense to preempt him saying that he didn't remember me from his school days, but it was the kind of thing that you obviously should have told me ahead of time. So what happened? You hadn't been planning to mention it at all, but then at the castle it suddenly occurred to you that I might find out from his parents that he had studied in London, and then it would be even worse."

Inês nodded gravely. "You're right, of course. We hardly even met in Portugal. Our families stayed apart, except to throw bombs. And then, by a twist of fate, there we both were, students in another old capital of an empire. The first year, we ignored each other. The second year, we fought like cats and dogs. The third year, we ignored each other again. The fourth year we fell in love."

"Forever," added Pedrinho, taking Inês's other hand.

Lacey gesticulated savagely. "Could everyone just stop holding hands? This is getting smarmy."

Inês reached apologetically for Lacey's hand, then, realizing what she was doing, recoiled as if from a viper. The two women caught each's other eyes and laughed despite themselves.

"The next thing also was at the castle. Both of you went missing at the same time and then showed up again at the same time. There was so much drama and confusion that night that I didn't put it all together at first, but when I gave it some thought it seemed plausible that you were off on a little tryst in some dark parapet or something. Enemies? Probably not. Lovebirds? Probably so." She said this scoffingly but without malice.

"It was a dark and stormy night and the air was full of romance. Can you blame us?" asked Inês.

"Whatever. But you're going to have to cover your tracks better if you want to go incognito in Brazil."

"Why will they have to go incognito in Brazil?" asked Daisy.

"Don't jump ahead, Mom. We'll get there. But first let's fill out this corner of the puzzle. After the castle, it was clear that there were all sorts of connections other than the Crooked Queen between your families. Dinis and Rui were into some kind of bad business, Leonor was into Beatriz's handbag, and the two of you were into each other. I have to admit that I didn't see it as soon as I should have. Frankly, Pedrinho, you gave me the willies. I now think that's because you were so much smoother than the rest of your family that I painted you as an evil puppet master. That day we met at the embassy, we almost broke through. You wanted me to know that you were on Inês's side, that you were a friend. But your dropping 'trade secrets' freaked me out. I thought you were spying on me, maybe working with whoever hired Black Jacket."

"I wasn't! I promise I was always trying to protect you."

"I know that. When I saw you outside my Airbnb, I still thought you were after me. Later, when I found out that you weren't working with Black Jacket, it seemed more likely that you were trying to watch out for me—although I have to say that my mom did a better job of that than you did."

Pedrinho grimaced, and Daisy beamed.

"Hey, I'm not criticizing. I missed a big one too. Etymology."

"Etymology?" asked Inês.

"What's that mean?" asked Daisy.

Lacey ignored her mother and focused on Inês. "Do you remember the rule of paradox?"

Inês searched her mind, then snapped her fingers. "The less hidden, the more hidden."

"Exactly! That's true for the physical world, and it's true for language. I didn't see it until after Coimbra, where everything started and ended, not just today but six hundred years ago. You are Inês, and this is Pedrinho. *Inho* makes the diminutive in Portuguese. No one would ever formally be named Pedrinho; it's just a nickname. Pedrinho is a little rock, a little Pedro. He is Pedro, and you are Inês. It was fated like fado, wasn't it?"

"Yes, yes," agreed Inês. "Fated like fado. Our names—how could our parents have given those to us by chance? Of course Coimbra ran through all of their blood. It was their beginning, and the source of their conflicts. We were born just a few weeks apart and of course our families did not share such news. When our parents found out that they had given us these names—names with such power to bind, power to heal, power to kill—their rage at each other flared worse than ever. With my name, there was not much to do. But Pedro could be diminished to Pedrinho, and with it the linkage broken. Or so his parents imagined. Fate is stronger than imagination."

"Lacey, Mrs. Papparin, you must understand," implored Pedrinho. "Our families are not all bad. Even mine, which is the worse."

"And yet you had to hide your love from them and plot for years to run away," said Lacey.

Inês and Pedrinho nodded sadly. "Yes, it's true," admitted Inês. "They would never have accepted our love. The war would have raged until everything was destroyed. We would have lost them and probably each other too. We were doomed to be Pedro and Inês. Doomed, but could we break the curse? We dared to dream that we could."

"Dreamed. Plotted. Planned." Lacey's shoulders had relaxed. The cadence of her words had slowed.

"*Sim, sim,*" agreed Inês. "For many years."

"And the centerpiece of your plan was to steal the Crooked Queen."

"Steal?" asked the lovers in unison.

Lacey shot her mother a surprised glance. "Why, yes. You took it, didn't you?"

"Yes, of course we did," said Inês. "But we did not think of it as stealing. The Queen was tearing apart our families. It belonged to neither of them and both of them. It belonged to us as much as anyone. We could take the Queen and sell it, and with the money start our new lives together in a faraway place."

"I'm not sure about your logic. It was a very bad plan, wasn't it?"

Inês and Pedrinho nodded vigorously. "My mother," said Pedrinho sadly. "I didn't imagine how cruel she had become. By the time we found out that she was blackmailing Mr. Fonseca, asking him to do the impossible and return what he hadn't stolen, it was too late. He had disappeared into the ocean."

"But you knew he hadn't really," protested Lacey.

"No, not at first," answered Inês. "Not for many years. We thought he had died, at his own hand or in a violent spat with Alfonso. We could not leave our families then. Nor could we admit what we had done. Those were black, black years."

"When did you realize? It must have been before I showed up."

"Yes, barely. Just a few weeks ago it was approaching the fifth anniversary of his death that I began to go back over everything again.

The postcard. The disappearance of the money. Aleister Crowley. Mousie, do you remember what Saint Anthony is the patron saint of?"

"Lost things."

"Yes, lost things. He's the patron saint of lost things. On the day of Saint Anthony's feast, I went alone to the Boca do Inferno to think it all over, and suddenly it just clicked. My father wasn't dead. He was lost. And two days later, you showed up."

"How convenient," said Lacey dryly.

"How fated," said Inês with conviction.

"But then why didn't you ask me to help you find your father?"

"Oh, Mousie, I'm sorry. Yes, I should have done that. But that would have required telling you everything about Pedrinho and me, about our taking the Crooked Queen, about your plans to leave. I didn't know you. You showed up suddenly, a gift from the hand of fate. I wanted you to find my father, to bring him back so that Pedrinho and I could leave. I asked you to find the Queen because I thought that would lead you to my father."

"And so it did."

"I'm sorry. I didn't imagine the danger that would put you in."

"That's OK. Danger's my day job. But did you really think I wouldn't discover the truth?"

"Maybe the problem is that I really didn't think. I thought I was riding fate. And I didn't know that we were leaving so many crumbs."

"Oh yeah, lots of bread crumbs."

Pedrinho's brow furrowed. "But I still don't understand. How did you figure it out? We were so careful."

Pedrinho, Inês, and Daisy all looked intently at Lacey. Would she invoke trade secret protection? The Mouse looked down uncomfortably at the table, then began to bite a fingernail.

"Stop that!" said her mother and Inês like a Greek chorus, both slapping at Lacey's hand. The hand-to-hand contact seemed to stun Lacey into a decision. "OK, OK," she muttered, not making clear whether she meant to comply with manners or disclosure. Her audience opportunistically interpreted it as the latter. With nowhere to run from the three expectant faces, she sighed deeply and began.

"Well, I knew pretty much from the beginning that you were keeping things from me. Fools, lies, and skeletons, indeed! At first, I thought that you were trying to protect someone, maybe your father. You clearly didn't want him accused of taking the Queen. After I figured out that the skull wasn't his and that he was probably alive, I began to wonder whether you had known that all along. It even crossed my mind that you had been behind Black Jacket's attack at São Roque."

"No, please, Mousie," protested Inês in a hurt voice. "You couldn't think that of me."

"No, I didn't think *that* of you," answered Lacey, a bit coldly. "I said that it crossed my mind. It was something to be considered and weighed. But it didn't make any sense. You were right near me when it happened. I saw your face. You were genuinely frightened and worried for me. More to the point, you needed me then still. You needed me to find your father."

"Please don't think that I was just using you, Mousie. I thought that you would enjoy the adventure. And I meant to tell you everything later, once Pedrinho and I were safely away. Honestly, I did."

"Yeah, yeah." It was a neutral "yeah, yeah," neither quite "yes, yes" or "no, no." "Anyway, the only way to bring things to a close was to find your father. When I went back for my hat, Miguel at Lunar Tiles gave me the name of the dealer who had bought up all your dad's tiles—Cisterno Vazio. That obviously wasn't a real name."

"How did you know that, sweetie?" asked Daisy. "It sounds perfectly Portuguese to me."

"It is Portuguese, Mom, but it isn't someone's name. It means *dry well*, which is what Fonseca means too. Mr. Fonseca liked to play with words. It was clearly him. I just had to find him in Coimbra. And I did. That's when things picked up. Inês, you had followed me to Coimbra and were watching when I went into the *Passeio Lusitano* and met your father."

"How did you see me?" exclaimed Inês. "I was so well hidden."

"I didn't see you, but there are other ways to leave breadcrumbs. You called and told me to meet you at the Quinta das Lágrimas. The time you gave yourself to arrive from Lisbon was plenty to drive, and just enough to come by train if the schedule worked out, but it didn't. I checked. There was no way that you could have come by train and arrived as early as you did, but the first thing you told me at the Quinta was that you had come by train. So what really happened? After I left the *Passeio,* you went in and found your father. What exactly you said, I don't know, but the upshot was that he promised to come out of hiding. And then you were done with me. I had served my purpose, and any more digging around might have led to the truth. It was time to get rid of me."

"Please don't say that!" begged Inês. "Yes, it's true that I met my father, as you say. And, yes, I wanted you to drop the case. But I was worried about you. Dinis had already shown himself to be a brute. If you got closer to the truth, who knows what could have happened? I was so worried about you, Mousie. I sent Pedrinho to watch for you when you returned to Lisbon. I never wanted you to be hurt. I'm so sorry I put you in danger."

"We've been over that," said Lacey curtly. "I don't hold Black Jacket or Dinis against you, or you either, Pedrinho, even though he's your freaking brother. And I can't say I blame you for wanting to get away from that family of yours. But you, Inês, you really pulled one over me at the Quinta."

"Exactly what did she pull?" asked Daisy.

"She wanted me to think I was losing my mind. It was the perfect setup. The legend of the ghost of Inês de Castro. From the moment I walked into the hotel, I was primed to see a ghost. The clerk at the front desk told me of encountering the ghost. The painting in the room would give anyone nightmares. And then our walk to the Fountain of Tears in the afternoon. Everything was slightly off. Everything was a shade of the macabre. The indecipherable poem. The creeping banyan. The Judas tree. The blood-stained rocks at the fountain. Then the same walk by night. Why did you want to go again so much? To leave me alone at the fountain. Your mom didn't call you along the trail. That was a lie. You didn't do your homework. I did. There's no cell coverage there. You slipped away when I didn't notice so I could enjoy the hallucinations on my own."

"Hallucinations?" asked Daisy with concern. Inês had buried her face in her hands again.

"Oh yeah, that was a trip. Over supper, Inês accidentally"—Lacey made rabbit ears—"knocked a drink onto my lap. While I changed, she had the opportunity to slip something into my drink. Something that grows in the Quinta's herb garden, part of its international botanical collection. I have a little sample here." Lacey reached into a pocket and produced a sandwich bag. Inside were a handful of dried green leaves. "*Psychotria viridis,* or *chacruna* to the people of the Amazon rainforests. It produces a powerful hallucinogenic tea called *ayahuasca*. She wouldn't have had the time to brew it properly, but a small rough batch mixed with my port would have had quite an effect. Enough to make me start seeing some interesting things that I was already primed to see."

"I'm so sorry," sniffed Inês. She sounded so genuinely contrite that Lacey finally relented and offered some forgiveness.

"Forget about it. It was quite an experience, that's for sure. And, in the end, it gave me one of the final pieces to the puzzle. That, and the visit to the chapel with your rude friend Santiago."

"He's actually a nice guy," protested Inês. "He was very kind to Pedrinho and me when our families were fighting. He was the only one who knew our secret."

"Yeah, he kinda had to, since he took the Queen for you."

"How did you figure that out?"

"Because he was lying about the chapel. He said that the hotel put a sensor and alarm around the place the Queen was displayed, but there's no electricity in the chapel. Also, there's no way anyone could have gone over those rickety rails on the balcony and come back up that way again. The rails would have broken right off with any weight on them. It was an inside job, through and through. So either Santiago took it for himself, or he took it for someone else. If he had taken it for himself, why was he still working at the Quinta five years later? And if he took it for someone else, who could it be? Ricardo? He denied it and I believed him. Donna Maria? She has no interest in *azulejos*. Alfonso? But he couldn't have helped showing off if he had it. Rui or Dinis?" Lacey made a guttural noise, somewhere between a cough and a neigh. "Leonor or Beatriz? Now those would have been interesting possibilities, but I put them to rest last week. Those two are another whole story, but I think that story is for them to tell if they want to. That left the two of you. When it didn't make sense that it was either of you individually, all of the pieces coalesced. It was the two of you together."

"Nothing gets by you, does it?" asked Pedrinho with a little smile.

Lacey blushed modestly. "Let's remember that this all started when Inês found me out. It took Mom to bail me out at the cathedral. And you, Pedrinho, gave me the most important piece on your mom and the tomb of St. James in Galicia."

"Still, I'm astonished that you put it all together, Mousie," said Inês. "You are an amazing person. It's a good thing you dropped out of law school. The law would not have been safe with you."

Lacey said nothing. Her mother saved her humiliation from further praise. "So you two are really going to run away from your families? Don't you think that will break their hearts?"

"No," said Pedrinho. "We will write them a letter explaining things—at least some things. They will not understand; they will be angry at first. But now things will have to change. Ricardo will return, and that will bring happiness to the Fonsecas. The finger-pointing over the Crooked Queen will end. When time has passed, maybe when there are little ones, we send back the doves. If they return with olive branches, then maybe we will come home."

"But what will you do in the meantime?"

"We will settle down in Brazil. We will find jobs and build a life together. But the first thing we will do in Rio is to find a priest and get married. Say, you will be landing in Rio too! You can be our witnesses and only guests."

"Yes, yes," chirped Inês. "It will make the wedding perfect."

"Sorry," broke in Lacey. "We're not going to Brazil with you. We'll be disembarking in the Canary Islands in two days. From there we'll catch a flight to Madrid and then on to New York."

Inês looked disappointed and perplexed. "But then why did you come after us in the boat? Why didn't you confront us before we left Lisbon?"

"Don't you see, Inês? I'm not here to confront you. I'm neither a cop nor a priest. Your life is your own business. We waited until we were far away from Portugal because I didn't want you to turn back. This was your choice, yours and Pedrinho's, and I don't think it's a crazy one."

"But then why did you come after us at all?"

"Because..." Lacey choked up despite herself. "Because, despite everything, you are a friend, and I wanted to say goodbye. Goodbye, bon voyage, and good luck."

In the Hollywood reel, this would have been the moment for soaring music, free-flowing tears, and a group hug. But that would have been far too smarmy an ending for Lacey Papparin, the Mouse. She did make a small accommodation and allowed Inês to seize her hand. Then she quickly brought things back to the practical.

"I am curious about one thing, though."

"Yes?" said Pedrinho.

"How did you manage to sell the Crooked Queen, and how much did you get for it?"

Inês and Pedrinho burst out into simultaneous denials. "No, no," said Pedrinho. "We never sold it. When we took it five years ago, that was our plan, so that we could raise money to elope. But after Ricardo disappeared, we couldn't bring ourselves to sell it. Now, five years later, we still can't bring ourselves to sell it. We've saved enough money between the two of us to get a start in Brazil."

"But then where is?"

"In our cabin," answered Inês. "Would you like to see it?"

"Would we like to see it? Is the Pope Catholic? Are pasteis delicious? Are you kidding?"

"Then let's go," said Pedrinho, pushing back from the table.

The foursome rose and adjourned from the Sugarcane Bar. They walked the ship's gaudy corridors in silence. There was so much more to say, so many more questions to ask, but also so much to ponder. The walk allowed their mood to turn inward. Even Daisy, who had no reason to feel the weight of the moment as the other three did, allowed reflection to prevail. Perhaps she had reflections of her own on her daughter and herself, and how the trip's revelations might change their relationship.

They arrived at the cabin shared by the elopers. It was exactly the same as Daisy and Lacey's, except maybe a wee bit tidier (despite the presence of a man). Inês seated the women at the table while Pedrinho went into the closet. He emerged carrying a heavy rectangular object about two by three feet, wrapped in white cloth. He placed the object on the table and unfastened the wrapping. The cloth rustled over the smooth surface of the tiles and disappeared from the table. There, in a montage of six *azulejos*, lay the Crooked Queen.

Lacey had seen photographs of it before, but what she saw on the table looked little like what she had seen in the pictures. It seemed older, more chipped and tattered, more careworn and weary. The furnace-glazed colors, dulled by the years, showed the queen of legend, sitting on a high-backed, gilded throne, crown erect on slumping head. But it was not the crookedness of the neck that attracted attention; it was the languor of the eyes. Undetectable from photographs but plain in person, the eyes were not fully closed as they should have been in death. The lids were open just a smidgen, just enough for the queen to look one more time on the royal court and those that had bowed as low in her death as they had held her low in her life. What expression lay in those veiled eyes was hard to tell, especially with the tarnishment of centuries. Was it malice, revenge, pride, sorrow, or just tiredness?

"What do you think?" asked Inês of Lacey.

Lacey paused before answering. "I'm not sure. It's different than I thought. Alfonso once said that to see the Crooked Queen is to become Portuguese. I guess I've now become Portuguese, and I'm not sure I like the way it makes me feel. Mostly just weary, like the weight of an old, decaying empire never left my shoulders. I wish that Grão Vasco had closed her eyes all of the way and given her the rest that she deserved."

"I wish that too," said Inês quietly, not making clear if she meant that for the queen, her country, or herself.

This turn in the conversation could have ended the gathering on a melancholy note, but Inês suddenly clapped her hands and jumped up from the table. "I've got it!" she announced with delight. She disappeared into the closet and remerged a moment later carrying a white cardboard box. She plunked it onto the middle of the Crooked Queen and opened the lid, revealing four shriveled *pasteis de nata*. "I was saving these for when we arrived in Brazil, to give us a last taste of home," she explained. "But they would be really stale by the time we arrived, and I can't imagine anything better than sharing them with you."

Now it was Lacey's turn to jump up in excitement. "Wait, wait!" she exclaimed, and disappeared out the cabin door. A few minutes later she was back, carrying an identical box of her own. "*Bolas de Berlim*," she explained, opening the box to reveal four fat blobs of dough sprinkled with coarse sugar and bursting with golden *crème pâtissière*. "I thought Mom and I could eat these back in the States as a final goodbye to Portugal. But you're right, they would be stale."

"You two are peas in a pod!" laughed Daisy, tugging both of the younger women by the hair.

"Coffee," said Lacey with urgency. "*Meia-de-leite*, if we can find some milk."

"Over there in the fridge," said Inês, bustling toward the coffee maker.

"It will be a feast!" exclaimed Pedrinho.

"We'll get fat!" cackled Daisy.

"Never, Mom," said Lacey as she scurried for the milk. "That's the magic of Portuguese pastries."

EPILOGUE

A few months after the events narrated in this story, Lacey was back at her mother's house in Iowa when she received the following letter from Inês, postmarked Belo Horizonte, Brazil.

Dear Mousie,

How are you? Did you and your mother make it back safely to America? Is she driving you crazy? I don't think she could. She seems very sweet, much more so than my mother.

Pedrinho and I arrived in Brazil and are doing well. First thing we were married by a priest, just the two of us in a little chapel by the sea. It was a little sad not having anyone with us, but also very romantic—just like Pedro and Inês's secret wedding of old. We've settled in the south of Brazil. We have a cute little apartment and both of us found jobs quickly. I have a little bump on my belly. Maybe I will have more news to send you soon. You should come and visit us sometime!

Beijinhos, menina!
Your friend,
Inês

P.S. There is something that I didn't tell you on the boat and that I have hesitated to tell you even now, but I think it is something that you should know. That night at the Quinta das Lágrimas, when you saw the ghost of Inês de Castro in the woods—well, I hadn't taken the ayahuasca, but I saw her too.

ABOUT THE AUTHOR

Daniel Crane is a law professor at the University of Michigan and a frequent commentator on legal affairs in national media outlets. His first novel, *Girl with Egg Basket*, was published by DartFrog Books in 2016.

Printed in the USA
CPSIA information can be obtained
at www.ICGtesting.com
LVHW041700190124
769098LV00003B/134